I0611331

Also by Ray Hobbs and published by Wingspan Press

An Act of Kindness

Following On

A Year From Now

A Rural Diversion

A Chance Sighting

Roses and Red Herrings

Happy Even After

The Right Direction

An Ideal World

Published Elsewhere

Second Wind (Spiderwize)

Lovingly Restored (New Generation Publishing)

MISCHIEF & MASQUERADE

RAY HOBBS

Wingspan Press

Published in the United States and the United Kingdom by WingSpan Press, Livermore, CA

The WingSpan name, logo and colophon are the trademarks of WingSpan Publishing.

ISBN 978-1-63683-000-1 (pbk.)
ISBN 978-1-63683-999-8 (ebook)

First edition 2021

Printed in the United States of America

www.wingspanpress.com

1 2 3 4 5 6 7 8 9 10

This book is dedicated to the memory of those who have kept past enemies guessing, and to those who, for all we know, may well perform a similar function today.

RH

Thanks are due, as ever, to my brother Chris, whose academic approach, ideas and arguments were invaluable in formulating the plot of this story.

Sources

Macintyre, B., *Double Cross* (London, Bloomsbury 2016)
Masterman, J.C., *The Double Cross System* (London, Spere Books Ltd 1973)
Wheatley, D., Stranger Than Fiction (London, Arrow 1976)

RH

Author's Note

The Royal Navy was founded when the 16th century and the English language as we know it were both in their infancy, and when William Shakespeare was yet to be born.

Ships were often at sea for a matter of years, resulting in sailors developing a language that bore little resemblance to that spoken ashore, and it became the service's universal parlance. Tradition being born of pride, it is little wonder that navalese is still the *lingua franca* of the Royal Navy. There are those who mock it, largely because, having no tradition of their own, they fail to understand the concept, but elements of that language have been in use for five hundred years, and that alone must be a measure of their worth.

Whilst I have kept naval terminology to a minimum in this book, I have decided to offer a fuller explanation than in the past, in the hope that truth will 'make all things plain,' where a mere glossary often leaves questions unanswered. I shall begin, oddly enough, with the term 'Eight Bells', which indicates the end of a four-hour watch.

The naval day is divided into watches: The First Watch 2000 – midnight, The Middle Watch midnight – 0400, The Morning Watch 0400 – 0800, The Forenoon Watch 0800 – 1200, The Afternoon Watch 1200 – 1600, The First Dog Watch 1600 – 1800, The Second Dog Watch 1800 – 2000.

Each half-hour was marked, until relatively recently, by the ringing of the ship's bell: one bell after thirty minutes, two bells rung as a pair after the first hour, three bells (a pair and a single) after an hour and a half, and so on. The end of the watch was signalled by eight bells rung in four pairs. Nowadays, use of the bell is largely ceremonial; sailors have wristwatches and mobile phones, but the language lingers on among those steeped in the tradition.

The more perceptive among you will have noticed that the two dog watches are of only two hours' duration. This is not an error on my part, but an official means of enabling all hands to have an evening meal.

The Wardroom is the naval officers' equivalent of a mess. In the eighteenth century it was called the 'Wardrobe', and it was used for storing prizes of war. For some reason, naval officers liked to congregate in it, possibly to keep an eye on their spoils and to remind themselves of the reason they joined in the first place.

The **RNVR**, or Royal Naval Volunteer Reserve, was, in peacetime, a part-time adjunct of the Royal Navy, just as the Territorial Army was to the regular army, and the Royal Air Force Volunteer Reserve was to the RAF. Those recruited for Hostilities Only during World War Two were also taken into the RNVR. There were several naval reserves at one time, each with its own unique purpose, e.g. the Royal Naval Volunteer (Special) Reserve, the Royal Naval Volunteer (Wireless) Reserve, the Royal Naval Minewatching Service, and the Royal Naval Reserve, which, at the time of this story, consisted of Merchant Navy personnel who had volunteered to serve with the Royal Navy. In the mid-1950s, however, the Admiralty drew all its reserves into one new Royal Naval Reserve, a force which could be mobilised at any time to reinforce the professional Royal Navy.

The battlecruiser was the result of an initiative on the part of the Admiralty in the early 20th century, to combine the firepower of the battleship with the superior speed of the cruiser. The economy of armour plate necessary to ensure that speed made such ships vulnerable to shellfire and, notably in the case of *HMS Repulse*, aerial attack. The *Scharnhorst*, which appears in this book, was and is often referred to as a battlecruiser, but in reality it was a fast battleship, a more practical type of ship altogether.

To **ease springs** before a social occasion and before the port and cigars is to relieve oneself. The nautical allusion is to the routine reduction in the tension of the 'springs', the lines that restrict a ship's fore and aft movement at its moorings.

Postings and Drafts are essentially the same thing. Officers receive a notice of posting, whereas ratings are given a draft chit. The difference is in the language, which is polite in one case, and simple and direct in the other. I imagine it is obvious to the reader which is which.

Good Conduct Badges. Ratings up to and including petty officer are given a chevron worn on the left arm for each four years' good conduct, up to a maximum of three, representing at least twelve years' satisfactory service, or, as the lower deck would have it, 'undetected crime'. A 'three badge' junior rating is therefore highly experienced, although his lack of enthusiasm for promotion is often seen as laziness and self-indulgence.

A **Pot Mess** is basically a stew made on a hob with any kind of meat. The term is also used to describe a scene of untidiness.

'Nelson's Bridge for boarding First Raters' wasn't really what William had in mind for an evening's diversion, but a tactic devised by Lord Nelson, which involved boarding and taking possession of the most valuable prize, an enemy battleship with three gun decks, or 'first-rate ship of the line', and then using that ship as a bridge for boarding another.

Whilst the foregoing are examples of an arcane official language, the slang of the lower deck is known familiarly as 'Jackspeak' and is simply impenetrable, although its use does seem to be on the wane, as sailors spend more time playing with their mobile phones than in conversation, but that seems to be the route society has taken.

RH

THE ADMIRALTY, LONDON

DECEMBER 1943

Room 33 had been William's home at the Admiralty since 1940, when he and Lucy Pendleton, his assistant, had been required, as newcomers to the work of the Deception Committee or, London Controlling Section, as it had become known, to form the nucleus of the Department of Maritime Zoological Warfare.

It was the perfect partnership; Lucy was completely supportive and always ready to offer ideas, usually from an unusual perspective and, almost inevitably, she'd become very much a part of William's personal life as well. The only problem now was that she'd disappeared, although not totally; there were those in authority who knew exactly where she was. Unfortunately, all William was allowed to know was that she was in the United States, where she was still engaged in deception.

His thoughts about her were interrupted when the telephone rang.

'Room Thirty-Three,' he answered. 'Lieutenant Commander Stamford speaking.'

'Hello, Stamford.' The voice was Captain Challock's. 'Will you come to my room? I have a visitor I want you to meet.'

'Aye-aye, sir.' William put down the telephone, picked up his cap and straightened his uniform before taking the stairs down to Room Twelve, which was Challock's office.

When, at Challock's invitation, he opened the door and stepped inside, he saw immediately that the other officer in the room wore a star above the four rings on his sleeve and was therefore a captain in the United States Navy. He was also wearing his cap, so William saluted him. His first words, however, were to Captain Challock.

'Good morning, sir. May I congratulate you on your promotion? I only heard about it this morning.'

'Thank you, Stamford.' Turning to his visitor, Challock said, 'Captain Boyle, I'd like you to meet Lieutenant Commander Stamford, one of our most valued officers. Captain Boyle has come to us as US Liaison Officer, Stamford.'

The two exchanged greetings, and Boyle took William's hand, but his features gave no indication of friendliness. Instead, he said, 'So you're the guy who convinced the Nazis you were using dolphins to hunt U-boats.'

'Porpoises, actually, sir.'

Boyle shrugged. 'They're the same kind of thing, I guess, but it beats me how they fell for a story that wouldn't fool a babe in the wood.'

Challock looked half amused. 'I take it you're not impressed,' he said.

'No, Captain Challock, I am not. Lieutenant Commander Stamford would have to invent something a whole lot better than that to take me for a ride.'

Still smiling, Challock told William, 'There's a challenge for you, Stamford, although I'm not inclined to place a bet on it.'

Boyle continued to look unimpressed. He was dark-haired, with a blue chin and heavy jowls that created a forbidding appearance.

'I'll do my best, sir,' said William, 'but I hardly know Captain Boyle, so it's rather like bowling at invisible stumps.'

'Like what?' Boyle's tone alone betrayed his impatience as well as his incomprehension.

'It's an allusion to cricket,' Challock explained. 'Stamford and I are both devotees of the game.'

'I guess cricket is what you guys play instead of baseball.'

'Except that cricket came first,' said William, adding generously, 'I did play baseball at school, sir.'

'You did?' It was an expression of semi-disbelief.

'It was nothing like Major League Baseball, of course, but we were a relatively small school. Having said that, though, we persuaded a number of schools to adopt the game and, before long, we were able to form a league. It became very popular. We even had our kit made at a factory in New Jersey.'

In spite of himself, Boyle was inquisitive. 'So, how did your school come to learn about baseball?'

'I introduced the game, sir.'

Captain Challock appeared to become vitally interested in the state of his thumbnail.

'*You* did?'

'My school was very forward-looking and open to new ideas. As a matter of fact, I first became enthusiastic about baseball when I visited my uncle in Philadelphia and watched the Phillies for the first time. The visit was a fifteenth birthday present for me, and one I'll never forget.'

'What year was that?'

'Nineteen-thirty-two, sir.'

'They came fifth in the National Series, I believe.'

'Are you sure, sir? I thought they were fourth.'

For the first time, Boyle seemed unsure of himself. 'Of course. I was maybe thinking of nineteen twenty-nine. Whereabouts in Philadelphia did your uncle live?'

'In Chestnut Hill. Do you know it, sir?'

'I know *of* it. Does your uncle still live there?'

'Regrettably not, sir. He suffered a fatal accident four years ago.'

'What happened?'

'He was hit by a streetcar, sir, when his bicycle wheel became jammed in the track. It's always a risk, I'm told, but it was a sad loss all the same.'

'I'm sorry to hear about your uncle, Stamford.'

'Thank you, sir.'

'Stamford,' said Captain Challock, still maintaining a straight face, 'If you care to join me in the wardroom at eight bells, I'd like to buy you and Hughes a drink to celebrate my promotion.'

'Thank you, sir. I shall certainly join you. I can't speak for Lieutenant Commander Hughes, but I've never known him refuse a drink, so I'm sure he'll be there.'

'Good. Now, Stamford, have you anything you need to ask me about?'

'Yes, sir.' The thought had been at the forefront of William's mind for the past three weeks. 'When am I going to see Miss Pendleton again?'

'Not for a while, I'm afraid, Stamford. I realise you've come to depend on her for a great deal, and I'm trying to find you a temporary assistant, but you'll have to be patient.'

'Thank you for that, sir. I must say it's very frustrating, not knowing where she is or for how long she'll be there.'

'It's out of the question while she's in the USA, Stamford. They won't disclose her whereabouts to anyone but those most closely involved.'

'That is correct,' agreed Boyle, 'we take security pretty damn' seriously in the US Navy.'

'I imagined that might be the case, sir.'

'You'd better believe it, mister.'

———◆I◆———

The gathering in the wardroom was pleasant enough despite Boyle's presence, and both William and Dai Hughes were able to demonstrate their genuine pleasure at Captain Challock's promotion.

Once Challock and Boyle had left the wardroom, Dai asked, 'What do you make of Boyle, William?'

'Anchor-faced to the point of caricature, and not at all impressed with my track record, I have to say.'

'He strikes me the same way. Believe it or not, he wanted to know why I'm still unfit for service with the fleet, although I don't know whether he was criticising me or the hospital.'

William nodded sympathetically. Dai's lungs had been affected by toxic gas when the submarine in which he was serving was damaged, and he was lucky to have survived the condition. 'Either way,' he said, 'the fault lies with the British.'

'He doesn't even make any allowance for the Welsh,' observed Dai glumly.

'Whereas we do as a matter of course.'

'I'd say that remark has just cost you a drink.'

'All right, I'll get them.' William beckoned the steward and ordered two gins. When they arrived, he signed for them and handed one to Dai. 'Mud in your eye,' he said, raising his glass.

'*Iechyd da.*' Good manners prompted Dai to ask, 'What did he have to say about your track record?'

'Just that he couldn't believe the enemy swallowed the DMZW. He said it would take something a lot more convincing than that to make a monkey out of him.'

'I hope you set him right, mun. It seems to me it was the reason you were put on this planet.'

'Yes, I convinced him that I'd played baseball, that I'd developed the passion for it when I was visiting my uncle in Philadelphia, and that, in a moment of carelessness, my uncle's life was brought to a premature and abrupt end when he was hit by a streetcar.'

'Good for you, mun.' Dai looked thoughtful for a second and asked, 'What's a streetcar?'

'A tram.'

'*Fy duw.* Why can't they speak English?'

William let that pass, and asked, 'How's the lovely Bea? I haven't seen her for a while.' Second Officer Beatrice Dean was Vice-Admiral Davies's secretary as well as his niece. She was also unofficially engaged to Dai.

'She's as lovely as ever, mun, and all set to come with me to North Wales to meet my family. That's if we ever get leave together.'

'Surely the admiral can swing it for you.'

'Ah, but he mustn't be seen bestowing favour on his niece.'

'Bad luck, Dai. I can see it's not the bed of roses it seems, being a flag officer's future nephew-in-law.'

Dai looked uncertain. 'Is there such a thing?'

'Be the first, Dai,' encouraged William. 'Strike a blow for Wales.'

'Buffoon. Anyway, have you heard when Lucy's likely to return?'

'Buy me a drink and I'll tell you.'

'Okay.' Dai went to the bar and returned a few minutes later with two gins. 'So,' he said, 'have you heard anything about Lucy?'

'Only that she's in America, which I already knew, and that her exact whereabouts are none of my business. Apparently, they take security pretty damn' seriously in the US Navy. You'd better believe it, mister.'

'Boyle?'

William nodded.

'Do you think he knows anything?'

'No, I doubt if the Americans trust him anymore than we do.' He put his glass down heavily and said, 'If we'd only got married when we first thought of it, she might have been excused whatever job they've lumbered her with.'

———— ►◄ ————

A few days later, Captain Challock ordered William to accompany him and Captain Boyle to a meeting with the Prime Minister. Challock declined to be drawn on the subject of the meeting, and the three proceeded in silence along the familiar passageway.

Having reached the stretch of corridor that led to the Prime Minister's office, they waited for the others to arrive, because, as William had suspected, the meeting was to be attended by the London Controlling Section.

First to arrive was Vice-Admiral Davies, a tall, spare man with dark, thinning hair that was beginning to show traces of grey. They shook hands, and the admiral spoke a few words with Boyle, having met him only briefly.

Before long, the others began to arrive. There were some whom William had not yet met, and Challock introduced him to them. One was a charming and immaculate RNVR officer called Fleming, who noticed William's medal ribbon and nodded his approval. The other was a tall man, who gave the appearance of being acquainted with the good life. He wore the uniform of an RAFVR officer, and William remembered hearing that he was the author of a number of popular novels.

Presently, the Prime Minister's secretary came to them and invited them to follow him. They entered the private office and penetrated a bank of cigar smoke to be greeted by the Prime Minister.

'Good afternoon, gentlemen. He consulted his notes and said, 'I believe we have the company of Captain Boyle of the United States Navy.' He scanned the assembled company. 'Where are you, Captain?'

Boyle took a pace forward and came to attention. 'Sir.'

'Stand easy, Captain. I only wish to welcome you, nothing more sinister than that.' He picked up a cigar from the box on his desk and added mischievously, 'At least, not yet.' His keen eye swept the room again and he said, 'Lieutenant Commander Stamford, thank goodness you're still with us. How are you coping without the services of the inestimable Miss Pendleton?' He struck a match and lit his cigar.

'With difficulty, sir. She left a vacuum in her wake.'

'Admirably put, Stamford, but I'm afraid her secondment was necessary, if not vital, to the conduct of the war.'

'I understand, sir.'

'Now, do be seated, all of you.' He waved his cigar in a familiar gesture. 'I have to tell you that the subject we are about to discuss is possibly the most sensitive of the whole war.' He paused to let his words take effect. 'I have just returned from a conference with President Roosevelt and the Soviet leader, Mr, er, Stalin, at which we were able to reach agreement that the Western Allies would mount an invasion of Europe....' He teased them with a dramatic pause before breaking the suspense. 'Next year.'

There was a shocked silence. Everyone knew the invasion must happen eventually, but the decision still took them unawares.

'I need hardly impress upon you the need for total secrecy. Only a small number of senior officers is aware of the development, and I intend to keep it so. Now, you all have Ultra Clearance and each of you is essential to the operation. That is why you are here.' A raised hand caused a flicker of annoyance to cross the Prime Minister's face. 'Yes, Captain Boyle, what is it?'

'With all due respect, sir, the Prime Minister has referred to a small number of senior officers, but this gathering includes a junior officer.'

'Yes?'

'I am wondering, sir, what the Prime Minister's explanation is for including him in such a high-level briefing as this.'

William tensed himself for the Prime Minister's response, and he sensed that others were doing the same. When Mr Churchill spoke, however, it was not the angry outburst they expected, but a reproof of icy disapproval.

'I take it you are referring to Lieutenant Commander Stamford, Boyle. Is that so?'

'Yes, sir.'

'Firstly, I do not make a practice of explaining my decisions, but you are a newcomer to this gathering, so I shall make an isolated exception in your case. The second thing you should know is that a lieutenant commander in the Royal Navy is classed as a senior officer. Thirdly, Lieutenant Commander Stamford has proved himself to be invaluable and is present at my invitation because I shall require his services yet again. Do I make myself clear?'

'Yes, sir.'

'Good, and there is one more thing, Captain. I prefer not to be addressed in the third person. I feel as if I am being discussed in my absence. You may, of course, wish to do that later; in fact, I should be disappointed if you did not. It would mean that I had failed to make a lasting impression, and heaven forbid that such a state of affairs should ever be allowed to exist.' His last remark provoked polite laughter from the gathering. 'I shall acquaint you with your orders in due course, gentlemen. Meanwhile, thank you all for attending. Vice-Admiral Davies and Lieutenant Commander Stamford, please remain behind for one moment.'

The admiral and William waited until the others were gone.

'Vice-Admiral Davies, I want you to arrange the promotion of Lieutenant Commander Stamford to Commander with immediate effect.'

'Aye-aye, sir.'

'As he is a part of this enormous undertaking, he should hold a rank commensurate with his responsibility.' Mr Churchill gave the admiral a mischievous look and said, 'He will also be a senior officer in the eyes of our allies as well as in ours.'

'Just so, sir.'

'I'm most grateful, sir,' said William. 'Thank you very much.'

'I shall be asking a great deal of you, Stamford. Until then, carry on, both of you.'

'Aye-aye, sir.'

'Aye-aye, sir.'

2

Captain Challock was alone when he sent for William, although the shadow of Captain Boyle was never far away.

'I had to let the cat out of the bag, Stamford,' said Challock. 'He was keen to find out which schools took part in your baseball league. I think he wanted to send the story home, to *The New York Herald Tribune*, no less.'

'That could have been embarrassing, sir,' agreed William.

'Did you ever play baseball, Stamford? Before you answer, bear in mind the importance of good relations with our allies.'

'Never, sir.'

'Never visited the USA?' Challock shook his head as he asked the question.

'No, sir.'

'And I suppose you never had an uncle in Philadelphia?'

'Not as far as I'm aware, sir.'

'Then how on earth did you know that the Philadelphia whatever-they-were-called came fourth in the National Series?'

'I didn't, sir. I just took a chance on Captain Boyle being similarly vague on the subject. The details about Philadelphia I learned from a novel I once read. It was very boring, and I now wish I hadn't persevered with it.'

Challock nodded. 'I'll smooth things over,' he said. 'It was my fault for egging you on, although what Captain Boyle said was as good as a challenge.' After some thought, he said, 'I shouldn't say this, Stamford, but the Atlantic Ocean has a mysterious property.'

'Has it, sir?'

'Oh yes, you see, ships have been able, since Viking times, to cross from east to west and make the return voyage. What is more, within the past twenty-five years, aeroplanes have followed their example. At a price, even telephone calls can be made to and from the USA. It all seems so easy nowadays, but there is one human trait that, despite mankind's most earnest efforts, remains incapable of making the transatlantic crossing.'

William was well-acquainted with Challock's propensity for creating suspense and he was inclined to be patient. 'What is that, sir?'

'Humour, Stamford.'

'I'm inclined to agree, sir.' The answer was unexpected but rational enough.

'And it's a two-way impediment.' Challock was warming to his argument. 'It's not simply a case of the Americans being obtuse; it affects both nationalities equally. Take the actor George Burns as an example. Now, he has a reputation in the USA as a comedian, although his talent is apparently lost on us. Whilst we're searching his patter for some concealed nuance that may hold the key to a latent or advanced form of humour, the Americans are already laughing themselves silly at every sentence he utters.'

'I find his humour elusive too, sir.'

'Good. I'm glad it's not just me. You know, Stamford, one day, psychiatrists may hit on a solution to the problem, but they currently have their hands full with casualties from this war, so let's not expect too much too soon.'

'Of course not, sir.'

'Meanwhile, the war continues.' He leaned forward with his hands together, almost in an attitude of prayer. 'If you wanted to entice the *Scharnhorst* from its berth in God-knows-what Fjord, how would you go about it?'

'Always provided capital ships were available to administer the knockout blow, I suppose I'd let the Nazi High Command know of the whereabouts of a nice, juicy convoy, sir.'

Challock nodded slowly. 'There would be a risk attached,' he said.

'From aircraft and U-boats, sir?'

'Yes, at least from U-boats. The weather is currently not on the side of the *Luftwaffe*.'

'It would call for a heavy screen of destroyers. Also, what heavy units would be available, sir?'

'A cruiser squadron and the battleship *Duke of York*.'

'Oh, if the *Scharnhorst* could be coaxed into coming within range of the *Duke of York*'s guns....' It was an appealing image. The battlecruiser *Scharnhorst* had been a powerful but elusive threat for far too long.

'Prepare a report, Stamford. Concentrate on how *Scharnhorst* and the Nazi High Command could best be tempted and be as quick as you like. As we speak, convoy JW 55B is on course for Murmansk and is due to dock there shortly after Christmas.'

———◆◀———

From William's point of view, the task was an easy one. He was as familiar as anyone with the nature of *Operation Ostfront*, the *Kriegsmarine*'s plan to intercept and sink convoys before they could re-supply the Soviet army and air force, and he knew what must be uppermost in the minds of the Nazi High Command.

He delivered his report to Captain Challock that afternoon.

'Things have been going badly for the Nazis since the Battle of Stalingrad, sir,' he reminded him, 'and it's now more than ever vital for them that they prevent supplies from reaching the Soviet forces. That alone should be sufficient to make the Nazi High Command take the baited hook.'

'We know, though, that Hitler is disillusioned with his surface fleet. The loss of *Bismarck* did the *Kriegsmarine*'s standing no good at all, and therefore there's the question of whether or not he'll countenance another foray by *Scharnhorst*.'

'I think we have to consider the *Kriegsmarine*'s point of view, sir. They must be desperate, by this time, to convince Hitler of the surface fleet's worth. I think they'll order *Scharnhorst* to attack the convoy.'

Challock closed the report and put it into his briefcase. 'I'll put this before the LCS,' he said. 'I think they'll give it their approval.'

'I take it the information will be passed to the enemy via the usual channels, sir?'

'Yes, Stamford. The Nazis have an agent in Rosyth, someone we're keeping under surveillance. She'll pass it to a double agent there, and he'll transmit the goods to Berlin. I'm told it will be as good as whispering in Hitler's ear.'

'And then we can stand by for the main event, sir.'

Challock held up a cautionary hand. '*If* the High Command take the bait, *if* they give the task to *Scharnhorst*, and *if* the Commander-in-Chief can lure her into his trap, that's when we can expect something to happen.'

———◂▸◂———

Later that night, at his flat in Clapham, William sat at the piano. In his haste to move to alternative accommodation, the owner of the flat had left the Bechstein and several other luxuries behind, and William had been quick to appreciate them.

His current project was the piano part of the Sonata in A for Violin and Piano by Brahms. Lucy had presented him with it shortly before being whisked away, and now he was keeping faith with her by practising it for her return. He was a highly capable sight reader, but Lucy had convinced him of the need to practise in order to appreciate and execute hidden facets that might otherwise escape his notice.

It was a beautiful piece, and William, who had played very little by Brahms, felt that he'd been introduced to a new friend. He worked on, completely absorbed, until the chiming clock told him it was ten o'clock and time for a drink.

He poured gin and Indian tonic water, courtesy of one of the wardroom stewards, into a tumbler. All it lacked was a slice of lime or lemon, but those luxuries, like many others, were a pre-war memory, so he drank it without.

As he drank, he wondered if the London Controlling Section had seen his report. From what Captain Challock had told him, it seemed that time was almost as scarce as exotic fruit.

———◂▸◂———

Challock summoned him the following afternoon.

'I have three things to tell you, Stamford,' he said. 'The first is that the LCS gave your report their unanimous approval.'

'That's excellent news, sir.'

'The second is that the information is about to be fed to the enemy, if it has not already been, er, communicated.'

'That's even better, sir.'

'Quite. The third is that I've spoken with Captain Boyle and poured a quantity of oil on his troubled waters. It actually cost me a small fortune in something called bourbon, apparently pronounced "burben", so "oil" is possibly not the most appropriate word to use.'

'I know what you mean, sir, and that's what matters.'

Challock looked puzzled. 'What is "Bourbon", Stamford? Do you know? Until last evening, I thought it was a French dynasty, albeit with different pronunciation.'

'I believe it's a kind of spirit distilled from rye, sir. Apparently, the Red Indians called it "firewater".'

'I'm not surprised. I tried it and it tasted like TCP, not that I'd ever consider gargling with it.'

William was more concerned with the outcome of the drinking session. 'What was Captain Boyle's attitude in the end, sir?'

'He was quite affable.' Challock considered that assessment and said, 'At least, as affable as could be expected. Unfortunately, you are still less than popular. There is a limit to my powers.'

'I'm sure you did your best, sir.'

'Oh, I did, Stamford.' Clearly still nursing a hangover, Challock closed his eyes to gain what relief he could. Then he opened them, apparently having remembered something. 'There was a fourth thing I had to tell you, Stamford,' he said.

'Yes, sir?' William braced himself.

'I heard tell of an old acquaintance of yours this morning.'

'Who was that, sir?' Drawing information from Captain Challock required time and patience.

'Cast your mind back, Stamford, to your early days at the Admiralty, when you were fallible and naïve. I'm referring to none other than Commander Bonnington. He's currently serving in Sheerness.'

'Good grief.' It was no wonder the news evoked a startled reaction. In response to an unintentional slight, Bonnington had demanded William's return to the fleet. Only Lucy's influence and intervention had saved him.

Challock was clearly amused. 'You look as though you've seen a ghost, Stamford,' he said.

'Worse than that, sir, I'm reminded of the time my days in Naval Intelligence almost came to a premature end.'

'It would never have happened. Vice-Admiral Davies would have given you an avuncular reprimand and returned you to your duties. Take it from me.'

'I didn't know that, sir.' The shock of hearing Bonnington's name was beginning to recede. 'Is he still a commander, sir?'

'He is, and is likely to remain so until he exchanges his uniform cap for a bowler.'

'In any case, our paths are unlikely to cross again.'

His remark caused Challock to smile. 'You can never say that with any certainty, Stamford. The Royal Navy is a small world and a large family.'

3

North Queensferry, Fife

Thomas Gael wrapped his scarf more firmly around his neck and throat, and shivered in spite of his heavy, tweed overcoat. He resented the order that had sent him to Scotland. Ireland was wet, it was true, but Scotland was much colder, and the Scots were welcome to it.

He had to meet *Agentin Elster*, who had secret intelligence for him. He was told to wait at the junction of Ferry Lane and Ferry Road, where *Elster* would carry out the introduction with a coded greeting. He shivered and continued to wait. He knew quite a lot about *Agentin Elster*, although he was about to meet her for the first time.

It was a deserted spot, which was probably why *Elster* had chosen it. The only sounds Gael could hear were the buffeting wind and the cry of the seagulls. A car approached, but its driver took no interest in him. It continued to the top of Ferry Lane.

After a while, another sound came to his ears, and he identified it as the crunch of tyres on gravel. He turned and saw a woman, wrapped as he was, in tweeds, and on a bicycle, but he had to wait for the coded greeting.

The woman came closer and stopped beside him. 'Good afternoon,' she said. Her accent was English. 'Can you direct me to the Food Office?'

The coded greeting came as a surprise; he hadn't expected *Agentin Elster* to arrive on a bicycle, but he responded immediately.

'The nearest food office is in Edinburgh.'

She sighed. 'Such a long way.'

'On a bicycle, yes.'

'But a bicycle is very convenient.'

'I'm charmed to make your acquaintance, *Agentin Elster*,' said Gael. 'I believe you have something for me.'

'Yes.' She took a package wrapped in oilskin from her basket and handed it to him, saying, 'The information in this file must go to Berlin immediately.'

'All right, I'll see to it.'

'Good, and there's one more thing.'

'What's that?'

A gust of wind blew her coat lapel across her face, and she removed it irritably. 'My time at Rosyth is over. They've posted me to Chatham.'

'And just where on God's earth would that be?'

'It's a huge naval base and dockyard in North Kent, you Irish clot.'

'Sure, if I didn't know whose side you were on, I could take exception to that remark.'

'Just wait for your orders, but get that information to Berlin straight away.'

'Okay.'

She gave him a brief nod and cycled away.

He watched her with a hint of regret. As far as he could see, she was a fine-looking woman. It was just a pity she felt the way she did about the Irish. Still, they'd warned him about that. He walked back gratefully to his lodgings. It was only half-past three, and his landlady would be out until five. He would have ample time to read the document and send the message to Berlin.

———◆◄———

'Will you be going home for Christmas, Stamford?'

'Yes, sir. Will you?'

'Yes, and I'm looking forward to it. One of the good things about serving in a stone frigate is that the usual festivities can be observed.' Challock had never made a secret of the fact that his preference would have been a sea-going appointment. He was a professional naval officer, and his normal function was to be at sea, but he was also sensible enough to realise that his current appointment was possibly of greater value to the allied cause.

'I wonder how many more Christmases this war will see.'

'Oh, don't start that game, Stamford. There's nothing to be gained by it. Just be patient.'

'I'm impatient for cricket to be resumed, sir.'

'So am I. Did you hear, by the way, that Hedley Verity was killed earlier this year?'

'No, sir, I didn't. That's a tragedy.'

'Of course, you don't read the papers, do you? He was with the army in Italy.'

William could only shake his head in sorrow.

'And Bill Bowes was taken prisoner last year.'

'I did hear about that, sir. What have the Germans got against Yorkshire's bowling attack, or the MCC's, if it comes to that? They don't even play cricket.'

'You tell me, Stamford. You're the expert on how the enemy thinks.'

———— ◆►◄ ————

Marguerite Werner was tired. The journey from Edinburgh to London had taken far too long, and she still had to face the onward journey to Chatham. She reached up for her suitcase, but a voice behind her said, 'Allow me.' It was the captain in the Essex Regiment who, since Grantham, had been trying somewhat clumsily to disguise his interest in her. He lifted the case down for her.

'How very kind of you. Thank you.'

'Have you far to go?'

'Victoria Station.' She smiled. 'I have someone waiting for me.'

'Of course.' He picked up his grip and concealed his disappointment as far as he could. 'Cheerio.'

'Cheerio.' She followed him and the others as they left the train at King's Cross Station. There was a queue for the ticket barrier, but at least she was less than an hour from her destination, so she waited patiently.

Eventually, she gave up her ticket at the gate and was continuing towards the exit when a man appeared at her right-hand side. As she turned to avoid him, another appeared on her left.

The first man asked, 'Miss Marguerite Werner?'

'What do you want?'

'We want you to come with us.'

'Who are you?'

'We are police officers. Just do as I ask.'

'This is ridiculous.'

With no alternative, she allowed them to take her through the exit to a car waiting outside. One of the men put her suitcase in the boot and the other guided her firmly into the back seat of the car.

'Where are we going?'

Her fellow occupant on the back seat said, 'To New Scotland Yard.'

'This is nonsense.'

They drove on in silence. Marguerite was anxious to protest her innocence of any charge they might want to bring against her, but she was equally reluctant to say too much.

The car entered Victoria Embankment and drew up inside the portals of New Scotland Yard, where the two detectives ushered her inside. After some procedure at the desk, they took her down a passage to an empty room painted drab green. An unshaded light bulb hung over a plain, deal table and three wooden chairs. An empty Wills cigarette tin evidently served as an ashtray.

One of them asked, 'Would you like a cup of tea, Miss Werner?'

'That's the least you can offer me.'

'Milk and sugar?'

'No sugar, thank you.'

'Sit down. I shan't be a minute.'

'Good, and then you can tell me what this ridiculous charade is all about.'

After a few minutes, the officer returned with three cups of tea, which he placed on the table. 'Now, Miss Werner,' he said, 'or maybe you prefer to be called *"Agentin Elster"*, let's have a little chat about the work you've been doing for the *Abwehr*. You won't need to tell us very much, because we've been watching you for some time, and we know you're a Nazi spy.'

'I'm a British citizen.'

'We know, and we also know about your German father and his Nazi sympathies.'

'Leave my father out of this.'

'Oh, but we can't possibly do that. You see, he also has been questioned by the police, and is proving rather more co-operative than you.'

'I don't believe you.'

The detective took out a silver cigarette case and opened it. 'Cigarette?'

She made no reply, but took one and accepted a light.

'What was your work at Rosyth Naval Base?'

'I was a secretary. Look, surely I'm allowed legal representation. I want to see a solicitor.'

'You can see a solicitor when we charge you. These proceedings come under the Emergency Powers Defence Act of Nineteen Thirty-Nine, and you don't enjoy the same rights as you would if it were a normal criminal investigation.'

'How awful. What kind of country has this become?'

'An infinitely more liberal one than that for which you've been spying.'

The other detective, who had so far been quiet, said, 'You know the penalty for spying for an enemy power, don't you, Miss Werner, not to mention an act of treason?'

'No, I don't, and I'm only British because I was born here.'

'The same can be said of most of us, *Agentin Elster*.'

'You know what I mean, and I don't know why you're calling me that.'

'Don't you, Miss Werner?'

'No, I don't.' She eyed the two detectives resentfully. They were both smartly dressed in sober suits, white shirts, and one of them wore an MCC tie. Otherwise, they could have blended into the background anywhere. She regretted not having done so herself.

'We know a great deal about you, but a confession would help your cause immeasurably. You understand that, don't you?'

The first detective stubbed out his cigarette and said, 'You were seen removing a Top Secret file from your Commanding Officer's desk. Why did you take it?'

'When was this supposed to happen?'

'Two days ago. You returned the file later in the day, presumably having made a fair copy. You were then seen in the company of a known enemy agent at the junction of Ferry Road and Ferry Lane, North Queensferry. You handed a packet to him. What did it contain?'

'It's impossible.'

'Did you imagine you were unobserved?'

'There was no one th…. It never happened.'

'Drink your tea before it gets cold, Miss Werner.'

The first detective offered her another cigarette, which she took with a shaking hand.

The interrogation continued for a further hour with the detectives repeatedly going over the allegations.

'You were seen taking the file and returning it, and you were also seen in Ferry Lane, handing a packet to Thomas Gael. We have photographic evidence. I think it's time for you to come clean and tell us everything.'

'I've nothing to tell you,' she said wearily. 'It's all nonsense.'

'If you want to avoid the hangman's rope, Miss Werner, and it is still possible to do so, you'd better spend some time alone, thinking about the situation in which you find yourself.' Turning to his colleague, he said, 'Take her down to the cells.'

———◆┃◆———

Once again, Captain Challock invited William and Dai, this time joined by Bea, to meet him in the wardroom.

'I just want to buy you all a drink, to thank you for your efforts throughout the year, and to wish you all a very happy Christmas.' He raised his glass. 'Happy Christmas.'

'Happy Christmas, sir,' they chorused.

'Well, I know Stamford's going home to Kent, but what are you two doing this Christmas?'

'We're going to visit Bea's family,' Dai told him, 'and then we're going to Wales.'

'Well, I hope you have a marvellous time. Is this when you make the engagement official?'

'That's right, sir,' confirmed Bea self-consciously.

'In that case, let me offer you my heartiest congratulations and best wishes.'

'Thank you, sir.'

'Thank you, sir.'

'I'd like to offer you mine, as well,' said William, deeply conscious of Lucy's absence, 'and Lucy's on her behalf.'

'Lucy will be back,' said Bea perceptively, 'you'll see.'

'I hope so.' William glanced at Captain Challock, who appeared to be vitally interested in a nineteenth century print of the Battle of Trafalgar. It was clear to William that he knew more than he was prepared to divulge.

'How's the chest, Hughes?' Challock asked the question, presumably to change the subject.

'A lot better, thank you, sir. Before very long, I should be "in all respects ready for sea and for war", as they say.'

'I should hope not,' said Bea. 'You've done your share.'

'He has, Miss Dean,' agreed Captain Challock, 'but you can't blame him for being dedicated.'

'I remember how keen I was in nineteen-forty,' said William, 'and I also remember Vice-Admiral Davies's words to me on that occasion.'

'But when you thought Commander Bonnington was going to send you back to sea,' said Challock, 'you realised you were converted. At least, that's how I remember it.'

'That's right, sir.

'And you know the admiral was right.'

'Yes, sir, he was.' William made his reply almost without thinking. The Trafalgar print had prompted thoughts of the fleet, which were difficult to dispel, because the curtain was about to rise on a naval engagement of supreme importance.

Marguerite Werner's reply was little more than a broken whisper. 'I took the file and copied it. I gave the film to Gael.'

'Marguerite Werner,' said the first detective formally, 'I am arresting you for espionage and treason under the Treachery Act of nineteen-forty. You may call a legal adviser, but I think we should first bring in one of our military colleagues to discuss the possibility of clemency.'

For the first time since being confined to her cell, Marguerite lifted her head. Tears coursed down her cheeks as she asked, 'How can I expect clemency?'

'By co-operating with the Allies.'

4

William arrived home expecting to find his sister Jane alternately agitated and indulgent as she coped with two over-excited children. Instead, the house was deserted, so he dropped his bag and walked round to the chemist's shop.

The girl on the counter was unfamiliar to him, but he was aware that young women were frequently directed into the forces or other war work, so it was no surprise that the girl he knew had moved on.

'Good afternoon,' he said, removing his cap. 'Is my mother about?'

The girl gave him a strange look and asked, 'Who's your mother, then?'

'Mrs Stamford. Unless things have changed since her last letter, she owns this shop.'

'Well, I didn't know she was your mother. She's in the back.'

'In the pharmacy?'

'Yeah.' She delivered her reply as if to a silly question, which, he had to admit, it was.

'You're new, obviously.'

'I'm temporary.' She looked at the clock and said, 'Until six o'clock. The usual girl will be back on the twenty-ninth. She's had the 'flu.'

'I'm sorry to hear that.'

The girl peered at the epaulettes on his greatcoat and asked, 'What are you, then?'

'I'm the Commissionaire at the Odeon Cinema in Leicester Square.'

She appeared to find the information fascinating. ''Ere,' she said, 'do you get in to see the pictures for noffink?'

24

He shrugged. 'Yes.'

'You don't sound very excited about it.'

'You can get used to anything after a while.'

'I wouldn't mind a job like that,' she said wistfully.

'What are you going to do after Christmas?'

'I'm going in the ATS.'

'Good luck.' With an unhelpful attitude like hers, she would need it.

He was spared further dealings with her when his mother came through from the pharmacy.

'William,' she said, 'I thought it was your voice I heard just now.' She lifted the hinged section of the counter to join him.

'Hello, Mum.' He drew her into a long hug. They hadn't seen each other for a long time. 'There was no one at home, so I came round here.'

'I meant to leave a note for you. George arrived home this morning. He's got a longer leave than we expected, and they're all over at their house. They're coming to us tomorrow.' She looked up at the clock and saw that it was ten minutes to six. 'Doris,' she said to the girl, 'you can go now if you like.' Returning to the other side of the counter, she opened the cash till and took two one-pound notes and several coins. 'Here are your wages. Thank you, have a happy Christmas and good luck in the ATS.'

'Fanks. Merry Christmas, then.' She took the money and left.

'That girl is to charm what Jane is to modesty,' observed William, 'and I'm talking about the cartoon character, not my sister.'

'I should hope not.' His mother looked at him sharply and asked, 'Have you taken to reading the *Daily Mirror*?'

'I don't read any paper, Mum. They're all too depressing.'

'Well, how do you know about Jane?'

'Blokes have told me about her. It's shameful, the way she goes on, taking off her clothes and parading in her underwear.'

His mother shook her head. 'I never know when to take you seriously,' she said.

'Never mind, Mum. Neither does anyone else.'

———✦———

In keeping with family tradition, William and his mother saw Christmas in with Holy Communion at Christchurch. Counter assistants might come and go, but some things never changed.

Christmas Day and Boxing Day were as they'd always been, with the added pleasure of George's extended company. For the past three years, his Christmas leave had been all too brief, but now the children had their dad for the whole of the Christmas season, although that didn't deter Harry from asking an embarrassing question.

'Dad, how is it that Uncle William's a commander, and you're only a squadron leader, and you're older than he is?'

'I don't think age has anything to do with it, Harry. What do you think, William?'

'I think I've just been lucky. The Prime Minister likes to be surrounded by senior officers, and that meant he had to promote me.'

'I bet you've never even met the Prime Minister,' said Harry.

'Oh, I go down to his office from time to time. We have been known to have an occasional glass of champagne together.'

It was too much for Pamela. 'You should grow a long nose, like Pinocchio,' she said, 'for telling whoppers.'

'Oh, is that what it is?' William felt the end of his nose. 'It's certainly longer than it was yesterday. I noticed it when I was shaving.' The children laughed, and William was happy. No one ever believed the truth when he told it.

His sister Jane's curiosity was of a more romantic kind. 'I haven't had time to ask you until now, William. Are you still seeing Lucy?'

'Yes and no.'

'Well, which is it?'

'There's nothing wrong between us. It's just that she's been posted away and I haven't seen her for several weeks.'

Jane was incredulous. 'Haven't you written to her?'

'We're not allowed to communicate with each other. Security, you know.'

'Nonsense.'

'Security,' said George. 'They speak of little else. I wonder if we'll all be so reticent when the war's over. Somehow, I doubt it.'

'She's a lovely girl as well,' said Jane, convinced that the separation was her brother's fault. 'Do you remember Christmas in the Blitz? That was when she got all the children singing in the air raid shelter.'

William preferred not to be tormented by the memory, but there was little he could say.

Jane's curiosity was undiminished. 'Have you spoken to her family? They'd know where she is.'

'No, they don't, Jane. They're just as much in the dark as I am. All we know is that she's in America.'

'America?' Harry was instantly excited. 'Is Auntie Lucy in America?'

'Yes, Harry. For all I know, she might be hunting buffalo or roping steers.' In the interests of credibility, he said, 'Not today, of course. They celebrate Christmas there as well.'

'I'm sure you could find out her address if you tried, especially now you've been promoted.'

'Jane,' he told her quietly, 'if I could write to her, I would. The fact is, I'm missing her like hell, and I don't want to argue about it; in fact, I'd rather not talk about it at all.'

'Fair comment,' said George. 'Let's talk about something else.'

'Well, I think it's ridiculous,' said Jane.

'That's your freedom,' said her husband. 'We're missing the one o'clock news.'

William got up and switched on the wireless set.

'It takes ages to warm up,' said his mother. 'I think there's something wrong with it.'

'They'll read the headlines again at the end,' Jane reminded her.

When the sound came up, they recognised the voice of Roy Rich. It was the briefest of bulletins, simply because there was no real news apart from a reference to the fighting in Russia, which continued to go in Stalin's favour. The harsh Russian winter had set in, and Hitler's retreating army was defending itself against the weather as well as the Red Army.

'History's repeating itself,' observed George with some satisfaction. 'Hitler's paying the same penalty as Bonaparte.'

William thought about the cargoes he'd described for the *Kriegsmarine*'s benefit: fuel, ammunition, fighter and ground attack aircraft. If the message had reached Berlin, his ruse must have taken effect.

George continued to voice his thoughts on the subject. 'I have to wonder why Hitler was stupid enough to invade Russia in the first place.'

'I just can't imagine,' said William, thinking about the report he and Lucy had produced back in 1940.

'The man must have no imagination at all, to think he could stretch his supply lines over that distance.'

'Obsession leaves no room for imagination or analysis,' said William. 'The extremes of politics are too simplistic for mature consideration of any kind.'

'That's rather a deep observation,' said Jane with a hint of surprise.

'Maybe it was that sort of thing that made them promote him to commander,' said George good-naturedly.

It seemed to William that George's observation was a little too close to the mark. 'No,' he said, 'I've already told you. The Prime Minister likes to be surrounded by senior officers.'

'It's not what you know, but who you know,' observed Jane.

'That's just what I said to Mr Attlee only last week,' said William, 'and he agreed with me.'

'You never know when he's being serious,' said Jane to her husband.

'The safest way is never to believe him, Jane.'

It was good advice, although William was hopeful that the Nazi High Command would remain as gullible as ever.

———◆◄◆———

On the morning of the 27th, William rubbed his eyes and looked at the clock beside his bed. It was a little after seven, which meant that he'd missed the beginning of the news. Hurriedly, he grabbed his dressing gown and went downstairs to switch on the wireless set.

He waited impatiently for the set to warm up. There was the usual hum, which stopped when the announcer's voice became audible.

'....was finally sunk with torpedoes by the accompanying destroyer force. It is reported that there were only thirty-nine survivors.

'The Prime Minister has sent his personal congratulations to Vice-Admiral Sir Bruce Fraser.' There were several pieces of unimportant news, but William could only deduce that *Scharnhorst* had been sunk. Admiral Fraser was Commander-in-Chief of the Home Fleet, and that made it almost certain that they were talking about *Scharnhorst*. Eagerly, he waited for the headlines to be repeated and, at the end of the bulletin, he was rewarded.

'The German battlecruiser *Scharnhorst* has been sunk. These are the facts so far in our possession. The German ship was steaming north from her base in Norway to attack a British convoy bound for Murmansk when she was sighted by three cruisers of the Home Fleet, who opened fire, inflicting some damage. They drove her towards the battleship *HMS Duke of York*, which opened fire, reducing *Scharnhorst's* speed and ability to return fire. After suffering colossal damage inflicted by the British flagship, *Scharnhorst* was finally sunk with torpedoes by the accompanying destroyer force. It is reported that there were only thirty-nine survivors....'

They'd done it. After four years of cat-and-mouse frustration, they'd finally sunk the *Scharnhorst*.

5

William found Captain Challock similarly relieved.
'With *Tirpitz* out of action and *Scharnhorst* gone, we can breathe more easily,' he said.

'How badly was *Tirpitz* damaged, sir?' William had taken no part in the previous September's operation by midget submarines, so he knew little about it.

'The information we've gleaned from enemy transmissions suggests that the damage is critical, but that doesn't mean it can't be repaired. We're keeping our finger on the pulse.'

'Naturally, sir.'

Captain Challock leaned forward and placed his hands together. It was a familiar pose, and William knew he was about to hear something of importance, presumably unconnected with *Tirpitz* or any other enemy warship.

'I should remind you again of the need for absolute secrecy regarding *Operation Overlord*, Stamford.'

'Of course, sir.' William had learned only recently that *Overlord* was the codename for the invasion of Europe. As a junior member of the team, he was seldom included in the briefings of the LCS. Instead, most communications came to him via Captain Challock.

'There has been considerable discussion as to where the invasion is to take place. As you can imagine, there were several possibilities. I imagine you may have given the matter some thought.'

'Yes, sir. The favourites must be Calais, the South of France, the Low Countries – although that's questionable – and possibly Normandy.'

'Good thinking, Stamford. The Pas de Calais would involve

only the shortest of crossings, which would facilitate not only the assault itself, but air cover and logistics.'

'The South of France has possibilities, sir. The assault could be mounted from North Africa, as those on Sicily and Italy were, and it would take place in the Unoccupied Zone, where the enemy are thin on the ground.'

'What about the Low Countries, Stamford? They are the direct route to the nerve centre in Berlin.'

William was unconvinced. 'My preference is the Pas de Calais, sir, if only for the reasons you've given.'

Challock allowed himself a knowing smile. 'It's a fascinating game, isn't it, Stamford? The fact is that, whilst the plan is yet to be confirmed, the invasion zone that has been chosen is Normandy.'

'Normandy, sir?' William had considered it, but not seriously.

'There are several good reasons for the choice, absolutely none of which should concern us, because our task is to throw the enemy off the scent.'

'Where do we want him to expect the invasion, sir?'

'Anywhere but in Normandy. We have to keep the bugger guessing.'

'That covers a wide field, sir.'

'It does, and that is why several officers have been charged with the task of misleading the enemy. The various options, as you guessed, will include Southern France and the Pas de Calais. One that, I believe, you have not considered is Norway.' He watched William's expression change from expectation to disbelief. 'Oh, yes.' he confirmed, 'Norway is to be treated as a possibility, but your task, Stamford, is to make the case for the Low Countries.'

For a moment, William suspected that he'd misheard his superior. 'The Low Countries, sir?'

'Holland and Belgium,' confirmed Challock. 'For the purpose of this operation, you can forget Luxembourg.'

'So the job I'm required to do is not completely silly, sir.'

'Holland and Belgium are possibilities,' insisted Challock, 'and you may be assured that the Teutonic mentality is unlikely to share the humour that you obviously find in such a prospect.' He added for good measure, 'I doubt, also, that it would appreciate your proclivity for sarcasm and irony any more than I do.'

'I'm sorry, sir, but I'm going to struggle to sell the idea to myself, never mind the enemy.'

Challock was relentless. 'If you advertising johnnies can persuade the nation's young women that a nightly dose of opening medicine will give them a slender figure, then you're quite capable of persuading Hitler that the Low countries are a feasible option.'

'I wasn't responsible for Bile Beans, sir. That account went to a rival agency.'

'The principle is the same, and an invasion via the Low Countries is entirely credible when compared to the Department of Maritime Zoological Warfare or, for that matter, carrots being the night-fighter pilot's indispensable aid to night vision.'

William was only partly mollified. 'I still think I've drawn the short straw, sir.'

'Nonsense. We both know the short straw was Norway. Consider the poor bugger who drew that one.'

'He has my sympathy, sir, whoever he is.'

'Good. I'll convey your condolences to Captain Boyle when I see him.'

'Thank you, sir.' William struggled to maintain a straight face.

'Of course, you're not alone in this subterfuge, although you're unlikely to come into contact with your accomplices. One is an Irishman, an enemy agent whom we caught and successfully turned some time ago. The other was also working for the enemy until shortly before Christmas, when Special Branch caught up with her.'

'She doesn't sound very reliable, sir.'

'She's agreed to espouse the Allied cause, but it will be some time before we know we can trust her,' admitted Challock.

'Espionage is another world,' said William, thankful that he had no place in it.

'Agreed, Stamford, but on a lighter note, you will be at the wardroom dinner, won't you?'

'Dinner, sir?' William's thoughts were still with the clandestine, shadowy world of espionage.

'Tomorrow evening.'

'Oh, of course.' It was his duty to attend the dinner, although he had little enthusiasm for it.

'You're still moping about Miss Pendleton's absence, aren't you?'

'As I told the Prime Minister, sir, she left a vacuum in her stead.'

'I believe you and she are more than just colleagues. Isn't that so?'

'Yes, sir.' It was pointless to deny it. Challock was too perceptive for that.

'There's nothing wrong with that, Stamford, as long as you ensure that what happens ashore stays ashore.'

'Of course, sir.'

'In wartime, men are parted from their wives and sweethearts, often for long periods; even before the war, we were away for two or even three years, but you'll see her again, Stamford.'

———◆ㅐ◆———

William got to work on the project, making notes, adding to them and sometimes crossing them out altogether. He'd relied for so long on Lucy's input that working on his own was more difficult than he could have foreseen. He had to make the enemy suspect that an Allied assault on the Low Countries was not only feasible but likely, and he hadn't yet convinced himself.

At this point, Lucy would have made a remark or asked a question that would spark off a new idea. She might have asked something as innocent as, 'What is it like over there? I've never been to Holland.' What would he have told her? That it was very flat, much of it below sea level, and that the waters of the Rhine and Meuse were kept at bay by a system of dikes? There was a pumping system, as he recalled, powered at one time by windmills. The Dutch had attempted to stop the German advance in 1940 by flooding the countryside ahead of them, but the invading army came equipped for a waterborne assault, and the measure turned out to be completely ineffective.

That made him think. Wouldn't the Nazis use water as an obstacle? Their minds would presumably be open to any kind of seaborne or land-based obstruction or impediment that might hinder an Allied landing.

He remembered Lucy telling him at the time of the ill-conceived assault on Dieppe, that the first amphibious landings were made by the Ancient Greeks and Persians 3,000 years previously, with a similar lack of success. Much had been learned since then, however, and the US Marine Corps had since made a science of amphibious techniques involving special vehicles, which they were using in the Pacific. That set him thinking again, and he began to make notes.

———— ◆►◄ ————

'I don't know what the American amphibious vehicles are called, sir, but I know they're being deployed in the Pacific, and I imagine they'll be used in *Overlord*.'

'What do you have in mind, Stamford?'

'Reports of the movement of amphibious transport to the east coast would certainly raise a few Nazi eyebrows, but I wonder if it might be better to begin by dropping subtle hints, such as the requisitioning of large quantities of heavy axle grease and lead oxide paint.'

'Just to whet their appetites, eh?' Challock was clearly impressed.

'Yes, sir, and another idea came to me, although it first came to me more than three years ago, when we were trying to persuade Hitler to stay at home.'

'Trot it out, then.'

'At the time, I suggested that dredgers might be seen in the relatively shallow waters of harbours not normally associated with capital ships, sir. If the enemy were to suspect that those harbours were going to be used for increased traffic, that might also start them wondering.'

Challock was nodding, as if assimilating the idea. 'It's worth considering,' he said. 'The only foreseeable problem with the dredger idea is the risk of impeding normal harbour operations. Still, as I said, it's worth considering. Let me have a report and I'll put it to the LCS.'

'Aye-aye, sir.'

'If there's nothing else, Stamford, I'll see you this evening at the wardroom dinner.'

———◆◄◆———

William changed into mess undress uniform and made his way to the wardroom anteroom, where everyone was gathering before dinner.

He was delighted to find Dai and Bea there already. He shook hands with them both, aware that a degree of formality must be observed, although that didn't prevent him from asking, 'Bea, how do you do it?'

'How do I do what, sir?' There was fun in her eyes.

'How do you continue, despite the deprivation and restrictions of war, to be as glamorous as ever?'

'You're too kind, sir.'

'What I want to know,' said Dai, 'is why I can never frame a compliment in quite the same way that you do.'

'You have to work at it, Dai,' said William, 'although I'm sure Bea finds pleasure in every compliment you pay her.'

'I wouldn't go as far as that,' said Bea, with a mischievous smile that told Dai his efforts were no less appreciated. 'I'm going to leave you for a few minutes,' she told them.

'Bea's a game girl,' said Dai. 'She's learning Welsh now. She says it's so that she knows what my family are saying about her, but that's just her little joke.' An incident evidently came to mind, because he added, 'Mind you, I had to keep reminding them to speak English while we were there, Welsh being so much a part of everyday life.'

'But you both had a good Christmas, I imagine?'

'Excellent, mun. I showed her the sights, at least as far as I could in the time we had, and she was quite enchanted by them.' As he was reminded of another occurrence, he said, 'She was quite tearful when I showed her Gelert's grave and told her the story of Prince Llewelyn and his dog.'

'As our American allies say, Dai, you sure know how to show a girl a good time.'

'It was a bit of local colour, that's all.' He peered over William's shoulder and said, 'Speaking of American Allies, I see that Captain Boyle has been invited to this bunfight.'

'I suppose good manners had to prevail, and it'll give him something to criticise, so he'll be happy, just so long as no one makes a joke.'

'A joke, mun?'

'According to Captain Challock, about the only thing that's never been able to cross the Atlantic is humour.'

'I'd say he's right, there, mun.'

'What is he right about?' Bea re-joined them towards the end of the conversation.

'If you want to ease springs now, Dai, I'll explain things to Bea while I'm keeping her company.'

'Thanks, mun.'

'I'm not a delicate flower, sir. You don't really need to stand guard over me.'

'When you look so irresistible, Bea, believe me, I do.'

'Oh, you. What were you talking about just now?'

'Apparently, I'm *persona non grata* with Captain Boyle because of a silly story I told him.'

'Not you, sir. I don't believe it.'

'Yes, I thought he was throwing down the gauntlet, and I picked it up.' He explained the circumstances.

'They're not all like that, sir. At least, here's one who's not.'

William turned and saw that she was referring to a rear admiral in the US Navy. He was in the company of Vice-Admiral Davies and they were on their way, presumably to pay their compliments. They were both guests of the wardroom, as flag officers always were.

'Second Officer Dean,' said the American, beaming, 'how pleasant it is to see you again.'

'The pleasure is entirely mine, sir.'

They exchanged greetings and then Vice-Admiral Davies said, 'I'd like you to meet Commander Stamford, Rear Admiral. You may have heard his name mentioned recently. Stamford, this is Rear Admiral Farrell of the United States Navy.

'I'm pleased to make your acquaintance, Commander Stamford.'

'And I to make yours, sir.'

'I have heard your name mentioned, Commander, favourably, I have to say.'

'I'm relieved to hear it, sir.'

'You'll be hearing more of Commander Stamford,' said Vice-Admiral Davies. Meanwhile, we must circulate.' They took their leave, Vice-Admiral Davies favouring Bea with a wink that was almost imperceptible.

When they were called to take their places, William was pleased to find himself opposite Dai and Bea.

The meal was quite good, given wartime restrictions, and the formalities were not too intrusive. Eventually, the Mess President made the popular announcement, 'Gentlemen, you may smoke.'

Dai eyed the box of cigars and asked playfully, 'Are you going to choose one for me, Bea?'

'I think that might be a little insensitive in the circumstances.' She looked across at William, who had already observed Captain Boyle watching them from the top of the table.

'Not at all,' said William. 'Go ahead, Bea.'

'All right, if you don't mind, sir.'

Shyly aware that she was now the centre of everyone's attention, at least on their table, she took a corona and inspected it. First, she rolled it between her fingers along its length, then she held it to her ear to repeat the procedure before passing it beneath her nose to scent its aroma. Finally, she asked for a cigar cutter and took the nearest, which was Dai's. When she had cut the cigar, she handed it to Dai amid gentle applause. William was reminded of the first time Lucy had done the same thing, in response to a supercilious remark from a senior officer's wife, and the memory caused him to miss her all the more. Quietly, he took a cigar, cut it and lit it. There was always the possibility that Lucy would be back to accompany him to the next dinner, although he hardly dared hope.

Bea leaned forward to say, 'I hope that wasn't too insensitive of me, sir.'

'The formal part of the evening is over, Bea, so it's "William", not "sir", and you could never be insensitive if you were to practise for a whole year.'

6

When Captain Challock called at William's office, he was in a hurry.

'I have to leave in half-an-hour, Stamford, but I should be back before the month is out. Meanwhile, you'll report to Captain Boyle.'

'Aye, aye, sir.' William knew better than to enquire as to his superior's destination. Instead, he did his best to conceal his misgivings regarding Captain Boyle, although he was unlikely to fool Challock.

'Be on your best behaviour, Stamford.'

'Aye, aye, sir. Have a safe journey, sir.'

'Thank you. Goodbye.' Challock shook his hand and left the room.

That William had to report to Boyle was bad news, even though the arrangement was temporary, but he had to make the best of it. His best plan, he decided, was to keep his head down, and with that intention, he began work on a series of suggestions, which he would deliver to Challock on his return.

It was a sound plan, and it might have worked, had Captain Boyle been less enthusiastic about his role as deputy. In the event, scarcely an hour had passed before he summoned William to Room Twelve.

On the command 'Enter', William stepped inside, came to attention and saluted.

'Commander Stamford,' said Boyle, 'I've been reading a report you sent to Captain Challock, and it doesn't impress me at all.'

'I'm sorry to hear that, sir.'

'Oh, you are, are you? You could be a whole lot sorrier if you

38

can't think of something better than this.' He tapped the report several times with his middle finger.

'Is it the report itself that's the problem, sir, or something more specific?'

Boyle closed his eyes tightly, as if William's question were the most ridiculous he'd ever heard. When he opened them again, he asked, 'Just what do you think you're going to achieve with this shopping list?'

'Shopping list, sir?'

'Lead oxide paint and heavy axle grease.'

'Ah.' He knew what Boyle was talking about now. 'Lead oxide paint is used as a primer against rust, and thick grease is used to protect moving parts such as axles, bearings and the like against corrosion caused by salt water, sir.'

Boyle closed his eyes again. It seemed to be his pet signal that his patience was exhausted. 'I know what they're used for, Commander. What I want to know is, what do you expect the Germans to deduce from a list of items they could buy from any hardware store?'

'The intention is to present a clue, sir. The enemy are less likely to ask themselves why we are stockpiling goods obtainable from the local *Eisenwarengeschäft*, than to question the purpose of delivering such quantities to bases on the east coast.'

Boyle hit the desk with his closed fist. 'Don't get cute with me, Commander. I'm telling you that your disinformation, like your famous British understatement, is meaningless to them. Tell them we're moving tanks and landing craft and they'll start to take notice.'

'Other reports would follow, sir. For example, a consignment of couplings, or whatever they're called, for tank tracks would be reported, causing the enemy to ask the same question. The intention is to offer a series of clues, rather than hitting them with the blindingly obvious, thereby running the risk of giving the game away.' Sensing that anger had left Boyle temporarily bereft of speech, he pressed home his argument. 'They're no strangers to subtlety, sir. We're talking about the nation that produced Goethe, Schiller and Müller.'

At last, Boyle recovered the faculty of speech. 'Yeah? And when did those guys last pull an audience? The US produced the Marx

Brothers, but that doesn't mean we'd be fooled, even by a whole inventory of hardware.'

'I understand, sir.' It was all the same to William. Even if Boyle destroyed the report, he would write it again for Captain Challock's benefit.

'So we'll have no more of that subtlety bullshit. I want to see ideas that'll work. Do you read me, Commander?'

'Meticulously, sir.'

———◆◆———

'My impression,' said Dai when William joined him for a drink in the wardroom, 'is that he's a bird of passage. He's held several appointments since nineteen thirty-five, and none of them seagoing. I have the feeling that the Americans are just pushing him around until he decides to retire and shout at his roses.'

'I think he's an easily embittered man, Dai. He resents me because I fooled him over the baseball thing, and he despises what he calls "famous British understatement". I can't help wondering if he simply resents being posted here. It's a pity we can't swap him for Lucy.'

'I'm with you there, mun. She's much more fun to have around. For one thing, she'd put a smile on your face, and that would be an improvement.'

William had to agree.

———◆◆———

As the car turned into the drive, Captain Challock saw the house for the first time: large, three storeys and with gardens to the sides and most likely to the rear. There must be many such houses in Surrey, taken over by the military whilst their owners found alternative, temporary accommodation, and each used for a purpose that would remain a secret far into the future.

The driver parked on the circle at the front entrance and opened the car door for Challock.

'Thank you.' Challock returned the rating's salute. 'I'll carry my own bag. Carry on.'

'Aye-aye, sir.' The rating returned to the driving seat to take the car back to the depot, and Challock walked to the entrance, where a dark-haired man in a grey suit met him.

Challock showed his Naval Identity Card, and the man nodded.

'Good afternoon, sir,' he said. 'I'm Major Douglas, Intelligence Corps. I'll show you to your room. You've brought civilian clothing, I take it?'

'Yes.'

'Good. We like our guests to experience a relaxed atmosphere as far as possible, so we avoid uniform if we can.'

Challock followed Douglas up a flight of stairs to the first floor, where his host led him to the second of a row of four rooms.

'This is your room, sir,' he said, opening the door. 'When you've freshened up, perhaps you'd care to come down to the mess for a drink. It's the first room on the right, opposite the staircase.'

'Thank you, Major.'

It took Challock no more than a minute to unpack his case and familiarise himself with his room. He was pleased to find that he had a bathroom *en suite*, but was initially surprised when he noticed the iron bars outside the window. He doubted that the room had ever served as a nursery, and concluded that the bars had been added for security when one of Major Douglas's 'guests' occupied it.

Dressed, now, in a mid-grey, worsted, double-breasted suit, he went down to the room that Douglas had called the 'mess'. He found two officers there: Douglas himself and a man of sanguine features and ample proportions, whom Douglas introduced as Lieutenant-Colonel Selby, also of the Intelligence Corps. He was wearing a tweed suit, incredibly, with plus fours.

'Welcome to Safe House *Kestrel* sir,' said Selby. 'Lunch will be served at thirteen hundred hours. Perhaps in the meantime you would care for a drink?'

'Thank you. Gin would be most welcome.'

'By all means. Water or bitters, sir?'

'Oh, bitters, please.' The pink gin was a pleasant surprise.

Selby busied himself with the drinks. The practice made sense to Challock, who presumed that in a secure unit such as *Kestrel* a steward would have been an unnecessary risk.

Selby invited him to take a seat by the fire and proceeded to join him.

'We have, currently, two guests who will be of interest to you, sir,' said Selby. 'One, as you know, is Marguerite Werner, and the other is Georg Werner, her father. I should add that neither of them is aware of the other's presence here, although they do know of each other's capture.'

'Has Georg Werner agreed to co-operate? I know his daughter has.'

'He has, sir, although we are currently taking nothing about either of them for granted, and that is basically why we need your help. Essentially, we need fresh input, someone from outside this establishment, who will chat with these people and form an impression of their *bona fides*, so to speak.'

The last sentence caused Challock to feel a degree of unease. 'You do realise,' he said, 'that I'm not a trained interrogator?'

'We do realise that, sir, but it's only fair of us to give you an idea of the kind of people who might one day be working for you.'

'I appreciate that.' It was Challock's first visit to a safe-house, and he was curious. 'If Werner and his daughter are unaware of their mutual proximity,' he said, 'presumably, they're kept in solitary confinement.'

'Albeit of a somewhat luxurious kind,' confirmed Selby.

'In these relaxed circumstances,' said Douglas, who had so far remained silent, 'it's easy to forget, however fleetingly, that our guests are, in fact, prisoners.'

'Quite.' Challock had one important question to ask. 'When do you intend their reunion to take place?'

'When we are almost sure of their willingness to comply with our orders, we shall allow them to meet in a secure part of the grounds that is comprehensively wired for sound,' said Douglas. 'We hope that the excitement of their reunion will put them off their guard, so that any residual defiance is likely to emerge.'

'Couldn't you save time by bringing them together sooner?'

Selby shook his head confidently. 'It's very important,' he said, 'that we first make them believe that we're confident of their total compliance.'

'In fact, to lull them into a false sense of security?'

'Just so, sir.'

Challock was inclined to agree with young Stamford that espionage belonged to another world, and one with which his dealings were mercifully brief and infrequent.

———◆◆———

Boyle caught William as he was leaving the wardroom after lunch.

'Commander,' he said, 'I've been meaning to ask you about that party game you were playing last week.'

'Sir?'

'At the wardroom dinner. 'I'm talking about the charade with the cigar. What was it about?'

'Oh.' Now William knew what Boyle meant. 'Second Officer Dean was choosing a cigar for Lieutenant Commander Hughes, sir,' he explained. 'It's an old custom in some circles, but that was just a light-hearted moment between fellow-officers.'

'You have to be joking, Commander.'

'No, sir, the formal part of the dinner was over. It was a time for fun and relaxation.'

Boyle stared at him in disbelief. 'Fun and relaxation, you say? Don't you people know there's a war happening out there?'

'I think we've been aware of that for some considerable time, sir.'

Boyle's face darkened. 'I've told you before, Commander, don't get cute with me.'

'I'll try not to, sir.' William made a mental note to find out the exact meaning of 'cute.'

'In any case, what would a girl who's fresh out of high school, know about cigars?'

William wished he would simply accept the practice and leave the topic alone. 'Second Officer Dean is a mature and intelligent woman, sir, and she knows how to choose a cigar. As I said, it's an old custom. *Autre pays, autre moeurs*, as they say.'

'And what in Sam Hell does that mean?'

' "Other country, other customs", sir.'

'So why can't you speak plain English, Commander?'

'Ah well, sir, that's another English custom. A great many references to diplomacy and polite conduct are traditionally couched in French. I believe the Normans introduced them after the invasion of ten sixty-six.'

'So now you want to give me a history lesson. I've heard enough.' He gave William a dismissive look and left the wardroom.

Dai, who had been just within earshot and distant enough not to be caught up in the argument, came to William's side, 'Now, there's a man,' he said, 'who could benefit from lessons in polite conduct.'

———•►◄•———

Captain Challock was studying the files he'd been given.

Georg Werner had left Germany with his inherited fortune shortly after the previous war. His timing had been immaculate, escaping as he had, the economic disaster that ensued, and he had set up in London as a stockbroker. A chance meeting in 1938 with Joachim von Ribbentropp, Foreign Minister of Germany, resulted in his being recruited as a German agent, but he was not put to serious work until 1942, by which time MI5 were watching him closely and were able to feed him false information. He became increasingly active during 1943, and the decision was made to arrest him with a view to persuading him to become a double agent.

Marguerite's story interested Challock far more because, although she was Georg's daughter, her background, far from being that of an immigrant, was English upper-middle-class. Her interest in Nazi politics had begun shortly after Hitler's self-made appointment as *Führer*, when she was fifteen years old, although she tried to disguise her political convictions from her schoolfriends by adopting a *façade* of absent-minded foolishness.

On leaving school at the age of 18, she had spent some time in Germany, presumably in training for her career in intelligence. She had returned to England during the summer of 1939.

Challock was looking forward to meeting her the next morning.

7

Dai was happy. He would be seeing Bea that evening, and that alone would have been sufficient to make him happy, but he had an additional reason for celebration, and that was the result of his medical examination the previous day. The doctor had declared himself delighted with the way Dai's lungs were recovering, and saw no reason why, at the current rate of improvement, his patient should not be rated A-One fit within a matter of months. Dai had good reason to be happy, and when he was happy, being Welsh, he sang.

'O mor siriol, gwena seren,
Ar hyd y nos;
Loleuo'i chwaer ddaearen,
Ar hyd y nos—'

'What in Sam Hell kind of language is that, Lieutenant Commander?' It was unfortunate that Captain Boyle should arrive when Dai was partway through the second verse of 'All Through the Night.'

'Welsh, sir.' Dai deduced that Boyle was not a music lover. At least, it was either that or, more likely, that he disapproved of any language that was not American English.

'Do you usually sing in Welsh?'

'Whenever possible, sir. You might say that it's a national trait.'

'Surely, Welsh is a dead language, like Latin.'

'Certainly not, sir. Welsh is spoken in my part of Wales as our first language. Children in North Wales don't usually begin learning English until the age of eleven.'

'You don't say.' Captain Boyle sat down to assimilate the information. 'What does the British government have to say about that?'

'They don't seem to mind one way or the other, sir, although English audiences do pay to hear male-voice choirs sing in Welsh. Generally speaking, the English are not as musical as we are.'

'So, how do the Welsh feel about being ruled by the English?'

'Some resent it, sir, and there are those who would like to break free. Others take the line that we've lived next door to the English for a long time now, and it doesn't seem so bad.'

'How about you, Lieutenant Commander? How do you feel about your country being ruled as a colony?'

Dai bridled in spite of himself. 'Wales is not a colony, sir. It's a principality that's a part of Great Britain, and I hold the King's Commission. In common with every other Welshman who's fighting in this war, sir, I'm happy to say that my loyalty is beyond question.'

Boyle retired, shaking his head. 'I guess I'll never understand this crazy country and its people,' he said.

———◆I◆———

Thirty-four miles away, in Surrey, Captain Challock tapped on Marguerite Werner's door and, in response to a somewhat curt invitation to enter, he turned the knob and pushed open the door.

'Good morning, Miss Werner,' he said. 'I'm Henry Challock.'

'How do you do, Mr Challock. Are you with the military or the police?' She was dark-haired and very attractive, with deep brown eyes that gave the impression of calculated thought, and Challock suspected that there would be little intimation as to the nature of that thought.

'I'm a naval officer.'

'I see.' She indicated an armchair, inviting him to be seated. 'Your name, Mr Challock, calls to mind a village in Kent. Is that your family home?'

'It was,' he confirmed, 'generations ago.' Then, conscious that he was supposed to be asking the questions rather than answering them, he opened his briefcase and took out the file labelled

Marguerite Alexandra Werner. 'Miss Werner,' he said, 'I know you've been questioned several times since your arrest, but there are just a few details of your past that I should like to discuss with you.'

'After all this time, I shall be surprised if there is the minutest detail from my past that you people don't already know.'

'Even so, Miss Werner, let's begin.' He consulted the document from the file. 'You attended Bunbury Girls' School, I believe, from nineteen thirty-one until nineteen thirty-eight. Which house were you in, Miss Werner?'

'Latimer House.' She delivered her answer with an air of boredom, as Challock had anticipated.

'I appreciate that this is tiresome for you,' he said, 'but I'm sure you'll agree that it's preferable to facing the hangman.'

'As you people keep reminding me. Look, I've agreed to work for British Intelligence. What more do you want from me?'

'Bear with me, Miss Werner.' He glanced at the document again. 'You played hockey for Latimer House. Did you play cricket?'

'Only in games lessons.'

'What about lacrosse?'

'Again, in games lessons.'

'You enjoyed hockey, presumably?'

'Of course.' The shrewd look returned to her eyes.

'Not cricket?'

'For what it's worth, Mr Challock, I am no different from thousands of others in this country, who find cricket the most boring game ever devised. If that makes me an ardent Nazi, then others who share my persuasion must also share that description.'

'It's your freedom to express your dislike of the game, however popular it is with others.' He smiled at the thought. 'Cricket is played with unbridled enthusiasm in India, the West Indies, South Africa—'

She snorted. 'A game fit for those people. What a civilised nation such as the English see in it is beyond me.'

'You said you played lacrosse.'

'Only in games lessons,' she reminded him.

'Didn't it appeal to you?'

'Of course not. It was invented by....'

'By an inferior race?'

'Who can deny...?' Again, she hesitated.

He nodded, noticing the alarm that showed in her eyes. 'Who can deny what, Miss Werner?'

'I was going to say, who can deny any nation the right to play whatever games it chooses? All I'm saying is that we don't all have to share their enthusiasm.'

'I agree. Games have been played in this country that no one would countenance nowadays. No one in their right mind, anyway.'

'Such as?' Now that the alarm was past, she was ready to argue again. It seemed an odd habit for a woman of her political persuasion.

He shrugged. 'Cock fighting, dog fighting, quail fighting, bull baiting, badger baiting, any kind of baiting, I suppose.'

Her eyes flashed again. 'You're trying to trick me, Mr Challock. You want me to forget myself and say something that reveals my National Socialist sympathies.'

'No, Miss Werner, that's not what I want at all. I want you to demonstrate that you're prepared to renounce Hitler and all his works, and to espouse the Allied cause.'

'So you all keep saying.'

Challock was watching her eye movement, and he surmised that she was looking for a way to change the subject. A moment later, he was proved right.

'Mr Challock,' she said, 'it seems wrong to call you "Mr", when you're a naval officer. What is your rank?'

'Captain.' He said it casually, as if it were of no importance.

'You should be proud of your rank, Captain. You shouldn't hide it away.'

'Miss Werner,' he said, ignoring her observation, 'I wonder what people will say in generations to come, about Hitler's record of inhumanity, about the burning of the synagogues, for instance, and the deportation of countless innocent people to labour camps.'

With only the merest eye movement, she asked, 'How can we know what they will say, Captain Challock? No one holds the key to the future.'

———— ►◄ ————

That afternoon, he visited Georg Werner in his room.

Having introduced himself, this time by rank and name, he went straight to the point. 'I'd like to know your opinion,' he said.

'Regarding what, Captain?'

'What should we do with Hitler, Himmler, Goering, Goebbels and the rest, after the war? Should we hang them or shoot them, or should we make the punishment, as far as possible, mirror the crime? I'm sure their offences will be reported in detail when the time comes, so we'll have a few ideas by the time we need them.'

Werner appeared unmoved. It was possible that his self-control was superior to his daughter's. 'I've always been led to believe,' he said, 'that the British pride themselves on their tradition of "fair play". Surely, you would exact punishment without barbarity.'

'Your English is excellent, *Herr* Werner.'

'It should be, Captain. I have lived here for twenty-five years.'

'You were recruited for the *Abwehr* in nineteen thirty-eight by Joachim von Ribbentropp, I believe?'

'I have told you that many times.'

'Oh, not me personally, *Herr* Werner. I'm new to your case, so you have to make allowances.' He went on. 'The Nazi hierarchy held von Ribbentropp in low esteem, didn't they?'

'There is rivalry in any political party.'

'But in the Nazi party, isn't rivalry a deadly game?'

'I believe it can be, Captain.'

'For example,' said Challock, 'imagine what might happen if one party member overheard a rival member suggest that the Nazi cause was doomed and that the Allies were going to win the war. What then, *Herr* Werner?'

'The outcome is obvious.'

'Do you mean the outcome of the war?'

'No, the outcome you suggested. One would denounce the other.'

'Bad form.' Challock shook his head in disapproval. 'Just for interest's sake, *Herr* Werner, who do you think will win the war?'

Werner hesitated. Eventually, he said, 'I should say it is too early, at this stage, for anyone to make an accurate prediction.

———◆◆———

Captain Challock reported his findings to Lieutenant-Colonel Selby later that day.

'At this stage, Selby, I don't trust them. Werner's playing a clever game. He's trying not to look rattled, but he is. I asked him who he thought would win the war. He was carefully non-committal, but his eyes gave the game away. He was too scared to tell me what he really thought.'

'What about her, sir?'

'She's a chip off the old block, but she hasn't quite got the idea of masking her feelings yet.'

'What do you want to do now?'

'I'd like to see them both again, Selby.'

———— ►◄ ————

'I don't mind telling you, Bea, I'll be relieved to see Captain Challock back in harness.'

'You too, Dai? Captain Boyle was downright rude to me this morning.'

They were sharing the double bed at Dai's flat, which they had made their temporary home, although Bea kept her address purely for appearances' sake.

'He's treating you the same as everyone else, then.'

'Apparently.' She ran her fingers through the stubble on his chin. Dai had discontinued shaving two days previously, and she'd still not decided whether she favoured a set or preferred him clean-shaven. 'As a junior Wren officer, I suppose I should take it as a compliment.'

'Yes, we shouldn't grumble. All the signs are that he's made William his whipping boy.'

'Poor William.'

'He can take it, Bea, just as we must. After all, how much damage can Boyle do in such a short time?'

8

Lieutenant Commander Wheelwright held the telephone a few inches away from his ear and winced. He'd only taken up his position in Postings and Drafts a few days previously, and already he was caught up in a major row. Rear Admiral Heywood at *HMS Pembroke*, otherwise Chatham Naval Base, was venting his anger about a posting that meant nothing to Wheelwright.

'I do see, sir,' said Wheelwright. 'The reason I know nothing about it is that I've only been here since Monday.'

'I don't care where you've been, or how long you've been there, Wheelwright. Because of some ridiculous mix-up, I am now without an intelligence officer, and I expect you to do something about it.'

'I shall, sir.'

'As a matter of urgency, I hope.'

'Aye-aye, sir.' Wheelwright heard the telephone go down at the other end and knew it was safe to do the same.

'Can I do anything to help, sir?' The offer came from Second Officer Chorley, who occupied the other desk in the room.

'I doubt it, Miss Chorley. Someone's posted Chatham's intelligence officer to Sheerness, of all places, and Rear Admiral Heywood is naturally upset.'

'Has he no one else who can take on the responsibility, sir?'

'Apparently not.'

'We could try speaking to Captain Challock, sir. He may know of someone.'

Wheelwright looked up in surprise. 'You know, Miss Chorley,' he said, 'that's not a bad idea.'

Second Officer Chorley smiled happily from behind her round, tortoiseshell spectacles before thumbing through the Admiralty directory. Lieutenant Commander Wheelwright was one of the few men who had shown any interest in her, and she was eager to please him. 'Captain Challock is in Room Twelve, sir,' she reported.

'Thank you, Miss Chorley.' He picked up the telephone and asked to be connected with Room 12.

A gruff American voice came on the line. It said, 'Room Twelve. Captain Boyle here.'

'I beg your pardon, sir. I thought I was through to Captain Challock.'

'Ordinarily, this is his office. He's on detachment right now, and I've taken over his duties. Who are you?'

'Lieutenant Commander Wheelwright, sir, Postings and Drafts.'

'Okay. What do you want?'

'You see, sir, there was a bit of a mix-up before my arrival here, and somehow, the intelligence officer at Chatham was posted to Sheerness, although no one seems to know why, and the Commodore at Chatham is understandably displeased about the whole business.' He removed his spectacles and struggled to extricate a handkerchief from a tight trouser pocket so that he could mop his brow.

'So, what do you expect me to do about it?'

'I was wondering, sir, if you knew of an officer who might be available to fill the vacancy. I'm clutching at straws here, as you can imagine.'

There was a moment's silence at the other end, and then Boyle spoke. 'It sounds to me,' he said, 'like just another example of the kind of chaos I've come to expect from this boy scout troop you people call a navy.' He was silent again, and then, in a surprisingly reasonable tone, he said, 'You know, Lieutenant Commander, I think I may have just the man for you.'

'Really, sir?' Wheelwright inserted two fingers inside his collar to ease the tightness against his throat.

'Yes, I can spare Commander William Stamford.'

'If you're sure about that, sir.'

'Yes, the Commodore at Chatham is welcome to his services.'

With a huge feeling of relief, Wheelwright said, 'Thank you, sir.

I'll find you a replacement for Commander Stamford as soon as I can.'

'You do that, Lieutenant Commander.'

———— ►◄ ————

HMS Wildfire, Sheerness-on-Sea, was a bleak and cheerless establishment, and particularly so in winter, but Captain Daniels, RN, Assistant to the Commodore, now had reason to be in good spirits. Not only did he have the services of an excellent intelligence officer, recently arrived from Chatham, but he now had the opportunity to grant Postings and Drafts a small favour whilst relieving himself of an officer he had disliked from the day of his arrival.

'Bonnington,' he said, 'you were involved in intelligence work at the Admiralty at one time, I believe?'

'That is correct, sir.'

Daniels tried not to sound too satisfied when he said, 'In that case, you'll be treading a familiar path.'

'Sir?'

'Pack your bags, Bonnington. You're going back to the Admiralty. You're to report to Captain Boyle in Room Twelve.' He allowed himself a smile. 'He's American, I believe.'

———— ►◄ ————

'I don't believe it, Dai.' William was packing the few personal effects he kept in Room 33 into his grip.

'Neither do I, mun. It's a crazy thing for Boyle to do, because Captain Challock will go off half-cocked when he finds out what he's done.'

'You know why he's done it, don't you?'

'Because of that story you told him about playing... rounders, wasn't it?'

'Baseball, yes.' He smiled briefly at the memory of the incident and said, 'If he can't take a joke, he shouldn't have joined.'

'I just hope this thing isn't the start of something much bigger.

Boyle has a lot of clout behind him.' Dai watched William pack the webbing belt, holster and pistol he'd had since 1940, when invasion seemed likely. He asked, 'Did you never return that revolver, William?'

William shook his head. 'No one asked me for it. Anyway, it's not a revolver.' He unfastened the flap on the large holster and withdrew a semi-automatic pistol. 'I think they were short of revolvers after Dunkirk,' he said. 'It's a Webley four-five-five, and as far as I know it hasn't been fired since it was proved, although Boyle doesn't realise how lucky he is that I haven't brought it out of mothballs before now.'

'Shooting is too good for him,' said Dai. 'I'll let you know how it goes,' he promised.

William offered his hand. 'Let's hope we'll see each other before long, Dai.'

'Let's hope so, mun. *Pob lwc, fy ffrind.*'

'What?'

'Good luck, my friend.'

'All the best, Dai.'

They shook hands and parted.

——— ►◄ ———

Challock found Marguerite Werner in a sceptical mood.

'What's on the agenda today, Captain? Are you going to trick me into giving the Hitler salute, or will you just persuade me to dismiss certain games as fit only for savages?'

'Neither, Miss Werner. As you no doubt realise, I'm not a trained interrogator, although I'm interested that you should mention games, just now. Did you have a particular game in mind?'

She gave something approaching a shrug. 'I thought you wanted me to say, yesterday, that lacrosse was invented by an inferior race, and that cricket is a game suitable only for the subject-races of the British Empire.'

'On the contrary, I should be appalled to hear anyone make those judgements.'

'There are many British people who hold similar views, Captain, but that does not make them disciples of the *Führer.*'

'Regrettably, there are,' he agreed. 'Are you still a devotee of Hitler?'

Her look was weary, although whether it were genuine or contrived, it was impossible to say. 'Of course not. I'm working for the Allies now – at least, I would be if I were allowed out of this... elaborate confinement.'

'When did you first become drawn to the Nazis?'

'In nineteen thirty-three, when the *Führer* became Chancellor. I was very young.'

He glanced at his notes. 'Thirteen, in fact, but you say you're no longer a devotee of Hitler.'

'Quite right.'

'Yet you still refer to him as "the *Führer*".'

'Ten years is a long time, Captain, but old habits die hard.'

'You didn't speak of "the *Führer*" at school, did you?'

Once again, those expressive eyes betrayed surprise before she collected herself. 'How do you know I didn't. I may have, for all you know.'

'We have an extremely detailed dossier on Bunbury School, Miss Werner, and on you in particular. We know, for example, that you hid your Nazi sympathies behind a façade of empty-headed silliness.'

'What, if I did? Anyway, it's the same kind of thing when someone gets married. She takes her husband's name, but her friends refer to her by her maiden name for long enough afterwards. It's what they're used to.'

'I see. You're no longer a dedicated Nazi, but you believe in racial superiority. I refrain deliberately from calling it "racial purity". You lack, after all, the highly-prized blonde hair, blue eyes and high cheekbones of the *Übermensch*.'

'In case you haven't noticed, Captain, so does the *Fü*.... I beg your pardon. I should say, "Hitler".'

Her barbed irony told him nothing. He continued. 'You despise the Irish, I believe?'

'Who told you that?'

'One of your old school friends.'

'You people really are too Machiavellian for words. In fact, you're despicable.'

'There are failings on both sides, Miss Werner, but we don't burn synagogues and deport innocent people to labour camps. Neither do we shoot our own people when we can no longer control them.'

Surprisingly, she made no response.

'Until tomorrow, Miss Werner.'

Challock was still disinclined to trust her completely. He felt that he needed to interview her again.

———◆◆———

'We have a new intelligence officer arriving tomorrow, Hughes.' For once, Boyle was in a reasonably cheerful mood.

'What's his name, sir? It's just possible that I know him.'

'I doubt that. He's called Commander Bonnington.'

For the second time that day, Dai was in a state of disbelief. 'Not Commander F. C. Bonnington, sir?'

'I believe so. Wait a minute.' Boyle looked down at the document on his desk and said, 'Yes, Commander F.C. Bonnington, Royal Navy.' He looked sourly at the wavy rings on Dai's sleeve and said, 'At least he's a genuine naval officer. Anyway, how do you come to know him?'

'He was here in nineteen-forty, sir.'

'What happened to him?'

'He was posted, sir.' It was as much as Dai was prepared to tell him. The circumstances were none of Boyle's business.

'Obviously.' Boyle seemed to revert to his normal, disagreeable self. He asked, 'How am I going to get to see Vice-Admiral Davies, when each time I try, I get blocked by that smart-ass secretary of his. Let me tell you, Lieutenant Commander, it's high time some guy screwed that dame and put a smile on her face. It might also make her more amenable to work with.'

Dai was controlling his anger with difficulty. 'If you'll let me make a suggestion, sir,' he said, 'as one who's been here since nineteen-forty, maybe I can help.'

'Okay, tell me. I need to inform Vice-Admiral Davies about the changes I've made today, and to do that, I need to get past Miss Iceberg 'Forty-Four.'

Reluctant though Dai was to offer assistance, he knew it was nevertheless his duty to do so. 'If you don't mind my saying so, sir, you're going about it the wrong way. This is a bureaucratic organisation, and the Service Memo is the procedure to which we all conform.'

'You don't say.'

'I do, sir. You should communicate your message in a Memo. Then, when you've done that, you should seal it in an envelope. I'll address it for you if you wish.'

'Good thinking, Lieutenant Commander. Where do I get one of these memos?'

'They're in your right-hand drawer, sir, and the envelopes are beneath them.'

——— ►◄ ———

It was 1900, and well after dark when William arrived at *HMS Pembroke*. He showed his identity card to the men on the main gate and asked to be directed to the wireless station. He had to report to Commander Bray.

'It's about two hundred yards up the main drag, sir,' one of them told him, 'and it's signed to the left. You can't miss it.'

'Thank you.' He returned the seamen's salutes and continued on his way. It was all very well to talk about signs; it was almost impossible to see anything in the blackout.

Someone hailed him from a few yards away. 'Have you got a "glim", mate?'

William felt in his pocket. He didn't smoke, but he usually carried a box of matches for lighting the fire and the stove at his flat. The figure came closer, and William struck a match, cupping it between his hands. As he did so, he saw that the request had come from a very young ordinary seaman, who realised his mistake.

'I'm sorry, sir,' he said, saluting hurriedly. 'I didn't realise you was an officer.' He looked mortified.

'Obviously not. Take a light, anyway.' He struck another match, and the sailor lit his cigarette, shaking as he did so.

'Thank you, sir. Sorry, sir.'

'That's all right, but be more careful in future. I might have been a sub-lieutenant, and then you'd have been in trouble.'

The sailor laughed. 'Aye-aye, sir. Goodnight, sir.'

'Goodnight.'

William found the sign to the wireless station by stumbling against it. Gratefully, he opened the door and walked in.

A petty officer telegraphist stood in his way. He asked, 'Can I help you, sir?'

'I hope so. I'm Commander Stamford.' He showed his identity card. 'I'm supposed to find Commander Bray.'

'He's just gone off-watch, sir. The Duty Officer is Lieutenant Atkinson. Would you like to see him, sir?'

'I suppose I'd better if there's no one else.'

'Follow me, sir.' The PO led him past two doors and then knocked on a third. On hearing an invitation to enter, he pushed open the door and announced William's arrival to the Duty Officer.

'Ah, come inside, sir.' The lieutenant got up from his desk to introduce himself. 'I'm Atkinson, sir.'

William shook the DO's hand.

'I'm afraid Commander Bray went off-watch over an hour ago, sir. My relief will be here by twenty hundred, and I'll be able to take you over to the wardroom then. In the meantime, would you like a cup of tea?'

'It would be very welcome, Atkinson. I've had nothing since lunchtime.'

Atkinson turned to the PO telegraphist, who was awaiting further orders, and asked, 'Can you organise that, PO? See if you can find some biscuits as well, will you?'

'Aye-aye, sir.'

'As it's so late, sir,' said Atkinson, 'I think the best plan will be to organise accommodation for you, and leave the joining routine for tomorrow morning.'

There was a knock on the door, and a diminutive Wren with dark, curly hair stepped in carrying a tray loaded with two cups of tea and a plate of biscuits.

'Thank you, Maggie,' said Lieutenant Atkinson. 'You've just earned your first good conduct badge. You'll get it in less than four years' time.' It was an old joke, but the grin on the Wren's face showed that she appreciated it.

'Will there be anything else, sir?'

'No thanks, Maggie. Carry on.'

'Aye-aye, sir.'

William smiled. 'Yours is a happy watch, I take it, Atkinson?'

'Yes, sir. As I see it, we're all in this together, so we may as well be civil towards one another.'

William had to agree. It was his first impression of *Pembroke*, and he liked what he saw.

9

Dai had endured a night of frustration. He wanted, quite naturally, to warn Bea of the strong likelihood that Boyle had made an official complaint against her, but circumstances had rendered it impossible. Bea had gone to her parents' home in Bromley to celebrate her younger sister's birthday, and had decided to stay the night and catch the early train to work in the morning. He'd considered telephoning her at home, but to do that would blight an otherwise happy occasion. The idea, which had been his only one so far, was unthinkable. He would simply have to wait until morning, when he would try to speak to her before the admiral could open his internal mail. He would need to report at 0800, as usual, to Captain Boyle, hoping that Boyle wouldn't delay him, and then cut along to Bea's office a quickly as he could.

Unfortunately, when he arrived at Room 12 the next morning, he found that Boyle was not alone. The other officer in the room was a Commander, RN, and when he turned, on hearing the door, Dai recognised him immediately. He saluted both officers, but it was Bonnington who spoke first.

'Hughes, isn't it? Still recovering from that cough, are you?'

'Yes, sir, although I'm told I should soon be fit to re-join the fleet.'

'Good.' He smiled briefly at Captain Boyle and said, 'Things are looking up here, now that the Admiralty has come to its senses and got rid of that insubordinate fool Stamford.'

'The postings are yet to be confirmed, Commander,' Boyle reminded him, 'but that is how things stand.' He picked up an envelope from his desk and said, 'Deliver this memo to Vice-Admiral Davies, Hughes.'

'Aye-aye, sir.' Dai took the envelope from him, relieved, if only for the moment, that the memo wasn't already in the admiral's hands.

As he made his way to the admiral's office, he reflected that the four years or so that Bonnington had spent in Sheerness had left him completely unchanged. He was as disagreeable as ever. Dai could only hope that, on his return, Captain Challock might be able to persuade the admiral to get rid of him, as well as reversing some of the other damage Boyle had done.

With that thought, he took the stairs to the next floor and arrived at Bea's office, where he knocked on the frosted pane of her door.

'Come in.' The invitation was, as usual, business-like but pleasant. He pushed the door open and stepped inside.

'Dai,' she said, what brings you here? Don't tell me you can't get enough of me.'

'You know I can't, Bea, but this is official business.' He looked nervously towards the adjoining door that led to Vice-Admiral Davies's office.

'You can speak up. He has an appointment elsewhere. He won't be in until this afternoon.'

'Oh, good.' It was a temporary delay, but first of all, good manners prompted him to ask, 'Did you and Clarissa have a good time last evening?'

'Very pleasant, thank you. I passed on your birthday greetings.' She looked at him strangely. 'Dai, is something the matter?'

He produced the envelope and said, 'I have a memo for the admiral. It's from Captain Boyle.'

'I'm not surprised. He's kept turning up here, expecting to be ushered in, and turning nasty when it wasn't convenient.'

Dai nodded. 'I suspect,' he said, 'that he's written something unpleasant about you in the memo.'

'Oh, that wouldn't surprise me. That's the kind of unpleasant behaviour I would expect of such an unpleasant man.' She took the envelope and disappeared with it into the admiral's office.

'I just wanted you to know about it beforehand, you know, so that it doesn't come as a complete shock.'

She returned, closing the door behind her. 'That was really sweet of you, Dai, but you'll have to excuse me. I have an awful lot to do.' She threw him a kiss.

"Bye, then. Just so long as you know.'

"Bye, darling. Thank you for warning me.'

Dai made the return journey to Room 12, reflecting that the matter troubled him much more than it seemed to worry Bea. After turning it over in his mind, he put it down to the phlegmatic nature of the English. Bea apart, they could be a cold lot, which was probably why he'd never heard an English male voice choir.

———— ◆◆◆ ————

Commander Bray ushered William into his office and invited him to take a seat. 'I'm sorry I wasn't around to welcome you last evening, old man,' he said. 'The fact is, no one told me you were coming.'

'It's been a mix-up all round,' observed William.

'And another mystery, old chap, is why they've seen fit to send a commander, when a junior officer could cope with things here.' He added hastily, 'Not that you're any less welcome for that.'

'Thank you. I suspect skulduggery in certain quarters.' He saw Bray smile, and said, 'Seriously, there's a captain in the US Navy, who's taken a dislike to me over something quite trivial, and I shouldn't be surprised to find that he's behind this.'

'I take it you're not altogether happy with the posting.'

'I'm not unhappy. From what I've seen so far, this is an excellent establishment, but the fact remains that there's important work waiting to be done at the Admiralty.'

Bray absorbed the information. He was an RN officer, maybe in his forties, and therefore most likely passed over, who might easily be happy to see out his career in a desk job. 'I see, but you're likely to be with us for a while, so maybe you'd like some coffee.'

'That would be most welcome.'

'I agree.' Bray opened the door and called into the next office, 'Joan, will you get one of the girls to organise coffee for Commander Stamford and me?'

William heard a distant 'Aye-aye, sir,' and then Bray returned, closing the door behind him.

'I'm temporarily without the services of my secretary this morning,' he said. 'She has an appointment ashore but she'll be back this afternoon. Anyway, when we've had coffee, I'll show you round the place.'

'Excellent.'

'How are your sleeping quarters?'

'Basic, but bearable.'

'I suppose that's as much as you can reasonably expect, old man.'

———————

Vice-Admiral Davies went through the items Bea had opened on his behalf, before coming to an envelope marked *Private & Confidential*. Taking the seaman's clasp knife he'd carried as a midshipman and now used as a paper knife, he slit open the envelope and took out the memo he found inside it.

His eyes narrowed as he read the originator's name, and then they opened wide with alarm. He opened the adjoining door and asked, 'Bea?'

'Yes, sir?'

'Do you know if Commander Stamford has left yet for Chatham?'

'Yes, sir, he left yesterday forenoon.'

'Damn.' He closed his eyes in frustration. 'Will you see if you can get Captain Challock on the telephone? I'll get you the number.' Returning to his office, he referred to the list of telephone numbers he kept locked in his desk drawer and wrote down the number of the house in Surrey. 'This is the number,' he told Bea. 'Whatever Captain Challock is doing, I want him to break off and come to the telephone. Put him through to me.'

'Aye-aye, sir.' Bea dialled the number and waited. It rang several times before someone picked it up.

'Douglas here.'

'Hello, this is Vice-Admiral Davies's secretary. He wishes to speak to Captain Challock.'

'Wait. I'll find him.'

Bea waited for maybe two minutes, and then she heard Captain Challock's voice.'

'Good afternoon, sir. I'm putting you through to Vice-Admiral Davies.'

The admiral nodded and went to his telephone.

'Challock?'

'Yes, sir.'

'Let's go to "Scramble".' He pushed the appropriate button on his telephone, ensuring that their conversation would be secure. 'Challock,' he said, 'that overbearing fool Boyle has had Stamford posted to Chatham.'

'Oh, no.'

'Have you much left to do where you are?'

'No, sir. I've made an assessment of these people. I can leave now.'

'Good. I'll send a car for you. I want you to go to Chatham and prepare Stamford, assess the situation and do whatever is necessary.'

'Aye-aye, sir. Do you want Stamford to return to Whitehall?'

'No, leave him there for now. If it's not too late, he could be very useful. When you're finished at *Pembroke*, come back here.'

'Aye-aye, sir.'

'I'll speak to you when you arrive. Goodbye, Challock.'

'Goodbye, sir.'

When he'd put the telephone down, he called Bea again. 'Bea, will you call Rear Admiral Farrell and ask him if he will spare a little of his precious time? I need him to be here when I speak to one of his officers.'

'Aye-aye, sir.'

The admiral left her to perform that duty while he read the memo again. He found that its contents were no less distasteful than before.

Bea called, 'Rear Admiral Farrell is on his way, sir.'

'Thank you, Bea.'

Bea looked at him uncertainly and asked, 'Did Captain Boyle's memo contain a complaint about me, sir?'

'About you, Bea?' The admiral's thoughts seemed elsewhere. 'Yes, but I shouldn't be inclined to worry about it.'

'Thank you, sir.'

'Not at all, Bea. Will you tell Captain Boyle that I require his immediate attendance?'

'Aye-aye, sir.'

First to arrive was Rear Admiral Farrell, who greeted Bea courteously before being welcomed into the inner office.

The admiral asked Bea to organise coffee for Farrell and tea for himself, which she did, taking it into the office herself.

'Thank you, Bea.' The admiral waited for her to leave, and then went to his desk. 'This is why I asked you to come, Farrell.' The admiral passed him the memo.

Farrell read it and returned it. 'I see. He's exceeded his authority in doing this,' he said.

'Worse than that, he's just jeopardised a vital intelligence operation, although I think we'll keep that to ourselves. Are you happy for me to speak to him first?'

'You're the senior officer, sir, and I appreciate your courtesy. Please feel free to roast him on a spit.'

'Thank you.' He was aware that Bea was hovering just outside the door. 'What is it, Bea?'

'Captain Boyle is here, sir.'

'Thank you. Send him in.'

Boyle stepped inside and saluted.

'Come inside, Boyle,' said the admiral, sitting down.

'I presume you want to discuss the contents of my memo, sir,' said Boyle.

' "Discuss" is hardly the word. I should like to know what gives you the authority to arrange postings, Captain.'

Boyle seemed unabashed. 'Sir, in the absence of a more senior officer, I acted on my own initiative because I believed that the urgency of the situation demanded immediate action.'

'What was urgent about *HMS Pembroke* being temporarily without an intelligence officer, Boyle?'

'I was led to believe that the Commodore at Chatham was most displeased, sir.'

'He can't have been half as displeased as I am at this moment. You had no right to do that, Boyle. Furthermore, you posted one of my most valued officers to *HMS Pembroke*. I believe that there has been some friction between you and Commander Stamford. Is that the case?'

'He was disrespectful to me on our first meeting, sir.'

Vice-Admiral Davies was losing patience. 'Are you referring to a story he told you? Something about playing basketball or rounders, perhaps?'

'It was baseball, sir, but the Vice-Admiral is otherwise correct.'

'Commander Challock told me about that. Apparently, you expressed surprise that Stamford had successfully carried out a certain deception, and you threw doubt on his ability to pull the wool over your eyes.'

'Yes, sir.'

'It was tantamount to a challenge.'

'I guess so, sir.'

'And so, to punish him for proving you wrong, you had him posted to Chatham.'

Boyle stood his ground. 'He was available, sir, and Chatham needed an intelligence officer.'

'He was not available, Boyle, because he was, and still is, required here to carry out a most important operation.'

Boyle looked uncertainly to Rear Admiral Farrell, possibly for support, but none was forthcoming.

'Your second offence, Boyle, was to have Commander Bonnington posted here to fill Stamford's place. It may surprise you to learn that, in nineteen-forty, the Prime Minister ordered me to have Bonnington posted somewhere where he could do no further harm. You see, Boyle, you may derive a little comfort from the knowledge that you're not the only liability in this establishment. Commander Bonnington can run you a damned good second!'

Boyle was clearly nettled. 'With all due respect, sir—'

'You've shown no respect to anyone since you set foot on these shores, Boyle. I don't think you understand the concept, and I would advise you to remain silent, because I haven't finished with you yet.' The admiral consulted the memo again. 'Ah, yes,' he reminded himself, 'not content with reorganising the Directorate of Naval Intelligence without reference to higher authority, you penned a scurrilous and unwarranted attack on one of my officers, who was performing her duty by shielding me from interruption. How dare you, Boyle!'

For the first time, Boyle remained silent. It was now Rear Admiral Farrell's turn.

'Captain Boyle,' he said, 'As an officer of the United States Navy, I am deeply embarrassed by your behaviour. In addition to the instances Vice-Admiral Davies has listed, I have received reports of your many anti-British utterances. It seems that you are fighting the War of Independence all over again. Well, let me tell you, there is no room for that attitude in this war. We are all in it together, and we have to get along.'

'With all due respect, sir—'

'As Vice-Admiral Davies has already told you, Captain, you and respect are complete strangers. I am going to recommend your return to the United States, where your record will precede you. Until then, you are suspended from your duties. Dismiss, Captain.'

'Sir—'

'Dismiss!'

When Boyle and Rear Admiral Farrell had gone, the admiral opened the adjoining door to ask Bea for more tea.

'Thank you for taking my side, sir,' she said as she went to pick up the tray.

'Do you imagine I would ever countenance a slur on one of my beloved nieces, Bea?'

'No, Uncle Edgar. You were very fierce just now.'

'Good. I needed to be.'

When Bea had gone, he sat in thought. Where could he send Bonnington this time?' He looked around the office and his eye fell on the calendar. The picture for January was of sheep in snow, and it gave him an idea.

William had seen *Pembroke*'s wireless station at work and spoken with various officers and ratings, all of whom seemed happy in their allotted tasks.

'Let me show you your office, now, Stamford,' said Bray.

They walked together along the passage that ran alongside the wireless room, the way the PO telegraphist had taken William the previous evening, until they passed Bray's office and came to one that was two doors further along.

'This is it,' said Bray, opening the door for him.

William looked inside. It was quite small, as was its one window. Its furniture comprised a desk and two wooden chairs. With the exception of the tiny window, it was very much like his first room at the Admiralty. He gave it his tacit approval.

'One more thing,' said Commander Bray. 'You'll share a secretary with me. I'll introduce you if I can find her. She's a willing girl, if a trifle hazy about the rudiments. Oh, and she has a German-sounding surname from way back, but we pronounce it the English way.' He called down the corridor, 'Marguerite? Are you there?'

William heard a door open and then a woman's footsteps on the passage.

'Come and meet Commander Stamford, Marguerite.' Turning to William, he said, 'Stamford, I'd like you to meet our shared secretary, Miss Marguerite Werner.'

William tried not to stare. Instead, he offered his hand. 'How do you do, Miss Werner?'

'How do you do, Commander?' She took his hand, looking straight into his eyes.

'I'm looking forward to working with you, Miss Werner.'

'In that case, perhaps you should follow Commander Bray's example and call me "Marguerite".'

'I shall.' At that moment, he could think of nothing else to say, because the young woman whose hand he had just shaken, and who, for some reason, had taken a spurious identity, was none other than Lucy.

10

C aptain Challock showed his identity card to the rating who challenged him, and the gate opened to allow the car access to *HMS Pembroke*.

'Drive up to the wireless station,' he told the driver. 'As I remember, it's not far up here and on the left.'

As the car pulled in beside the sign that read *Wireless Station*, he looked at the luminous dial of his watch. It was 1650. 'Park here,' he said. 'I'll be probably the best part of an hour, so see if you can get a meal. If they won't serve you because you haven't got a station card, get something in the NAAFI.' He handed him a half-crown piece.

'Thank you, sir.' The driver's surprise was evident in his response.

'You're welcome. A bacon sandwich isn't ideal, but it beats starvation.' He climbed out and looked for the entrance to the wireless station.

A Wren telegraphist, possibly returning from an errand, saluted him and asked, 'Can I help you, sir?'

'You can,' he said, returning her salute. 'I'm looking for Commander Bray. Do you know where I might find him?'

'Yes, sir. If you'll identify yourself, I'll take you to him.'

'Of course. I'm Captain Challock from the Admiralty.' He showed her his identity card.

'I see, sir. Please come this way.'

'Thank you.' He followed the Wren into the station, where she showed him to Bray's office and tapped on the door.

At Bray's invitation, she opened the door and said, 'You have a visitor, sir. Captain Challock.' She looked at Challock and said, 'That's right, isn't it, sir?'

'Absolutely right.' He shook Bray's hand and said, 'This Wren is to be commended, Commander Bray. Not only is she polite, helpful and resourceful, she is also punctilious about security.'

'Of course, sir. Well done, Wren Styles.'

'Thank you, sir.'

'Yes,' said Challock. 'Well done, and thank you for your help.'

'You're very welcome, sir.'

'Carry on.'

'Aye-aye, sir.'

'And now,' said Bray, 'how may I help you, sir?'

'I should like to speak to Commander Stamford.' He saw that Bray was holding his greatcoat. 'If you're about to go off-watch, there's no need for you to stay. Just point me in the direction of Stamford's office.'

'Of course, sir. Would you care to come this way?' Bray led him down the passage to William's office. His courtesy knock brought forth an invitation to enter.

'Commander Stamford, Captain Challock is here to see you.'

'Oh, thank you, Bray. Captain Challock, how are you, sir?'

'Chasing my tail, Stamford, but more of that later. How are you?'

'Well, thank you, sir.'

Challock waited until Bray was out of the office. 'I shan't beat about the bush,' he said, removing his cap and greatcoat. 'Is Marguerite Werner hereabouts? If so, will you find her before she goes off-watch?'

'Aye-aye, sir.' William went next door and knocked. 'Marguerite, will you come into my office, please?' He felt stupid using that name, but he imagined all would be made clear at some time. As she opened her door, he said, 'Captain Challock is here. He wants to speak to you.'

'Of course.' She accompanied him to his office.

'Come inside, my dear!' Challock shook her hand and closed the door.

'Take my chair, sir,' offered William, as there were only two in the office.

'Nonsense. I've been sitting on my backside all day, one way or another. Sit down, both of you. Now, I know you've met. How did it go?'

'It was fine, Captain,' Lucy told him. 'Neither of us gave the game away.'

'Good. That's what Vice-Admiral Davies was worried about when he heard you'd been posted here, Stamford.'

Lucy asked, 'Can I get you a cup of tea, Captain Challock?'

'Would you, my dear? That would be glorious after the day I've had.'

As Lucy left the office, William said, 'Sir, if it isn't asking too much, would you mind telling me why my assistant isn't in America after all, and why she has adopted an incognito?'

'Of course, Stamford. I'll tell you most of it when she returns, but just to put you in the picture, we told you she was in America to throw you deliberately off the scent. Miss Pendleton is engaged in vital intelligence work, and we didn't want you jeopardising the operation by trying to contact her. However, now that Captain Boyle has thrown a spanner, although I believe he would call it a "monkey wrench", into the works, I'm here to explain why you mustn't be heard, on any account, referring to or addressing Miss Pendleton by her real name.' He paused when Lucy came in with the tea things.

'Milk but no sugar, I believe, Captain?' Lucy poured his tea.

'What a memory you have, my dear.'

She poured William's without a word, but smiled and touched his hand as she gave it to him.

'Some time ago,' said Challock, 'Special Branch arrested a Nazi agent called Marguerite Werner, otherwise *Agentin Elster*. They'd been watching her carefully, as she was employed as a secretary at *HMS Lochinvar* in South Queensferry, and it soon became apparent that she was dangerous. We naturally kept her supplied with bogus information.'

'Where is she now, sir?'

'In a safe house, where I've spent the past three days trying to ascertain how genuine she is about working for the Allies.'

It still made little sense to William. 'So what is Miss Pendleton's involvement in this operation?'

'I'm coming to that, Stamford. After some preparation, Miss

Pendleton has taken over Marguerite Werner's identity until we know that the real Miss Werner can be trusted, or until it's decided that she must be kept in captivity. Now, you're obviously wondering why Miss Pendleton was chosen to perform this task, so I'll tell you. She bears a strong physical resemblance to Marguerite Werner, and they were at school together in Cheshire, so Miss Pendleton knows her quite well.' He paused to sip his tea. 'I described the resemblance as "physical" because I have to say that any likeness ends there. In all other respects, they could not be more different. Marguerite Werner believes confidently that the world is populated by superior and inferior races, although she argues that holding that belief does not necessarily make her an ardent Nazi. She is, nevertheless, one of the most disagreeable young women I have ever encountered.'

'She was like that at school,' said Lucy, joining the conversation for the first time, 'although she tried to hide her prejudices behind a cloak of silliness. Even then, they seldom remained hidden for long.' With a gesture of distaste, she added, 'People sometimes took us for sisters. That was until they realised how different we were.'

Challock nodded his silent agreement. 'When Vice-Admiral Davies learned that you'd been posted here, Stamford, he was naturally furious, but then he decided to leave you here, where you can communicate directly with Miss Pendleton. Your orders will come via me, and you will continue with your current task. Miss Pendleton will continue to be in regular contact with a double agent called Thomas Gael.'

William had the feeling he remembered from the early days in 1940, of being in a kind of Wonderland.

'Have you any questions, Stamford?'

'Yes, sir.' He put his feelings aside and made himself concentrate. 'You'll recall that I sent you a report shortly before you left the Admiralty.'

'Yes.'

'Captain Boyle dismissed my suggestions as too subtle for the Germans, sir. I think he may have destroyed the report.'

Challock closed his eyes momentarily. 'I'll see if I can retrieve it, Stamford. Otherwise, I'll have to ask you to re-submit it. Rest assured, it will not be dismissed again.'

'Thank you, sir.' William looked up at the bulkhead clock, and said, 'I don't know what arrangements you've made for dinner, Lucy, but I'd like to invite both you and Captain Challock to the wardroom.'

'Thank you, Stamford, but there's a seaman outside, waiting to drive me back to London. I hope he's had a meal, because I'm looking forward to mine.'

'If I'd known earlier, Captain, I'd have made you a sandwich, although....' Lucy stood up. 'I can do it now. I'll make one for your driver as well, in case he didn't get a meal.'

'Bless you, Miss Pendleton. I shall appreciate that, and so will my driver.'

Lucy disappeared. When the door was closed, Challock said, 'She's a remarkable young woman, Stamford, but you already know that, of course. Still, you mustn't let it cloud your judgement.'

'I'll try not to, sir.'

'What are your duties here?'

'Just the checking of intercepts, sir. It's not like a "Y" station, but they do pick up quite a lot of plain-language chatter.'

'You'll have time for your special duties, then?'

'Ample time, sir.'

'Good. I have to say that after the past few days, I'll be more than ready to resume work at the Admiralty.' He smiled as another thought occurred to him. 'I shouldn't say this, but I don't expect to find Captain Boyle there on my return. Vice-Admiral Davies was very terse on the telephone.'

'Good.'

There was a muffled knock on the door. William opened it to find Lucy with two packets of sandwiches.

'Sorry,' she said, 'my hands were full. There was only corned beef, so I hope that's all right, Captain.'

'It's more than all right,' said Challock. 'You've done us proud. Thank you, Miss Pendleton.' He opened his briefcase and put the sandwiches inside it.

'It was no trouble, Captain.'

'Let me show you out to your car, sir,' offered William.

'No, thank you. I've taken enough of your time already. Goodbye, both of you, good luck and thank you again, Miss... Werner. Let's get into practice.' He shook hands with them both and left.

As the door closed, William and Lucy fell into each other's arms and remained locked together for some time.

'I've missed you like hell,' he said eventually.

'So have I. It was the most delightful surprise, seeing you here this afternoon.'

'I was a touch taken aback, myself.' Conscious of the time, he asked, 'Do you know of any restaurants close by, Luc... Marguerite?'

'Yes, Percy, but we'd be better going a little further, although....'

'What?'

'Does it matter if we're seen together? As long as we keep my cover intact, we should be all right. We're only being sociable, after all.'

'You're right, but why did you call me "Percy"?'

'It's the "Marguerite" thing. "Look, Marguerite. England." '

'Of course, *The Scarlet Pimpernel.*'

'Let's get a taxi and ask the driver to take us to a good restaurant.'

'Let's.'

———◆◄———

The driver's choice was excellent; the restaurant was discreet, and the waiter even managed to find a bottle of acceptable, if somewhat expensive, wine. Even without the wine, of course, they would have been supremely happy to be back in each other's company.

Mindful of the need for reticence in a public place, William told her about the harmless nonsense that had taken place at the Admiralty in her absence, including the wardroom dinner and the cigar ceremony.

'So Bea chose a cigar for Dai,' he said. 'She did it ever so well, too, not as well as you do it, naturally, but she kept everyone entertained.' He held up a cautionary finger. 'I should say *almost* everyone, because Captain Boyle stopped me a week later, to ask what the process meant, and when I explained it to him, he was very scathing.

He wanted to know what a "girl fresh out of high school" knew about cigars.'

'He sounds horrid.'

'He probably is. What does "horrid" mean? It sounds like a word girls use.'

'It probably is. It means "Beastly", "tough" and "bristling with aggressiveness".'

'In that case, Marguerite, he is horrid, as you say, but Captain Challock doesn't expect to find him in SW One tomorrow. Apparently, Vice-Admiral Davies was less than pleased with him. I'll probably find out more from Dai or Bea.'

'Yes.' She looked a little wistful as she said, 'I was about to say, "Give them my love", but you mustn't, as you're not supposed to know where I am.' Changing the subject, she said, 'I never congratulated you on your promotion.' She ran her forefinger over the rings on his sleeve. 'It came as quite a surprise when Commander Bray introduced us.'

'The introduction was a bigger surprise for me,' he said, 'but I think we'll leave that subject alone for now.' He looked over his glass at her, still scarcely able to believe they were together again. 'I love you, Marguerite,' he said.

'I love you, too, Percy.'

'Where's your accommodation?'

'I have a flat in the town, but I can't invite you back. Not tonight, anyway.'

'Why not? Are you entertaining someone else? I'll run the blackguard through with my sword.'

'It's more practical than that, Percy. If you came back, one thing would be sure to lead to another, and... no can do, I'm afraid.'

'Oh, of course, that's understood.'

'No, it's not that. That was last week.' She put her hand on his and said, 'You see, I left my little bowler hat in the flat in London, so until I can get to a chemist, I'm a weeny bit vulnerable.'

William assumed a look that was reminiscent, he fancied, of Leslie Howard in the final scene of *The Scarlet Pimpernel*. 'Some things, Marguerite,' he said, 'are worth the wait.'

11

Captain Challock opened the door to Room Twelve to find an officer, a commander, seated at his desk. The visitor rose and came to attention.

'Bonnington, I presume? I took over your job in nineteen forty. My name's Challock.'

'How do you do, sir?'

Purely for the sake of common decency, Challock took Bonnington's outstretched hand.

'I rather expected Captain Boyle to be here this morning, sir.'

'He will not be here this morning or, for that matter, any morning, Bonnington. Captain Boyle is suspended from his duties and is currently at his London address, awaiting orders to return to the United States.' He picked up an envelope, saying, 'He left a note for you. I imagine he needs all the friends he can muster.'

Bonnington took the envelope but stared at him open-mouthed until he collected himself and said, 'I can't believe that, sir.'

'In that case, I'm sure Vice-Admiral Davies will be happy to confirm the news. He's expecting you now, so don't make yourself too comfortable.'

Again, Bonnington was incredulous. 'Vice-Admiral Davies? Is he still DNI?'

'Yes, Bonnington, he is still Director of Intelligence. I should hurry along if I were you, because he doesn't like to be kept waiting, as I'm sure you will recall.'

Bonnington hesitated.

'Now, Bonnington.'

Once more in possession of his office, Challock took his seat and opened first the left, and then the right, desk drawer. In the second, he found a manila file. He examined the contents briefly and recognised the report on the Low Countries as a potential invasion zone. Stamford would not have to rewrite the report after all.

Challock read it again as he would be required to present it to the London Controlling Section. In common with every previous report Stamford had submitted, it was considered, detailed and extremely well-argued. That Boyle had tried to get rid of him because of a petty grudge defied belief.

He worked on his submission to the Section, until the door opened and Bonnington reappeared. He saluted and said somewhat humbly, 'I am to remove my personal effects from this room, sir. I shall not be long.'

'Good. Have you got your official posting now?'

'Yes, sir. I am posted to Loch Ewe.'

Challock managed not to smile. Loch Ewe was in the far north-west of the Scottish Highlands, the point of departure for Russian convoys. Without posting him abroad or to Orkney or Shetland, the admiral had sent him as far as he could.

'I have everything now, sir,' Bonnington told him.

Again, Challock shook his hand as courtesy demanded. 'Let me give you one final piece of advice, Bonnington,' he said.

'Yes, sir?'

'Be sure to wrap up warmly. It's bloody cold up there.'

Bonnington closed the door after him, and with perfect timing, the telephone rang.

'Room Twelve. Captain Challock speaking.'

'Good morning, sir. This is Second Officer Dean. Vice-Admiral Davies would like to see you again, sir.'

'Thank you, Miss Dean. I'll be with him shortly.'

He made the short journey to the admiral's office and looked in on Bea, who reported his arrival.

'Ask him to come in, Bea.'

'Aye-aye, sir. The admiral will see you now, sir.'

'Thank you, Miss Dean.' Challock stepped inside the admiral's office and saluted.

'Come inside, Captain Challock. Bea, coffee, if you please.'

'Aye-aye, sir.'

The admiral sank into his chair. 'I think I can safely say,' he said, 'that the damage is now repaired. Director of Postings and Drafts has given a stern reprimand to the blockhead who set the whole thing in motion, and we can all breathe again.'

'I've just seen Bonnington, sir.' Challock smiled involuntarily. 'May I ask what made you think of Loch Ewe?'

The admiral pointed to the calendar with its wintry scene and woolly characters. 'Sometimes a picture can be an inspiration,' he said. Then, he became serious again. 'I'm sorry I had to rush our meeting this morning. I wanted to send that cross-grained malcontent on his way before he could do any damage. I really wanted to speak to you about *Agentin Elster.*'

'The consensus, sir, is that she is still hostile.'

'But she agreed to co-operate.'

'Who wouldn't, sir, when the alternative was the death penalty?'

'Quite. So, we keep our girl in the role. How was she?'

'In what sense, sir?'

'In good spirits?'

Challock smiled again. 'Yes, sir, and in even better spirits now that Stamford's around.'

'We must keep our fingers crossed that nothing goes wrong there.'

'Stamford's extremely reliable, sir. He won't compromise the girl's cover.' Smiling, he said, 'If he has a fault, it's his proclivity for telling tall but credible stories.'

'Quite, but that's why we recruited him in the first place.'

———◆►◄———

Commander Bray looked round William's door to ask, 'Stamford, have you seen Marguerite?'

'Yes, she's gone ashore to do some shopping. Do you need her?'

'Yes, I have some typing for her.' He looked momentarily thoughtful. 'I say, it's a bit of a liberty, isn't it, doing her shopping during working hours?'

'Women's needs are different from ours, Bray, and some things can't wait, so I'm told.' In truth, the shopping in question had required a medical prescription, and that had taken three days for her to obtain, as well as involving William and herself in a further period of celibacy, but that was none of Bray's business.

Censure became guilt. 'Of course, old man. I should have thought.'

'If I see her first, I'll tell her you've been looking for her,' promised William.

'Thanks, old chap. I don't want to make an issue of it. It doesn't call for a slap on the wrist or anything of that kind.'

'I'm sure she'll appreciate that.'

As Bray closed the door behind him, William couldn't help comparing the situation with the state of affairs that had existed at the Admiralty in 1940, when Lucy's superiors had made impossible demands and allowed her no leeway at all. By comparison, Chatham was a scene of rest and recuperation.

There was a knock on the door.

'Come in.'

The door opened, and a timid-looking Wren stood in the doorway, apparently wondering whether or not to nerve herself and take the final step.

'There's an intercept, sir,' she said uncertainly.

'Thank you.' He held out his hand to take the message form from her. 'Don't be afraid,' he told her. 'I only bite when I'm hungry.'

'No, sir.'

'All right, carry on.'

'Aye-aye, sir.' She withdrew gratefully and closed the door.

William studied the plain-language intercept carefully. It appeared to be an exchange between two stations, presumably small ships, as the Nazis were currently short of the other kind, and it concerned some temporary difficulty. He was reaching for a German dictionary, when the door opened and Lucy walked in.

'Hello, darling,' she said, waving her bag, which presumably contained her shopping. 'You can come back to my place tomorrow night.'

'Not tonight?'

'I'm afraid not. I have to meet my contact, and it could take some time, but don't worry, darling. We'll make up for it tomorrow night.'

'Wonderful, but wouldn't it be better if we stuck to "Marguerite" and "Commander Stamford" when we're on watch?'

'You're quite right. I was so pleased at getting what I needed, I quite forgot.' Somewhat belatedly, she placed a hand over her mouth.

'By the way, Commander Bray was looking for you earlier. He has some typing for you.'

Her look of excitement turned to disappointment. 'Oh rats,' she said, 'he would have.'

'Before you go, have you any idea what *zuknöpfen* means? *Knopf* sounds familiar, and the meaning's on the tip of my tongue, but just for now, I'm stumped.'

'*Zuknöpfen*? It means "to button up".'

'Of course.' He slapped his forehead impatiently. 'How could I forget?'

'It's easy enough, Percy, when you didn't have to *Mieder zuknöpfen* every morning against the Alpine winter, as we did.'

'Please don't talk about underwear, Marguerite. You know what it does to me.'

'All right, Percy.' She blew him a kiss and left the office.

He dispelled the image of Lucy and the other girls buttoning up their bodices, and concentrated again on the intercept. It went thus:

Station 1: What is the problem?
Station 2: I cannot button up for the day. Something is wrong.
Station 1: Are you using the correct key?
Station 2: Yes, it is not working correctly.
Station 1: For the sake of security, maintain silence.

Everything pointed to the first station's inability to operate the Enigma Shark encryption system, which was strange, when British Naval Intelligence were reading it without difficulty. William had no idea whether the incident might be important or not, but he made a note of the frequency on the top of the message form, and sealed it in an envelope to be sent to Bletchley Park for the experts to investigate.

He heard Lucy's door being opened and closed, so he dropped the envelope into his 'Out' basket and went to join her. He found her arranging carbons between sheets of paper preparatory to feeding them into her typewriter. He kissed her briefly and said, 'Move over, Marguerite.'

'Oh, thank you, Percy.' She vacated her chair for him.

There were two documents to be typed, neither of them complex, but typing had never been Lucy's greatest skill, so William set about them. After five minutes, he handed them both to her, saying, 'When you've taken these to Commander Bray and done what you have to do with them, will you come back to my office?'

She narrowed her eyes seductively. 'Of course I will,' she said.

'And behave yourself.'

'Aye-aye, sir.'

He spent the next ten minutes or so considering the on-going question of how he could best convince the Nazi high command that the Low Countries were under consideration as an invasion zone. It was still a monumental task, and he was no further forward when Lucy returned from Bray's office.

She closed the door behind her, took the chair opposite him and hunched forward across his desk, looking puzzled.

'What is it, Marguerite?'

'Nothing important, I'm sure, but Commander Bray has just told me to take things easy for the rest of the week. I must say he was looking a trifle embarrassed. I wonder what's on his mind.'

William smiled as he recalled his conversation with Bray that morning. 'I expect he's conscious that ladies, especially civilians, need gentle treatment. He strikes me as being very thoughtful in that way.'

'Yes, he is.' Apparently satisfied, Lucy dismissed the matter and asked, 'What do you want to speak to me about?'

'A very sensitive matter, not unlike the work we did in persuading the Nazis to invade Russia.'

'You know you can trust me, Percy.'

'Yes, I do. Have you ever visited the Low Countries?'

Lucy gave the question her brief consideration. 'I've never been to Holland or Belgium, but I have tuned in to Radio Luxembourg many times.'

'This is more serious than Ovaltine and a bedtime singalong, Marguerite.'

'I'll take your word for it, Percy.'

'What do Holland and Belgium mean to you?'

Lucy closed her eyes to aid recollection. 'Dutch masters, organists, Renaissance and Baroque composers....' She wrinkled her nose. 'They're not my cup of tea, really.' Closing her eyes again, she went on. 'Bulb fields, Dutch treats, Dutch caps, clogs, windmills, Belgian chocolates, Cesar Franck, Ysaÿe, Okeghem....' She broke off once more, to say, 'I'm not all that keen on him either.' She paused.

'Anything else?'

'Only the obvious features. Canals, dikes, the little boy who saved his country from flooding....'

'I think you may have something there. I've considered the possibility of crossing the terrain with the aid of amphibious vehicles, but the canals would still constitute a tremendous obstacle.'

The look of puzzlement returned to Lucy's face as she asked, 'Why do you want to cross the Low Countries?'

'I don't, but I want to make the Nazis think we're considering it.'

'As a place for invasion?'

'Yes, and I don't mind telling you, it's a mountainous task.'

Lucy became thoughtful again. 'You could call it an Herculean task.' With the look of someone who has just had a brainwave, she said, 'Maybe that's the answer.'

'What is?' He'd become used to Lucy's unusual thought processes, and he suspected that a stroke of brilliance might be in the making.

'The fifth labour of Hercules,' she said, 'was to muck out King Augeas's stables in a single day, and when you consider that Augeas owned thousands of animals, you can imagine the scale of the operation.'

'I can,' agreed William. 'Bullshit must have been a damned nuisance even in those days.'

'Really, Percy.'

'I'm sorry.' He gestured to her to continue.

'To proceed, hopefully without vulgar interruptions, Hercules first made two openings in the walls around the cattle yards, and then he diverted the Rivers Alpheus and Peneus so that they flowed through the stables, carrying all before them.'

Suddenly, William was enthusiastic. 'You've got something there, Luc... Marguerite. Instead of relying solely on the bombing of Nazi garrisons and installations, they could bomb the canal system so that the water would flood them. The Dutch tried it in 1940, but the Nazis anticipated it and brought inflatable whatsits....'

'*Gummiboote*,' suggested Lucy.

'Dinghies, yes, but this time, they would be taken by surprise, and all the time they were breaking out the dinghies and inflating them, the allies would be crossing the emptied canals with tanks.'

———◆◄———

He spent the remainder of the day working on his report, with the intention of sleeping on it before finally sending it in the morning by courier to Captain Challock.

When he arrived at the wireless station the next day, however, he found the outgoing Duty Officer outside his office, looking apologetic.

'Good morning,' said William. 'What can I do for you?'

'Good morning, sir. There are two civilians in your office. They insisted on waiting there for you.'

'Really?' Filled with curiosity, William opened the door to find two men in civilian clothes.

'One of them asked, 'Are you Commander William Stamford?'

'I am. Who are you?'

'We are police officers.'

'What do you want?'

'We want you to come with us.'

12

William sat in the back of the spacious saloon car beside one of his mysterious companions. He asked, 'Is either of you going to tell me what this nonsense is all about?'

The man next to him replied, 'You'll find out soon enough.'

'Now would be preferable. Where are you taking me?'

'New Scotland Yard. Now, be a good chap and stop asking questions.'

'Why?'

The man sighed impatiently. 'You don't want to make things worse for yourself. You could be in a lot of trouble.'

'So could you when Naval Intelligence find out about this pantomime performance.'

The driver spoke for the first time. 'Are you threatening us, Commander Stamford?'

'Only if you're threatening me. Are you?'

There was no reply, and William could only deduce that neither of them was skilled at repartee. He settled back into the leather seat and waited.

Quite soon, they reached Blackwall Tunnel. William said, 'You really are keeping me in the dark, aren't you?'

The man next to him said, 'This is no time for jokes, Commander Stamford.'

'In that case, why am I sharing a car with two of them?'

'Just keep quiet.'

'For all the intelligent conversation I'm likely to get out of you two, I might as well.' He contented himself for the time being by watching the London scenes as he passed them by.

Having negotiated their way through the busy streets of East

London, they eventually reached Victoria Embankment and drove into New Scotland Yard. The driver opened the rear door for his colleague, who broke his silence by saying, 'Come along, Commander Stamford.'

William had no choice but to comply.

His captors led him to what looked like a reception area, where they spoke to a man in uniform, and one of them made an entry in a book before ordering him to empty his pockets. He made an inventory of William's personal effects and then ushered him down a dim passage to a deserted and equally badly-lit room.

'Sit down.'

William sat on a wooden chair beside a plain wooden table. He asked, 'What happens now? Are you going to shine a bright light into my eyes?' He indicated the bare bulb that dangled from the ceiling rose. 'This one's not really up to it, I think you'll agree.'

'Be quiet and wait for the Chief Inspector.'

'Will he want to see my bus ticket?'

'Be quiet.'

'You people are no fun at all.'

The door opened and another man entered the room. He was tall and looked well-fed. He had a chubby face and an untidy moustache. William disliked him instantly on the basis that no one had any right to look well-fed while Britain was beset by rationing.

The man guarding William said, 'This is Commander Stamford, sir.'

'Oh, yes?' The newcomer looked William up and down.

William gave him a friendly nod and said, 'The uniform rather gives it away, doesn't it?'

'So we have a comedian in our midst.'

'Only one? I thought this place was full of them.'

'Kindly keep your jokes to yourself, Commander Stamford, and confine yourself to answering my questions.'

'First, tell me who you are.'

'I am Detective Chief Inspector Colman.'

'Is your family in the mustard business? You must be keen.'

'I'll ask the questions, Commander, and we'll begin with your drinking habits. I gather you're familiar with the cocktail bar of the Savoy Hotel.'

William shook his head. 'I wouldn't call myself familiar. I've only been there once, with a friend.'

Colman referred to his notes. 'And your friend wore a dark-grey, double-breasted suit and a thin moustache.'

'I should hope not. I'm happy to say I don't know a girl with a double-breasted suit or a moustache.'

'This person was a gentleman, Commander.'

'What *are* you suggesting?'

'That you were in the cocktail bar of the Savoy Hotel on the evening of the fourth of February, nineteen forty-four, and that you were in the company of the man I have described.'

'Wrong. I was at the Savoy about, oh, three months ago, and that was the only time I've ever been there. If you'd ever tried it, you'd know that their prices are absolutely scandalous.'

Colman looked again at his notes. 'You were seen there by two people, and you were overheard talking to the civilian I have described about your work at the Admiralty.'

For the first time, William scented real danger. 'Look,' he said, 'I have never spoken outside the Admiralty about my work there, and I have never discussed it with any civilian.'

'Two people saw and heard you.'

'In that case, they're mistaken. Who are these people, anyway?'

'They're fully-bound witnesses, and I'm not obliged to divulge their names.'

'If this farce is to continue, I think I'd better have legal representation.'

Colman was unmoved. 'There'll be time enough for that,' he said, 'when we charge you. In the meantime, you'd do yourself more good by making a clean breast of the whole thing. You can start by telling me who the civilian was.'

'How can I, when he doesn't bloody-well exist? Listen, if you phone the Admiralty and speak to Captain Challock, he'll set the record straight. He'll tell you I'd never do such a thing.'

'Captain Challock has been informed of your situation.'

The interview continued for what seemed a very long time,

with Colman repeating his questions and allegations. Eventually, Colman turned to the junior officer and said, 'This prisoner needs some time to himself. Maybe he'll come to his senses and make a full confession. Take him down to the cells.'

———————————

Captain Challock was irritated. He'd just come from a long, wrangling meeting of the LCS at which nothing had been resolved, and the reason, it seemed to him, was the self-importance of at least one of its members.

He opened the door to room 12 and saw a note on his desk. When he looked more closely, he saw that it was from Lieutenant Commander Hughes, to say that there had been a telephone call from Special Branch at New Scotland Yard, and that he was requested to return it.

He picked up the telephone and asked for the number. Maybe Special Branch had arrested another enemy agent. It would be interesting to find out.

The operator connected him with New Scotland Yard, who then set about finding the Detective Chief Inspector Colman who had tried to contact him.

Eventually, a voice said, 'DCI Colman here. Who's calling?'

'Captain Challock at the Admiralty. You tried telephoning me earlier this morning, I believe.'

'Yes, Captain Challock. It was to tell you that we have apprehended one of your officers, and that we are holding him for questioning under the Emergency Powers Defence Act of Nineteen Thirty-Nine.'

'What?'

'Just that, Captain. The officer in question is Commander William Stamford. We apprehended him at *HMS Pembroke* in Chatham earlier this morning.'

'You did what? This is a total nonsense!'

'We are holding him on suspicion of having passed classified information of a particularly sensitive kind to a civilian, whose identity is as yet unknown.'

Challock sat down heavily. 'Someone has made a big mistake,' he said.

'We are acting on information received, Captain. Our informant and an independent witness heard him speak to the civilian in question about his work at the Admiralty. He mentioned something he called "disinformation".'

At the mention of disinformation, Challock experienced the chill of an adrenalin rush. He asked, 'Where is this supposed to have taken place?'

'In the cocktail bar of the Savoy Hotel on the evening of the fourth of February, nineteen forty-four, Captain.'

Challock made a note of the details. 'And who are these people, who claim to have witnessed it?'

'We are not obliged to divulge their identity.'

'Oh, we'll see about that. Thank you for notifying me, Chief Inspector. We'll be in touch.'

He pressed the button on the cradle and asked to be connected with Vice-Admiral Davies's secretary.

Bea answered, 'Vice-Admiral Davies's office. Second Officer Dean speaking.'

'Miss Dean, this is Captain Challock. I must speak with Vice-Admiral Davies urgently.'

'I'm sorry, sir. Vice-Admiral Davies is at a meeting at the Air Ministry.'

'When is he likely to be back?'

'Much later, sir. It's difficult to say.'

Challock swore silently. 'When he returns, please arrange for me to see him, and impress upon him the fact that the matter is most urgent.'

'Aye-aye, sir.'

It would simply have to wait.

———◆◄◆———

William sat on his bunk, his thoughts going round in circles. He knew he hadn't been to the Savoy on the fourth. Damn it, it was less than a week ago. Those so-called witnesses must have been mistaken, but how? It was possible they'd seen an officer who looked like him, but who would discuss his work at the Admiralty with a civilian or, for that matter, anyone outside the Admiralty? It made no sense at all. He could only hope that Captain Challock would be able to bring his influence to bear, and bring the whole nonsensical business to an end.

———————▸◂———————

Lucy could stand it no longer. All she knew was that two civilians had taken William away and, according to Lieutenant Rogers, William did not look at all pleased about it. It made no sense at all.

She picked up the telephone and asked to be connected with the Admiralty.

'Admiralty.'

'Hello, will you put me through to Captain Challock in Room Twelve, please?'

'Room Twelve. A familiar voice asked, 'Is that Lucy Pendleton?'

'No, it's Marguerite Werner.' There had always been a risk involved.

'I beg your pardon, Miss Werner. Room Twelve, then.' The ringing tone sounded. Lucy hoped against hope that Captain Challock and not Dai Hughes would pick up the phone. If Dai answered, she would have to put down the receiver.

'Room Twelve. Captain Challock speaking.'

'Oh, Captain Challock, this is... Marguerite Werner calling from Chatham.'

'Hello, Miss Werner.' He sounded understandably surprised. 'What can I do for you?'

'Something awful has happened to Commander Stamford. Two civilians came this morning and took him away. I wondered if you might know anything about it.'

Challock hesitated. 'I know about it, Miss Werner, and I'm waiting to speak to Vice-Admiral Davies about it. He's safe, so there's no need to worry. I'll let you know as soon as I know anything more.'

'Thank you, Captain. I'm sorry to trouble you.'

'That's all right, my dear, but I must keep this line clear for the admiral. Don't call me again. I'll be in touch.'

'Of course. Goodbye, Captain.'

'Goodbye.'

At least, Captain Challock was doing something about it. She just had a horrible feeling that William was in danger, and this time there was nothing she could do to help him.

———— ►◄ ————

The junior detective pushed William back into the interview room and closed the door. Colman was waiting for him.

'Well,' he said, 'have you come to your senses?'

'There's nothing wrong with my senses. I know I wasn't at the Savoy on the date you mentioned, I know I have never spoken about my work to any unauthorised person, and I can only imagine your so-called witnesses saw someone else entirely and jumped to a ridiculous conclusion.'

Colman's expression remained unchanged. He asked, 'Do you know the penalty for what you've done?'

'I haven't done anything.'

'It's death by hanging. You've earned the death penalty, Commander Stamford. Just think about that.' He allowed his victim some time to reflect, before saying, 'But it could still be avoided. If you co-operate with us and make a full confession, we can put a word in on your behalf. Otherwise, it won't be long now. Treachery cases are tried in camera within weeks, and you could be making the acquaintance of the hangman by the end of next month, or even earlier.' He looked hard at William, possibly trying to gauge his reaction, and then said, 'If you insist on denying it, I have no alternative but to charge you under the Treachery Act of nineteen-forty with passing classified information to an unauthorised party.'

13

Captain Challock concluded his account of his conversation with Special Branch. 'It's a total nonsense, sir. Stamford is completely reliable. He'd never breathe a word of our work to an outsider.'

'The trouble is,' said Vice-Admiral Davies, 'we're dealing with Special Branch, and they behave as if they answer to no one. They're useful enough when they're operating with us; otherwise they function like a private army. Did you say this chap refused to give you the names of the informant and witness?'

'He was like a clam, sir.'

'Blast.' He opened the connecting door and said, 'Bea, will you get me Metropolitan Police Special Branch, please?'

'Aye-aye, sir.'

'What's the name of the officer in charge of the case, Challock?'

'Detective Chief Inspector Colman, sir. If you find him officious and overbearing, don't be too surprised. That was my impression of him also.'

After a few minutes, the telephone rang and Davies picked it up. 'Yes, Bea?'

Challock heard her say, 'I have Special Branch on the line.'

'Thank you, Bea.'

Challock could only follow the admiral's side of the conversation, which ran along similar lines to the one he'd taken part in earlier. From the admiral's questions and responses, however, he gathered that Chief Inspector Colman was being no more helpful than before, although he did provide one more piece of information.

'They've charged Stamford with passing classified information to an unauthorised party,' said the admiral, replacing the receiver. 'I don't know if Chief Inspector Colman is related to the people who produce mustard, but this business certainly leaves a nasty taste.'

Challock could only nod in agreement.

'We have to get to the bottom of this, Challock, because if we don't, an innocent young man stands to lose both his reputation and his life. In addition to that, we will lose a valuable officer, and one who will be almost impossible to replace.' He opened his desk drawer and retrieved a leather-bound book that appeared to be a personal directory. 'Before we do anything else,' he said, 'I must see to it that Stamford receives legal representation.'

———◆◆———

William's spirits had sunk to new depths. During the River Plate action, he knew that death might be imminent, and even later, as he lay helpless in the Sick Bay, he was aware that he might yet die of wounds, but that was one of the hazards of naval service in wartime. Now, he faced the death penalty for an act of treachery he had not committed, and whilst the outcome was the same, the circumstances were worsened by the injustice and shame involved.

He lay on the unyielding bunk, thinking of the life he was likely to forfeit. Never again would he know the joy of Lucy's company, nor would he ever see his mother and sister again. Instead, they would be left with the belief that he had betrayed his country and suffered the consequence.

Unable to sleep, he pondered those things endlessly until late afternoon, when one of his captors came to his cell.

'Up you get, Commander Stamford,' he said. 'Your legal team's here to see you.'

William followed him to the now grotesquely-familiar interview room, where he found two men in morning dress.

'Good afternoon, Commander Stamford,' said one, a short, dapper man with a receding hairline and a faint Scottish accent. 'My name is Jamieson. I'm a solicitor, and this is Mr Mallinson, the barrister who, if you're agreeable, will represent you at your trial.'

William shook hands with them both, and Mr Mallinson, a tall, determined-looking man invited him to be seated.

'I don't understand,' said William. 'Who arranged for you both to represent me?'

Almost brushing the matter aside, Mr Jamieson said, 'Vice-Admiral Davies is one of my firm's clients, but don't concern yourself with that. Let's concentrate instead on the matter in hand.' He sat back, at least, as far as the wooden chair would allow, and invited his companion by means of a gesture, to take over the conference.

'Commander Stamford,' said Mr Mallinson, 'firstly, I have to tell you some relatively good news, which is that the hearing has been postponed.' It was the first scrap of good news William had heard since his arrest, but he waited for the lawyer to continue.

'It appears that the prosecution are experiencing some difficulty in locating the witness, and until they do, they are unable to initiate proceedings.' He opened his briefcase and took out a foolscap booklet. 'Fortunately, it gives us more time for preparation.' Unscrewing the cap of his fountain pen, he said, 'Most importantly, Commander, I understand you have denied the accusation as put to you by Special Branch, that you passed classified information to an unauthorised person. Is that still the case?'

'Yes.'

'You are saying you are not guilty of the charge?'

'Absolutely.'

'Good.' He made a note before saying, 'You have told the police that you were not at the *locus in quo*, the cocktail bar of the Savoy Hotel, that is, on the evening of the fourth of February. Is that correct?'

'Yes.'

'Can you remember where you were, Commander? An alibi could be crucial.'

William had gone over the question a thousand times, each time knowing that he couldn't ask Lucy to testify that he was with her, however innocently, on that date.

'I was at the Nore restaurant in Chatham with a friend,' he said.

'And who was that friend?'

'I'm sorry. In the interests of National Security, I cannot divulge that information.' It was the ultimate irony that he had to give that reason, but Lucy couldn't give evidence under oath whilst posing as Marguerite Werner. To do so would risk compromising the operation, possibly with far-reaching consequences.

'It could mean the difference between a verdict of guilty and an acquittal,' prompted Mr Mallinson.

'I'm sorry. It's as important as that.'

'More important than your own life, Commander?'

William swallowed hard. 'I'm afraid so.'

Mallinson made another note. 'Very well,' he said, 'let's explore another route. When you are relaxing away from your place of work, I presume you wear your uniform?'

'Unless I'm at my flat in Clapham, yes.'

'But, in visiting a restaurant or bar, you would be in uniform, I take it?'

'Yes.'

Mallinson turned to the solicitor and said, 'We could cast doubt on the ability of the informant and witness to identify one naval officer among many. The American Bar is popular and often patronised by naval personnel to the extent that a special cocktail has been formulated for them, called the "Eight Bells".'

Mr Jamieson nodded enthusiastically.

'Also, a degree of relaxation caused by the intake of alcohol may have impaired their judgement.'

'Quite.'

'Having said that, an alibi would be preferable, in that it would come down to one person's word against that of another. Commander Stamford, would anyone else in the Nore Restaurant be likely to recall seeing you there?'

'I don't know anyone else there.'

'So we must rule out the alibi.' He made a note to that effect in his booklet. 'Cast your mind back, Commander, and tell me if you have ever spoken to anyone outside the Admiralty about your work there.'

'Never. I have the highest security clearance. That is the extent to which I am trusted at the Admiralty.' On reflection, he said, 'I'm a little surprised they haven't intervened in this nonsense before now.'

'Our presence here is a result of their intervention,' said Mr Jamieson.

'I'm sorry. I'm not thinking clearly.'

'It's not surprising, Commander Stamford.'

It was small comfort to know that someone, presumably Vice-Admiral Davies, had intervened on William's behalf, because the future remained less than promising.

———▸◂———

Lucy had spent the whole night wondering what had happened to William. In the absence of a clue or information of any kind, her only lifeline was the knowledge that Captain Challock was investigating the matter. Consequently, she arrived at work the next day, tired and anxious. Commander Bray noticed the change in her and even suggested that she might report sick, but she insisted on remaining at her workplace, waiting for the telephone to ring.

When it eventually did, it turned out to be a call for Commander Bray that had been put through to her office by mistake, so she had it transferred to his extension and returned to her vigil.

At noon, Commander Bray knocked on her door and came in. 'I wondered if you'd gone to lunch,' he said.

'No.'

'If you'd like to join the rest of us, Marguerite, you'd be most welcome.'

'That's very kind of you, Commander, but I'm not at all hungry. I'll give lunch a miss today.'

He shook his head reprovingly. 'That's never a good idea, you know. Still, you know best how you feel.'

'That's right, Commander.' She wished he would go away and leave her alone, but he wasn't to blame. He'd no idea what was tormenting her. He was only being sympathetic. 'I'm all right, Commander Bray,' she said, 'honestly.'

'Well, if I can be of any help, you know where to find me.'

'Thank you, Commander. I'll bear that in mind.'

He left, closing the door behind him.

Lucy remembered that he had a daughter of around her age or maybe a little younger, and his attentions were born of genuine concern for someone he regarded as one to be protected from life's unpleasantness. If only he had the power to do that.

———◆►◄———

Captain Challock picked up the telephone.

'Room Twelve. Captain Challock speaking.' He hoped it was the call he was waiting for.

'Good afternoon, sir,' said Bea. 'Vice-Admiral Davies wishes to see you.'

'Thank you, Miss Dean. I'm on my way.'

He walked briskly along the corridor and down the staircase to the admiral's office, where Bea greeted him and said, 'He says you're to go through, sir.'

'Thank you, Miss Dean.' He knocked on the glass panelled door, and Vice-Admiral Davies beckoned to him to enter. Challock stepped inside and saluted.

'Good afternoon, Captain Challock.'

'Good afternoon, sir.'

'Well, Challock, the matter is now out of our hands and we must wait. I do know, however, the identities of the informant and the witness.'

'Well, sir, I suppose that's progress.'

'Oh, it's a great deal more than that, Challock.'

———◆►◄———

Twenty-two hours later, William stood over the crazed earthenware bowl, relieving himself. He hated the primitive facilities in his cell, and the fact that privacy was an unknown luxury; in fact, he hated everything about his captivity, including his captors, the egregious DCI Colman and the two myopic and mysterious beings who had presumably mistaken him for someone else. He still found it incredible, however, that anyone he knew in Naval Intelligence would discuss intelligence matters with someone who might be connected with the enemy.

Mr Mallinson had given him some cause for optimism, but he was trying not to build up his hopes only for them to be dashed.

He flushed the bowl, fastened his fly and sat on the bunk. There were no hand-washing facilities in the cell, despite the fact that he was obliged to take his meals there.

The sound of a key in the lock interrupted his morbid deliberations, and he imagined that someone had come to take away his tray from lunchtime. If that were the case, they'd taken their time over it, although, deprived as he was of his wristwatch, he had no way of telling the time. The tray and its contents just seemed to have been there rather a long time.

The door swung open, and a young officer he didn't recognise said, 'Come with me, Commander Stamford.'

'What does Colman want now? He's charged me. What more does he want?'

'DCI Colman's gone. You won't see him again.' As William got up from his bunk, he said, 'Bring your stuff.'

The officer waited for William to pick up his jacket, cap and greatcoat, and then led him the length of the corridor until they came to the desk he'd noticed when he arrived. It was later than he'd imagined, because a large, art deco wall clock told him it was a little after 1430.

Another plain-clothes officer stood beside a cardboard box containing William's personal effects.

'Check them and sign here for them,' the officer told him.

'What's all this about?'

'It's your lucky day, Commander Stamford. You're a free man.'

William closed his eyes in disbelief. He felt light-headed, as if he were about to faint, and he held on to the desk while he signed for his property. When he could trust himself to speak, he asked, 'Where's DCI Colman?'

'You might well ask.' The officer grinned at his colleague. 'He's suspended from duty, pending a disciplinary hearing, and it seems we owe it to you.' He closed the book William had signed, and said, 'With any luck, they'll send him to another force, hopefully at the other end of the country.'

William picked up his wristwatch, fountain pen, wallet, loose change, Naval Identity Card, National Registration Identity Card, the key to his flat, the key to his office safe, and his penknife. He asked, 'What have I done?' It seemed a perennial question.

'It's not what you've done, so much as what's been done on your behalf, Commander Stamford. You must have a lot of influence.' The officer pointed towards the exit. 'At all events, you're free to go.'

In his shocked and confused state, William couldn't imagine how he might be responsible for Colman's fate, and he finished fastening his wristwatch before responding. As he turned to go, he said, 'It's a shame I missed Colman. It would have been nice if I could have told him what I really thought of him.'

'Yes, quite a few of us would have liked to do that. Anyway, goodbye, Commander.'

'Goodbye.' Still struggling to believe the change in his fortunes, William walked out of the building, pulling his greatcoat on. He was about to cross the forecourt to the pavement outside, where he could hail a taxi, when he noticed a Singer Roadster parked beside the exit. When he looked more closely, he saw that the driver was Captain Challock.

14

William saluted awkwardly, surprised to see his superior officer there.

'Jump in, Stamford,' said Captain Challock.

'This is very good of you, sir. I was about to hail a taxi.'

'Vice-Admiral Davies wants to see you before you go anywhere.' Challock waited for William to close the door, before moving off and turning into Victoria Embankment. He asked, 'How do you feel, Stamford?'

'When they told me I was free, it was like waking after a nightmare, sir, but now I don't know what I feel. I'm totally confused.' He felt his chin and said, 'I know I'd appreciate a shave, and a bath. A gin-and-tonic wouldn't come amiss, either.'

'You ask a lot, Stamford.' Challock turned right into Northumberland Avenue. Then, becoming serious again, he said, 'It must have been a hellish experience for you.'

'That's one way of putting it, sir. I still don't understand what led to my release any more than I know why I was arrested in the first place.' Another alarming thought occurred to him and he said, 'Lucy will be at her wits' end. I need to tell her I'm all right.'

'I telephoned her before I came for you, Stamford. She has been worried, but I've set her mind at rest.'

'Thank you, sir. I'm very grateful.'

'It was the least I could do.' Challock skirted Trafalgar Square before driving through Admiralty Arch and into the carpark beyond. 'Let's go and see Vice-Admiral Davies, and then all will be made known.'

As they entered the building, William felt particularly self-conscious about his dishevelled appearance, even though his embarrassment amounted to very little compared with his experiences during the past few days. He walked beside Captain Challock, almost shrinking into his uniform whenever they encountered anyone on the corridors and stairs.

When they reached their destination, Challock spoke to Bea, who gave William a surprised glance before notifying the admiral of their arrival. William shook his head minutely, indicating his current inability to explain his half-grown set and tousled appearance.

On receiving the invitation to enter, Captain Challock led the way into the admiral's office, but it was to William that Davies spoke first.

'My dear fellow,' he said, 'what a nightmare you've experienced. Come in and take a seat.' Then, going to the doorway, he asked Bea to organise tea for them all.

William waited for his superiors to be seated, and then took one of the remaining chairs.

The admiral leaned forward to register his concern. 'My dear boy,' he said, 'how are you feeling?'

'I'm very confused, sir.'

'Of course you are, and not without cause. We had no idea until yesterday afternoon that the whole business was a pathetic and despicable conspiracy.'

'A conspiracy, sir?' The mystery seemed to go ever deeper.

'Yes, Commander Bonnington made the allegation, and Captain Boyle agreed, initially, to endorse it. Boyle has since denied all knowledge of the plot, having realised in the cold light of day, one can only imagine, that it could only function as another nail in the coffin of his naval career.'

'But why, sir?' Even after the insanity of the past few days, it sounded too fantastic for words.

'Why did Bonnington do it? He blamed you for his original dismissal from this department in nineteen-forty, and when your name occurred again in connection with his posting from here to Loch Ewe, he must have been seized with an overwhelming urge to revenge himself on you.' He opened his hands in a gesture of innocent wonder. 'Unbelievable, isn't it? Rest assured, though, that Bonnington will face criminal proceedings as well as a court martial. His future is not to be envied.'

Challock, who had remained silent so far, asked, 'What is the situation with Boyle, sir?'

'If he continues to deny complicity, there's little we can do, and the Americans would be reluctant to extradite him anyway, as the whole thing would reflect badly on the US Navy.' He waved one hand dismissively and said, 'At all events, his career is basically at an end.'

William was still struggling to accept what he had just heard. 'What I can't believe, sir,' he said, 'is that Bonnington would have been happy to see me hanged for treason.'

'Oh, he knew it would be impossible for the authorities to get Boyle into court, and the charge would have to be withdrawn. All he wanted was to throw enough mud at you that you'd be an embarrassment to the Directorate and the Admiralty itself, and we'd have to get rid of you.'

William was shaking his head. 'I knew he was petty-minded, but I never expected anything like this.'

There was a knock at the door.

'Come in.'

The door opened to admit a Wren bearing a tray of tea things. Bea closed the door behind her.

'Thank you,' said the admiral as the Wren placed the tray on his desk.

Bea asked, 'Would you like me to pour, sir?'

'Yes, please, Miss Dean.' He caught the Wren's eye and said, 'Carry on, my dear.'

'Aye-aye, sir.' The Wren made her exit, closing the door behind her.

'Bea,' said the admiral, 'if anyone questions Commander Stamford's sudden and less than well-groomed appearance....'

'Yes, sir?'

'You can tell them simply that we're delighted to welcome him back.'

'Aye-aye, sir.' Bea left the office with a smile, knowing that the same response applied to her.

'One thing still puzzles me, sir,' said William, gratefully accepting a cup of tea. 'When I asked Mr Jamieson, the solicitor, how he and Mr Mallinson came to be involved, he mentioned your name.'

'Did he, by Jove? Well, it looked at the time as if you were going to need their help. That is all I'm prepared to say, and I should be grateful if you didn't raise the subject again.'

'The gratitude is all mine, sir. I can't thank you both enough.'

The admiral caught Challock's eye and he smiled faintly as he said, 'Captain Challock and I cannot possibly take the whole of the credit, Stamford. Some of it must go to the Prime Minister and the Home Secretary, both of whom intervened on your behalf.

———————

William made a short but necessary telephone call to Lucy before taking the tube to Clapham Common. Because he had no food at the flat, he took a welcome bath, shaved with the spare razor, and found a quiet restaurant, where he could eat without undue ceremony. Most of all, he needed sleep, and when he returned to the flat, he lost no time in undressing and sinking gratefully into bed.

———————

At his own request, he returned to Chatham the next morning. In addition to the obvious benefit of being near Lucy again, he wanted to demonstrate to everyone at the Wireless Station that his sudden disappearance had been the result of a misunderstanding now laid to rest, and that things were returned to normal.

The first person he saw there was Commander Bray, whose pleasure was characteristically genuine.

'My dear chap,' he said, shaking William's hand, 'I am delighted to see you again. Everything sorted out, I trust?'

'Everything, Bray. It was simply a case of mistaken identity.'

'I am infinitely relieved, as you must also be.'

'Thank you. Now, shall we put it behind us?'

'My thoughts exactly, Stamford.' Bray was about to take his

leave, but he hesitated for a moment. 'A word to the wise, old man. Marguerite has been a little out of sorts recently. I should be inclined to tread warily if I were you.'

'I shall, and thank you for the warning.'

'It's no trouble, old man. I'll see you later.' Bray went on his way, leaving William to let himself into his office.

He opened the safe and took out the draft report he'd prepared for Captain Challock before his unscheduled departure. Not surprisingly, he'd given it little thought during the past few days, and he wanted to refresh his memory. He was reading it when the door opened and Lucy walked in.

Hurriedly, she closed the door behind her. Then, joining him in the corner, out of sight of anyone looking through the window, she clung to him, kissing him urgently. Eventually, she said, 'I was frantic with worry until Captain Challock telephoned me. All I knew was that you'd been taken away somewhere, and that Captain Challock and Vice-Admiral Davies were trying to get you back.'

'And not just them. The Prime Minister and the Home Secretary got involved at some stage.'

'What?'

'Sit down and I'll explain. First, though, have I got lipstick all over my face?' There was no mirror in the office.

'No, I'm not wearing any today. As a matter of fact, the war's going on longer than I anticipated, and I'm running out of all kinds of things.'

'How awful for you.'

'Don't mock.' She gestured impatiently. 'Tell me what's been happening.'

He told her how he'd been taken away and charged with an act of treason. As he related his story, her eyes grew wide with horror, and when he told her the names of the informant and the witness, shock gave way to fury.

'That horrid man Bonnington,' she said. 'He's the one who should be locked up, not you.'

'By this time, he will be. He's facing a court martial as well as criminal charges.'

'Poor William,' she said, clasping his hands, 'what an awful time you've had.'

'I was okay, Lucy,' he told her heroically. 'Norwood Grammar School produce a rugged sort of chap.'

'How can you joke about it? The whole thing was so awful.'

'Not to be repeated,' he agreed, 'but retribution has caught up with Bonnington and DCI Colman, so the story has a proper ending.'

She looked lost. 'Who is DCI Colman?'

'He was the Special Branch detective in charge of my case. Apparently, he's due to face a disciplinary hearing at New Scotland Yard. It seems that mine isn't the only case he's mishandled.'

'There are so many villains in this case, it's like Ali Baba and the Forty Thieves.'

'Yes, boiling oil is certainly called for.'

'But I've got you back again.' She clasped his hands again.

'True, but we have to be careful. It's time to put "William" and "Lucy" away again, at least for the time being, and resurrect "Marguerite" and "Commander Stamford".'

She eyed him thoughtfully and said, 'You'll always be "Percy" as far as I'm concerned.'

'Can Percy and Marguerite get together tonight?'

'I have to meet my contact, but I'll be free by about eight o' clock.'

———— ◆◄◆ ————

Their conversation at the Nore restaurant was innocent and light-hearted. They were simply happy to be together again. In any case, 'shop' was no topic for a public place; they had ample time for that during working hours, when there was no risk of indiscretion. One question, however, occurred to William, and he put it to Lucy out of idle curiosity when they were walking along Manor Road to her flat.

'What sort of chap is your contact?'

'He's a double agent, an Irishman they caught early in the war. I thought you knew that.'

'I mean, what is he like?'

She gave the question some thought before replying. 'He's all right. He thinks I'm the real Marguerite Werner. He only met her once, very briefly, so he can't have formed much of an impression of her, other than that she has a low opinion of the Irish.'

'Charming. I suppose you have to live up to that.'

'To some extent. I was warned not to overdo it.'

He considered that information before saying, 'I suppose our people will be careful how much they tell him.'

'Yes. According to the man who briefed me, double agents are, by definition, not to be trusted completely.'

'Bugger!' He stopped momentarily, having collided with a hard object.

'What's the matter?'

'I just walked into a bus stop or some such thing.'

'That means we're nearly home. The bus stop is a landmark.'

William rubbed his forehead. 'It's left its mark on me,' he said.

'We're nearly there,' she told him, sounding like a parent with an impatient child.

She stopped at the next building and searched for her key. 'Here we are. There are four steps up to the door. Be careful.' She led the way, opening the door and closing it behind him before moving the blackout curtain to one side. A few seconds later, she switched on the electric light and led the way upstairs, whispering, 'This way.'

Adjusting his volume to match hers, he asked, 'Why are we whispering?'

'Because I don't want a reputation as a scarlet woman.'

'How many men have you had back here?'

'Only you, but you know what people are like for exaggerating.'

He followed her quietly to the landing, where she unlocked a door and opened it, switching on the light as she did so.

'I saw to the blackout before I came out,' she explained. 'Will you switch off the landing light?'

'With pleasure.' He returned the stairs and landing to darkness.

'Thank you.' She opened her bag and began rummaging in it. 'I think I'd better feed the gas meter before it runs out, and then we can have the fire on.'

William handed her a shilling piece.

'Thank you, darling.' She inserted it into the meter and then picked up a box of matches from the mantlepiece and disappeared into the next room.

'Is there anything I can do?' He was feeling a little spare.

'No,' she said, returning briefly. 'Back in a minute.' She kissed him and left the room, presumably to go to the bathroom.

William was impressed. The room was well-furnished, with two armchairs, a small sofa and something that looked like a drinks cabinet. He imagined the bedroom must be the next room.

He removed his greatcoat and draped it with his scarf and cap over the back of one of the armchairs.

Lucy returned, carrying her stockings and beckoning to him to follow her. 'It's a comfortable abode,' she said, unbuttoning her blouse, 'and home for as long as I have to maintain the pretence.' She motioned towards him. 'Come on,' she urged, 'don't be shy.'

Obediently, he followed her into the next room, which housed a double bed, a chest of drawers, a double wardrobe and two bedside tables.

'This place is very grand,' he said.

'It has to be, in case I have to bring a contact here. Marguerite Werner's father is a wealthy stockbroker. It would never do for his daughter to be seen living in a bedsitter. Come on,' she repeated, 'join in.'

He undressed, making a pile of his clothes on the ottoman beside the wardrobe.

She cast off her final layer and switched on a bedside reading lamp as she slid between the sheets. 'I'll leave you to switch off the main light, as you're nearer.'

He dropped his underwear on the pile, switched off the main light and made his way by the cosy illumination of the reading lamp to the bed. Easing himself into her waiting arms, he asked, 'Are you equipped with the necessary?' It wasn't the most romantic question he'd ever asked, but he could think of no other way of finding out.

'Of course.'

They lay still, holding each other and relishing the intimacy after months of separation.

'I love you, William,' she said. A few seconds later, she prompted him by saying, 'This where you're supposed to reassure me with protestations of your undying devotion.'

He faltered. 'Sorry, I'd forgotten who I was supposed to be.'

'Can we be William and Lucy just for tonight?'

'I think so.' He joined her in a lingering kiss. Eventually, he said, 'I love you, Lucy.'

With the horrors of the past week behind him, everything was right again.

15

Commander Bray called on William a week later. 'Stamford, old chap,' he said in his usual, good-natured way, 'I must say Marguerite seems to spend a lot of time ashore.'

'Not all that much,' William assured him, 'and she does have duties ashore.'

Bray bit his lower lip in thought. 'I know she does some work for Welfare as well as for you and me.'

'That's the answer, then. She has to serve three masters. It's not the best position to be in, you'll agree.'

'No, it's not.' Bray considered the matter and said, 'She received a "Staff in Confidence" this morning.'

'That'll be a Welfare matter,' confirmed William, wishing Bray would go away, but keen, also, to throw him off the scent.

'I didn't know they did that in Welfare. I've seen "Medical-in-Confidence" but never "Staff-in-Confidence".'

'With all the personnel cases they have to handle, I suppose it makes sense.'

'Hm. First I've heard of it, old man. Still, we live and learn.'

———◆◆———

Lucy heard the doorbell and looked at her wristwatch. It was twenty-past ten. Trust Thomas Gael to be late. She hurried down to the door and let him in.

He gave her a friendly smile. 'Good morning, Marguerite.'

'Good morning, Thomas. I have something for you, but I haven't much time. I was expecting you at ten.' She motioned to him to follow her up the stairs.

'I had things to do,' he said. 'Some jobs take longer than you expect, and don't forget that I should be in bed now. It's no joke, being back on the night-shift and at your beck and call as well.'

'You need to organise your life,' she said.

'You know that the Irish don't take readily to good order and discipline, Marguerite.'

'Yes, if you're a prime example, I know that only too well.' She let him into the flat, and he sank familiarly into one of the armchairs.

'Don't bother to make yourself at home,' she told him. 'I should have been back at work by now. Thanks to you, I'll have to think up a good excuse for being "adrift", as they call it.' She picked up the plain envelope. She had already destroyed the outer one, marked *Miss M. Werner. Staff-in-Confidence*. 'You're to send this to Berlin straight away, but don't mark it *Dringend*. As far as they're concerned, there's nothing urgent about it. It's just a piece of information you've picked up, that they may find useful. Have you got that, Thomas?'

'Sure I have, and it's a pleasure working with such a beautiful and clever woman such as yourself, although I think I've said so before now. You know, I think we should get together sometime and be sociable.' He reached for her hand. 'It might improve your opinion of the Irish.'

'Keep your mind on the job,' she reminded him, moving out of his reach. 'As I told you, I must get back to work, so I'd be obliged if you'd leave.'

'It's worth bearing in mind, though, isn't it? You can't deny that.' With an irrepressible smile, he went on his way.

Lucy picked up her coat and bag and followed him. With any luck, she might still catch the 10:30 bus to *HMS Pembroke*.

───── ◆◀◆ ─────

Commander Bray kept Lucy busy until about 1600, so it wasn't possible for her to speak privately to William until then, by which time it was obvious to him that something was causing her concern.

'Come in and talk to me, Marguerite,' he said. 'Whatever it is, it's better off your chest than on your mind.'

'Oh dear.' She came into the office and took her usual seat. 'When I took this assignment, I really didn't want to be weak and feeble, but something's come up that I'm not sure I can handle.'

'Is it something I should hear, or would it be better for you to speak to Captain Challock?'

She considered the question and said, 'There's no harm in telling you.'

He leaned against the back of his chair and waited.

'A few days ago,' she said eventually, 'you asked me about Thomas Gael, my contact.'

'I remember.'

'Good, because one thing I didn't tell you was that, as well as doing a fine line in Blarney, he seems to believe his purpose in life is to give pleasure to the female population.' She stopped awkwardly and said, 'You don't want to hear this, do you?'

'I do if it's causing you distress.'

'The thing is, Percy, he's made overtures to me on two occasions. Now, under normal circumstances, I'd have no difficulty in handling the situation. In this case, though, I'm concerned that tension between him and me is the last thing we need in this job. Do you see?'

'Yes, and I think you need to talk to Captain Challock.'

'Oh, crumbs. Must I?'

'There's no shame in what you've told me, and he's more sympathetic than most naval officers I know.' He picked up the telephone and asked for the Admiralty. When he was connected, he asked the operator for Room Twelve. There was a pause, and then he heard, 'Room Twelve. Lieutenant Commander Hughes speaking.'

'Hello Dai. How are you?'

'William, I'm fine, and your goodself?'

'Likewise. Is it possible for me to speak with Captain Challock?'

'I think that might be arranged. Wait one.' There was a pause of less than one minute, and Challock came on the line.

'Captain Challock here. Hello, Stamford. Is everything all right?'

'There's just a small hitch, sir, concerning a mutual acquaintance. Shall we go to "Scramble"?'

'Good idea.'

William pressed the button and waited to hear his superior's voice.

'Challock here again. Are you there, Stamford?'

'Yes, sir. Miss Werner is concerned about her relationship with her contact here. Apparently, he's rather taken with her, and she's worried that tension between them could rock a somewhat vulnerable and sensitive boat.'

'I see.' Challock was silent for a moment, and then he asked, 'Is Miss Werner with you?'

'Yes, sir. Would you like to speak to her?'

'I think that would be a good idea.'

William handed the receiver to Lucy, who took it from him nervously.

'Marguerite Werner here, Captain.'

William could only hear her side, but she seemed to be telling Challock much the same as she'd told him. There were some fragments of conversation, and then she handed the receiver back to him.

'Captain Challock wants to speak to you again,' she said.

'Stamford here, sir.'

'You and Miss Werner were quite right to bring this to my attention, Stamford, and she was right to be concerned. Now, the next time she has a meeting with Gael, which should be in a few days' time, you must accompany her, but in civilian clothing. The purpose is to let him know, before he gets too ambitious, that Miss Werner is beyond his reach, basically because she is involved with you. You are a civilian employed at the Dockyard.'

'I understand, sir.'

'By the way, I've read your report, and I'll be putting it before the LCS tomorrow. Well done.'

'Thank you, sir.'

'Not at all. Carry on, Stamford.'

'Aye-aye, sir.' William replaced the receiver.

'Just thinking about the flat, Percy,' said Lucy, 'I'd better give you the spare keys next time you're over, in case you arrive some time when I'm not around.'

'Good thinking, Marguerite, even though the idea of your not being around is too awful for words.'

———————

Lucy shuddered involuntarily. 'Darling,' she said, 'please don't do that when I'm trying to talk to you. You know it makes the words come out all funny.'

'Sorry.' William lay still beside her. 'What do you want to talk to me about?'

'Thomas.'

'The Gael chap?'

'Yes. You know, I really don't trust him.'

Her remark confirmed William's suspicion that she was more concerned about Gael than she'd admitted. 'You told me recently,' he said, 'that double agents are, by definition, not to be trusted.'

'That's right, but he's the only one I know, so I'm not exactly what you'd call experienced in this kind of work.'

'You really have been dropped in at the deep end,' he agreed. 'What makes you distrust Gael?'

After a moment's thought, she said, 'Just the little things he says.'

'Such as what?'

'When we exchange more than a few words, which isn't very often, he sometimes makes references to the other side. He talks disparagingly about Hitler and the Nazis in general. Now, when you consider that he started working for the *Abwehr* because he hated the British, because he couldn't wait for German tanks to roll into London, for Mr Churchill to be hanged and for the King and Queen to be shot, it doesn't exactly ring true.'

'You think he doth protest too much?'

'Yes.'

It sounded serious enough to William. 'Have you told Captain Challock about your suspicion?'

'No, I didn't want to speak too soon, in case I'd got it wrong.'

It was a familiar tale. 'It seems to me,' he said, 'that you've been told so often that you've got things wrong, you still don't trust yourself to get them right.'

She nodded. 'Even after four years of working with you.'

'I can't work miracles, Lucy, and there was a lot to be undone.' He turned on to his side and kissed her naked, flat midriff slowly and persuasively.

'Oh, but you're very good at some things,' she said, drawing him closer.

———▶◀———

Lucy replaced the receiver and said, 'Captain Challock says I have to be particularly guarded whenever I speak to Thomas. It's not difficult, as I don't care much for him, anyway.'

'Is that because of what he stands for, or is it simply a personal thing?'

'It's purely personal. It has nothing to do with his being an enemy agent or Irish or anything like that. Actually, I've nothing against the Irish, apart from the fact that they don't play cricket.'

'Ah, but that really is a mark against them,' he said somewhat absently.

'Oh, Percy, you're mocking me, but you know what I mean. There are accepted values and standards of behaviour that we've absorbed as a matter of course, but they don't apply to those who've not been brought up playing and watching the hallowed game.'

He nodded. 'Warning the batsman before running him out, for example. Doing the square thing, in fact.'

'That sort of thing, yes.'

'Did the real Marguerite Werner play cricket at school?'

'Yes, but grudgingly and very badly.'

'Oh, tut, tut.'

For all Lucy's weaknesses, one of her undoubted qualities was her perceptiveness, which prompted her to say, 'Something's on your mind, Percy. I can tell.'

'You're right, as usual, Marguerite. It's the ongoing question of how to persuade the enemy that the Low Countries are a workable option.'

'Man was never intended to be an invader.' It was a simple, unqualified statement.

'Is that a religious or a moral observation?'

'Neither. It's a common-sense one really. Invasions have been dogged by difficulty since man first coveted his neighbour's lands. In recent times, even Hitler decided against it in nineteen-forty, as you know, and invading Russia wasn't his wisest move either.'

'You're right, Marguerite. I'm still wondering why anyone would want to go to Berlin via the bulb fields.' He thought again about her reasoning and asked, 'What made you think along those lines?'

'What lines, Percy?'

'The difficulties in planning an invasion.'

'Oh, well, it's true, isn't it. I mean, there's the exchange of letters between Marcus Tullius Cicero and his brother Quintus, who accompanied Caesar to Britain in 54 BC.'

'Now, how could I have forgotten that?'

'There's no need for sarcasm, Percy.' Unabashed, Lucy went on. 'Quintus had written about the Romans' fear of tidal shores, and Marcus Tullius wrote of his relief at hearing that Quintus and everyone else had disembarked safely. They were so used to the negligible tides of the Mediterranean, that our shores represented a gigantic threat to their safety.'

An idea began to form in William's mind. Eventually, he said, 'You're right, you know. Tides are vitally important.'

'Caesar and his chums certainly thought so.'

'And they would be no less important to a modern invasion force. Its planners would need detailed tide tables for the appropriate stretch of coast. Also, with small landing craft involved, they'd need to know the currents inside out. We have to let the enemy know that we're studying those things in detail.' He sat back and beamed at his accomplice. 'Marguerite, you've done it again.'

16

William paid off the taxi and found the key to let himself into the building, glad to get out of the freezing March wind.

To preserve the pretence, he'd gone into the wireless station at the start of the forenoon watch and told Bray he was going to visit the dockyard. Bray knew better than to ask why.

Reaching the landing, William tapped on Lucy's door before turning the key in the lock.

'There's no need to knock,' said Lucy, opening the door.

'I was never one to take liberties,' he said, removing his cap to kiss her.

'Coffee?'

'Yes, please. Where on earth did you find it?'

'*HMS Pembroke*, of course.'

'You were always adept at that.' It evoked memories of working together at the Admiralty. Those days seemed long gone, but at least they were together again.

'You'd better change before he arrives, Percy.'

'Yes, I'll be back in a jiffy.' He took his grip into Lucy's bedroom and changed quickly into a civilian suit.

Joining her in the kitchen, he watched as she made coffee. 'I've been wondering about your family,' he said. 'Presumably, they haven't a clue, any more than I had, about what you're doing.'

'Captain Challock telephones my mother regularly and assures her that I'm all right. All she knows is that I'm engaged in vital work and that I'm unable to communicate with her, but I'll be home soon.'

'Captain Challock is proving to be a guardian angel. He got things moving when he heard I'd been arrested.'

'Yes, I have him on my provisional list of godfathers.'

'In case the Prime Minister's not available, presumably?'

Lucy lit the gas under the percolator and the kettle for extra hot water, and said, 'It's always a good idea to make provision for unforeseen difficulties.'

'When the war is over, people such as Captain Challock and Vice-Admiral Davies will be given knighthoods or elevated to the peerage, and they'll be terribly grand.'

'But not too grand for the likes of us, Percy. They'll still be approachable. At least, that's been my experience.'

'You know much more about it than I do, Marguerite.'

Lucy smiled mischievously and said, 'Bea sometimes refers to Vice-Admiral Davies as "Uncle Edgar". Isn't it a coincidence that he and my grandpa are both Edgars?'

'Yes, and it's quite right too. They're both good Edgars, and a good Edgar is even better than a good egg, especially when he gets me out of the clutches of Special Branch.'

'Oh, don't. Even the thought of it is too horrible for words.'

'The memory isn't exactly my fondest.'

After a while, the coffee was ready, and Lucy poured it out.

'I'll put some hot water in mine,' said William. 'I find it a little strong.'

'Me too.'

While Lucy brought the hot water, William stared out of the window in the direction of the Dockyard. 'It's inconceivable,' he said, 'that, faced with the Russians, the Americans and us, Hitler still believes he can win this war. The Nazi war machine is a force to be reckoned with, admittedly, but it must have its limits.'

' "Those whom the gods wish to destroy, they first drive mad." '

'Highly appropriate, Marguerite, but I'm used to hearing you trot out words of classical wisdom in Latin or Greek.'

'It's usually quoted, to use the word loosely, in Latin,' she told him, topping up the coffee with hot water, 'although that only goes back to the last century. The original observation is thought to have been made by Euripedes, but the exact wording is hard to find.'

'Forgive my ignorance, but was Euripides a philosopher?'

'Strictly speaking, no, he was a tragedian.' Seeing the look of incomprehension on his features, she explained, 'He wrote tragedies.'

'That must have been a depressing job.'

'They took their work seriously,' she agreed, 'but actually, the dramatists of Ancient Greece, like the playwrights of today, were philosophical people, so you were partly right.'

William was impressed, and not for the first time. 'Your understanding of these things defies belief,' he told her. 'If you'd been able to pass School Certificate maths, you could have matriculated and gone on to do great things.'

'And you and I would never have met.'

'That's true. Maybe it was preordained that you would struggle with algebra and trigonometry so that you'd be able to make your remarkable contribution to the war in this way.'

'And other things.'

'Yes, I haven't forgotten that you're excellent company and extremely good in bed, and that I want you and you alone to be the mother of my children.'

Their conversation was interrupted by the doorbell for the flat.

'That'll be Thomas,' she said. 'I'd better let him in.' She put the coffee things in the kitchen and went downstairs to the front door, returning a minute or so later with the caller. 'Darling, this is Thomas Gael, a business acquaintance of mine. Thomas, I'd like you to meet my *fiancé* William Stamford.'

That the news was a surprise to Gael was fleetingly apparent, but he recovered quickly. 'I am delighted to make your acquaintance, Mr Stamford. By the way, is that with an "n" or an "m"?'

'With an "m".'

'Of course. May I offer you both my congratulations?'

'Thank you.'

'Forgive my curiosity, but are you connected with *HMS Pembroke*?'

'No, the Dockyard, actually. I'm an inspector.' Dismissing the subject, he said, 'I'm sure you and Marguerite have business to discuss.' He walked over to the window again and resumed his survey of the town.

Lucy handed a file to Gael, looking covertly towards William and putting a cautionary finger to her lips. 'It's not urgent,' she said. 'Some time in the next forty-eight hours will do.'

'Leave it with me,' said Gael.

It seemed that with that simple transaction, Gael's visit was over. He picked up his hat and briefcase, into which he placed the file Lucy had given him. 'I should leave,' he said. 'I'm sure we all have things to do.' He offered his hand. 'Goodbye, Mr Stamford.'

'Goodbye, Mr Gael.'

'If we all leave now,' said Lucy, 'Thomas can catch his bus, and we can get the next one to *Pembroke* and the Dockyard.'

Later, back at *Pembroke*, William said, 'We need to keep an eye on Gael. You said you didn't trust him, and now I don't trust him either.'

'It didn't take you long to come to that conclusion, Percy.' She sat hunched over his desk, as she so often did, ready to hear what he had to say.

'It's just a feeling about the way he checked that he had my name right. He didn't need to.'

'Maybe he was just being polite. He is very polite, you know.'

'Even so, I smell a rat.'

'Also,' she said, 'he seems to know rather a lot about the real Marguerite Werner, although I don't know quite how.'

Suddenly, William felt uneasy. 'He's never met her, obviously.'

'They had one meeting, in Queensferry, before she came south to take up her post in Chatham, but you know what it's like when you've met someone only once. You see them again somewhere different and you don't always recognise them. Don't forget, also, that she and I are physically very much alike.'

'Do you think he's ever suspected anything?'

'If he has, I've never been aware of it.' Her eyes narrowed momentarily, and she said, 'He's not stupid, though. He wouldn't give anything away.'

'What has he said about Miss Werner?'

Lucy thought. Eventually, she said, 'There have been one or two occasions when he's mentioned their training in Berlin. He and she can't have been contemporaries there, but I imagine they might have known the same instructors.'

'How did you deal with it?'

'I told him that reminiscence was a peacetime luxury, and that we had to concentrate on the task in hand. It's the kind of thing Marguerite would have said when she wasn't playing the soppy half-wit.' With a dismissive gesture, she added, 'She could never stay in character for long.'

'Well done, Marguerite.' He was still uneasy, however. 'I think it's important for us to speak to Captain Challock about this,' he said, looking at the time. 'I'll try to get hold of him after lunch. He could be in a conference now. He usually is at this time.'

'I wonder,' she said.

'You wonder what?'

'Might it be a good idea for you to keep some civilian clothes at my flat. We don't want Gael to call when you're there, and see you in uniform.'

'You're right, Marguerite. It is a good idea.'

Lucy cocked an ear in the direction of the next office. 'Commander Bray's quiet,' she observed. 'He mustn't have anything for me to do. Have you?'

'Yes, I have. It's the usual thing.'

'The Low Countries thing?'

He nodded. 'We've dropped a few hints. Now, I think it's time to make it visual.'

'To give them something to look at?'

'Yes, but what?'

Together, they sank into deep thought.

After a while, William asked, 'Do you remember the early days, when we were persuading Hitler to take his summer holiday somewhere else?'

Now alerted, Lucy looked up.

'We resurrected the idea of disguising old merchantmen as battleships and making MTBs fiercer than ever.'

'Go on.'

'Plywood aircraft, tanks and landing craft, all cleverly painted, would create the illusion of preparation for an invasion.'

Now Lucy was enthused. 'They certainly would, and what about carefully-leaked photographs of eminent senior officers in various places?'

'If they could be persuaded, busy though they probably are, to appear in those places, I think it would be an excellent idea.'

'I wonder,' said Lucy tentatively.

'You *are* a wonder, Marguerite. Tell me what you're wondering now.' Now they were together again, their partnership was as productive as ever.

'Instead of just doing these things on the east coast, why not do them in, say, two adjacent places where an invasion might be launched? The sheer scope of it might convince the enemy that an invasion is being prepared there.'

Once again, William gave her full credit. 'That's an excellent idea,' he said. What made you think of it?'

She looked a little embarrassed. 'It's another of those ideas from the ancient world,' she admitted.

'Okay, it's not original, but who cares? Tell me about it.'

'There's not much to tell. Hannibal used the idea against the Romans at Lake Trasimene, and Alexander the Great did something very similar when he crossed the River Hydaspses.'

'When the Nazis destroyed the work of the intellectuals,' said William, 'they could have had no idea of the treasure they were discarding.'

———◆◀———

William submitted his report and applied himself to other matters, confident that he would hear from Captain Challock before long. The one thing he didn't expect, however, was to be summoned to the Admiralty. Naval Intelligence, of course, was full of surprises, so he gave it little thought, but simply reported at the appointed time.

Dai Hughes was as delighted as ever to see him, although their reunion had to be brief, considering the urgency of the proceedings. The pressure was apparent in the way Challock responded to William's knock.

'If that's Stamford,' he said, 'come in. I need to speak to you.'

William saluted and waited to be enlightened.

'Sit down, Stamford. I've read your report, and so have the Committee. It's been much criticised and debated, which means that they want to use your ideas, but they don't want to appear too eager. You'll find, also, that you'll get precious little credit for them, but you're used to that, aren't you?'

'I don't care who gets the credit, sir.'

'Good, because you'll have no say in the matter.' Challock made a sweeping gesture with his hand, suggesting that the subject was closed. 'I sent for you because of something even more important.'

William prepared himself for one of Challock's drawn-out introductions, and was surprised when his superior came straight to the point.

'A "Y" station – that's a listening station, in this case in Chatham, believe it or not – has picked up a signal from Berlin to Thomas Gael that opens up a real hornet's nest. It seems that your suspicions and Miss Pendleton's are right, that the fellow is not to be trusted. The signal, you see, refers to a mysterious *Agent Dohle*.'

'Is that d-o-h-l-e, sir?'

'Yes. I believe it means "jackdaw".'

'I believe it does, sir, but what do we know about *Agent Dohle*?'

Challock's expression was grim. 'Bugger all, Stamford, except that he's operating locally. The signal in question tells Gael to make contact with him, and that suggests physical proximity.'

'But surely, MI5 and Special Branch will be looking for him, sir.'

Challock snorted. 'That would make sense, wouldn't it? Unfortunately, there's a certain ambiguity in the wording of the signal – you know how German sentence construction lends itself to confusion – and because of that, MI5 are not convinced. If that weren't enough, Special Branch are, for once, in agreement with them.'

'Is *Dohle* definitely referred to as *Agent*, rather than *Agentin*, sir? The reason I ask is because *die Dohle* is a feminine noun, and it may suggest that the agent is female.'

'It may, but not necessarily, Stamford. An *Agent Taube* was caught in Portsmouth two years ago, and he was male enough, despite the gender of his codename, to make overtures to a Wren officer based at *HMS Nelson*. Fortunately, she had her wits about her and she alerted her superiors. He's working for us now, for what that's worth. Frankly, I can't bring myself to trust any of the blighters.'

'I can't blame you, sir.' William's thoughts had been pursuing their own journey, and he said, 'What I don't understand, sir, is why the enemy need two agents in Chatham. Surely, Marguerite Werner is sufficient.'

'Normally, I suppose she would be, but there's a lot at stake for both sides. We are keen, as you know, to keep the enemy from knowing where the invasion will take place, and they are just as keen to find out the truth. They're receiving contradictory intelligence that's no doubt driving them round the bend with confusion and disbelief, so they trust no one. I think they're playing off one agent against another, in the hope that they'll uncover false intelligence, and then, by process of elimination, they'll build a clearer picture of the possibilities.'

William could see now, how vitally important it was to discover the identity of *Agent Dohle*. Just one question remained. 'Where do I come into this, sir?'

'When we know who he is and where he lives, we'll decide what is to be done with him. Before we can do that, however, he has to be found, and that, Stamford, is your job.

17

William sat at his desk, staring into empty space. He preferred to look at Lucy when he was thinking, and not simply because of her obvious charms, but because he found that it stimulated his mental powers. Unfortunately, she was currently with Commander Bray.

The task he'd been set seemed impossible from the outset. Finding an enemy spy in an establishment the size of *Pembroke*, not to mention Chatham Dockyard as well, was like finding the finest of needles in a haystack afflicted with St Vitus' Dance. He continued to stare morosely until the door opened and Lucy came in. He was so lost in his deliberations that he hardly noticed her at first, until she came round the desk and kissed him slowly and promisingly.

'Someone will catch us one day,' he warned.

'If they've any decency, they'll look the other way.' Taking her usual seat opposite him, she asked, 'Have you had any joy with agent thingummybob yet?'

He shook his head. 'I don't even know where to begin.'

She furrowed her brow in thought. After a surprisingly short time, she said, 'When I'm stuck, which happens distressingly often, I usually write lists of the things I know, and the things I don't know. I find it sort of narrows things down and clarifies the problem.'

'A list,' he said, hitting his desk with the flat of his hand. 'That's what we need. Where would I be without you, Marguerite?'

'That has possibilities as a song lyric, you know. Tentatively, she sang, 'Where would I be without you, Marguerite?'

'You could work on it,' he suggested. 'Meanwhile, how can I lay my hands on a list of personnel currently at *Pembroke* and the dockyard?'

'Difficult.'

'But not impossible.' He picked up the telephone and asked the operator to connect him with Captain Challock at the Admiralty. He had to wait several minutes before a familiar voice came on the line.

'Room Twelve. Lieutenant Commander Hughes speaking.'

'Good morning, Dai. Is Captain Challock available for a quick word?'

'Not even for the quickest of words, William. He's in conference.' For some reason, Dai sounded less than his usual ebullient self.

'When he's free, will you ask him to telephone me at *Pembroke*, please?'

'By all means, William.'

'Thanks, Dai.'

'My pleasure, old friend.'

'Dai, is it my imagination, or are you ever so slightly out of sorts today?'

'More than ever so slightly, William. My request to return to the fleet has been rejected once and for all, on the grounds that I've missed out on a lot of experience, and that there's no place in the fleet for two-and-a-half rings and a mine of ignorance. I offered to forfeit the half-ring, but to no avail.'

Lucy was looking inquisitive, but she would have to wait.

'I'm sorry, Dai. I know it's a blow for an intrepid submariner like you, but try to think positively. Based where you are, you have almost unlimited access to the lovely Bea, and that's something you wouldn't have fifty fathoms beneath the Atlantic.'

'That's just, give or take a fathom, what the lovely Bea tells me.' Sounding more sorrowful than ever, he said, 'Women have no soul, William.'

'I couldn't agree less. It's because she has a soul that she's relieved to have you on dry land. Don't forget, the last time you went to sea, you filled your lungs with chlorine or some other evil substance, and life was touch and go for a while.'

'I'm not likely to forget it.' He paused, drawing the conversation to its close. 'Anyway, William, as one landlubber to another, I must away and attend to my duties, such as they are. If I don't log everything in sight and sign it all off, the war's as good as lost.'

'Cheerio, old son.'

'Goodbye for now, and don't worry, mun, I'll give Captain Challock your message.'

As soon as he'd put down the receiver, Lucy asked, 'Won't they let him go back to sea?'

'No. It was always doubtful, but Dai was determined. He'll get over it, though, when he's had time to consider the official argument and think about it in the cold light of day.' Dismissing the subject temporarily, he said, 'Meanwhile, we still have a problem to solve.'

'Yes, we have.' Lucy leaned forward in her customary way to discuss the problem. 'What are you going to do with the lists when you get them, Percy?'

'All I can do for now is make a note of anyone of non-British parentage. It's crude, but it's a start.'

'We should pay attention to Thomas Gael as well,' she suggested.

'In what way?' They were already keeping a general eye on him, but William wondered if Lucy had something more particular in mind.

'I only mean that, when we visit his place, we should keep an eye out for anything suspicious, anything that might link him with activities unconnected with our side.'

'Agreed.'

'Good.' Her tone brightened, and she said, 'I'm beginning to feel like a spy catcher already.'

'I wish I was.'

'Don't you mean you wish you *were*?'

'Sorry, Marguerite.' He wondered again how he could possibly function without her.

———— ▸◂ ————

It was mid-afternoon when Captain Challock telephoned. William took the call and came straight to the point.

'Shall we go to "Scramble", sir?'

'I think so.'

With the necessary equipment connected, Challock asked, 'What's the problem, Stamford?'

'I need lists of everyone currently serving here at *Pembroke*, sir, and at the Naval Dockyard.'

'I thought you might, and they're on their way to you by hand of naval rating. You should have them by the end of the first dogwatch.'

'Thank you, sir. That's excellent.'

'Hm. Make sure the rating gets a square meal. He's missing lunch to make the delivery. It would be too bad if he missed supper as well.'

'Aye-aye, sir.'

'By the way, Stamford, did you pick up some civilian clothing when you were in London?'

'Yes, sir.'

'Good. If you're snooping around, it's always better not to advertise the fact that you're a-servin' of 'Is Majesty the King. Anyway, if there's nothing else, I'll hear from you later. Carry on, and good hunting.'

'Aye-aye, sir. Thank you, sir.' William put the phone down and put Lucy in the picture. 'Captain Challock was way ahead of us, and the lists will arrive later today. A rating's bringing them, and the good captain has asked me to make sure he gets a meal. Apparently, he missed lunch to do this.'

'Poor boy. Yes, he must have a meal.'

'The "poor boy", Marguerite, may turn out to be a hairy, tattooed, three-badge leading telegraphist.'

'Well,' she reasoned, 'he'll still be hungry.'

'So he will.' Another thought came to him. 'Does Captain Challock strike you as a man who's read Kipling?'

'Well, he's a man of many parts. How did you learn that about him?'

'He quoted, or rather, *misquoted Gunga Din.*'

'Tut-tut.' She frowned.

'Well, he had to, really.'

'We're at war, Percy. We all have to do things we wouldn't normally do.'

'I mean, he had to because he was referring to His Majesty the King, rather than the Queen.'

'So he's up to date with his monarchs as well. He really does deserve a place on my provisional list of godfathers.'

William leaned forward to say, 'Let's do something special tonight, Marguerite.'

'Oh.' Her interest was aroused. 'Are we going to do it with the light on?'

'If you like, but first, I'll book a table at the Estuary Restaurant.'

'Lovely. Why?'

'Because I've just remembered several of the reasons why I want you to bear my children and to love, honour and obey me in what spare time maternal duties allow.'

Lucy considered his explanation and asked, 'How many reasons are there altogether?'

'Too many to count, although there could be more.'

'You're quite committed, then?'

'Totally committed.'

'In that case, Percy, I'd better think of a few reasons why I want you to sire my brood, because I really do. I have to say, though, I'm not all that keen on the "obey" angle. I've always been something of an individual, as you know.'

'I shan't make unreasonable demands, Marguerite.'

'In that case, it should be all right.'

A knock on the door interrupted their negotiations.

'Come in.'

A Wren opened the door, saluted and said, 'There's a dispatch rider outside, sir, asking to see you in person.'

'Send him in, will you?'

'Aye-aye, sir. By the way, sir, the dispatch rider is a Wren.' She added, 'I thought I should tell you.'

'To prepare me for the shock? Thank you for that, but she's no less welcome. Carry on.'

'Aye-aye, sir.' The girl saluted again and left the office.

A moment later, a Wren dressed in motorcycle leathers and a crash helmet came to the door. She wore her goggles over her brow, and her face was pink from riding into the cold wind. She saluted and asked, 'Are you Commander Stamford, sir?'

'Yes, I am.' He showed her his identity card.

'Thank you, sir. I have a dispatch from....' She checked her documentation. 'It's from Captain Challock, sir.' She handed William an oilskin-wrapped folder.

'Thank you.' He signed the receipt and asked, 'What's your name?' As the girl opened her mouth to speak, he said, 'Don't worry about your number. Just your name will do.'

'Wren Thompson, sir.'

'And when did you last eat, Wren Thompson?' As he asked the question, he was reminded of Lucy's insistence on correct grammar, and he clarified it for her, 'That's "When did you last eat – verb intransitive – Wren Thompson?" not "When did you last eat Wren Thompson? – accusative, as if encouraging a cannibal to recall a gastronomic experience.'

'I realised that, Percy.'

The girl rolled her eyes. 'This morning, sir, at breakfast.' She was hungry, and that was more important to her than English grammar.

'In that case,' he said, locking the folder in the safe, 'I'll take you across to the Junior Ratings' Canteen, and you can fortify yourself before returning.'

'Thank you, sir, but I haven't got a station card for *HMS Pembroke*.'

'No one should be made to starve, Wren Thompson.' He pulled his greatcoat on and reached for his cap. 'Back in two shakes, Marguerite,' he said. 'Now, Wren Thompson, let's get you fed before you fade away.'

He led her to the block that housed the Junior Ratings' Canteen and asked for the Senior Rate of the Watch, whose office was close by. A chief petty officer came out and saluted.

'Chief, I want this Wren to be given supper.'

'Has she got a station card, sir?'

'No, I am her station card.'

The chief petty officer looked uneasy and said, 'It's a bit irregular, sir.'

'The poor girl hasn't eaten since breakfast, and I consider that *highly* irregular.'

The CPO shuffled uncertainly. 'Well,' he said, 'if you put it like that, sir, I'll see to it that she gets a meal.'

'Thank you. Carry on, please, Chief.'

'Aye-aye, sir.' The chief petty officer saluted him and then addressed the Wren. 'Come along o' me, m' dear. It's Spam fritters tonight, just for a change, but I reckon you won't mind that, not if you're hungry.'

William left them and returned to his office.

'Just imagine, Marguerite,' he said, 'our dispatch rider is a tiny scrap of a girl, and she tears along the highways and by-ways with five-hundred cc's thundering beneath her vitals.'

'I think the image does more for you than it does for me, darling.'

'Anyway, she's now stoking up on Spam fritters and chips, bless her. When I speak to Captain Challock again, I'll put a word in for her. After our conversation about children, I feel almost fatherly towards her.'

'You'd be seven, or possibly eight, when she was born, Percy.'

'I said "*almost* fatherly".'

———◆▸◂———

In the morning, William trawled the lists of personnel at HMS Pembroke and Chatham Dockyard, and identified thirty-seven ethnically diverse names that might bear closer scrutiny. It was a start.

18

APRIL

A security check on William's thirty-seven names yielded nothing more helpful than the information that the officers, ratings and civilian workers concerned had been through the vetting process and were deemed to pose no risk. William was completely frustrated, and Captain Challock shared his exasperation, a fact he disclosed during William's next visit to the Admiralty.

'That Gael chap never gives us a clue as to Dohle's identity or his whereabouts,' he complained.

'Is his signal traffic being monitored all the time, sir?'

'Absolutely, but he's a wily fellow, you know.'

'I suppose he has to be, sir, working both ends, as he does, towards the middle.'

'I suppose so, Stamford.' Turning to a more pleasing topic, Challock said, 'You'll be pleased to know that the suggestions you put forward in your last report are being implemented, almost as we speak.'

'Thank you for telling me that, sir. Naturally, we shan't know for some time yet how successful all this has been, but what you've told me gives me some satisfaction in the short term.'

Even though there was no risk of his being overheard, Challock lowered his voice confidingly. 'Enjoy the satisfaction while you can, Stamford,' he said. 'As I told you earlier, the egos in a certain quarter won't hesitate to share in the credit.'

———◆◄◆———

The first person William saw on his return to *HMS Pembroke* was Commander Bray, who greeted him in his usual, affable manner.

When the two officers had exchanged greetings, Bray said, 'You chose the right time to be away, Stamford. This last couple of days have been damned difficult. Most of the time, I couldn't hear myself think.'

'What's been happening?'

'They've been overhauling the sprinkler system. Still, I suppose our block is now assured of protection against fire.'

William found Lucy similarly relieved to be able to work in peace and relative quiet.

'It's been awful,' she said. 'Those dockyard people just don't understand. I suppose it's not all that surprising.'

'How many of them were there?'

'Oh, only one, but he made enough noise for twenty.' She looked up at his handiwork and adopted Bray's line. 'Still, if there's a fire, we'll know the sprinkler's up to date.'

'I'm not sure,' said William, looking at the sprinkler head. 'Just a minute.' He placed the spare wooden chair beneath the sprinkler head and stepped up to examine it. After a close inspection, he said, 'This is the same type as we had in *Exeter*, and I don't know what he was supposed to be doing with it, but the pipe is covered in dust. Were you here when any of this work was being done?'

'No fear. I got out of his way.'

William stepped down. 'If he didn't replace this one, what, I wonder, did he actually do?'

'Search me, Percy. I don't understand any of it.'

'Neither do I, yet.' He left the office and tapped on Bray's door before opening it.

'Hello, old man. What can I do for you?'

'Do you mind if I have a look at your sprinkler?'

Bray was understandably surprised. 'Of course, old man. Help yourself.'

Again, William took the spare chair and mounted it to examine the sprinkler head. 'I just want to know that they've done a thorough job,' he said.

'Of course.'

He found, again, that the sprinkler was one of the old pattern, and that the supply pipe was as dusty as Lucy's.

'Satisfied, old chap?' Bray appeared to be humouring him.

'Not yet.' William went to his own office and repeated the procedure, to find the same curious conundrum. Returning to Bray's office, he asked, 'What's in the roof void, Bray?'

'Why, nothing. It's storage space, where they put the old equipment until they decide what to do with it.'

'Is the compartment usually locked?'

'Not as far as I know.' By this time, Bray was nonplussed. 'What is this about, old chap?'

'The sprinklers haven't been replaced. I'm just wondering what that chap actually did, apart from making a lot of noise.'

'Odd.'

William was inclined to agree, but instead of staying to discuss the matter, he took the torch from his office, walked down the passage and climbed the fixed ladder to the roof void.

By the light from his torch, he located the electric light switch and illuminated the entire space, which had been floorboarded and was being used, as Bray had told him, as a depository for equipment that appeared to have been left over from the previous war.

He found sawdust, no doubt from where a floorboard had been removed and replaced. The board was easy to identify, and he used his penknife to prise it up. As he suspected, the sprinkler heads were the old type, probably installed before the war, but there was an addition to each one, with two wires running beneath the loose floorboard, and he had to look closely to discover the purpose of the arrangement. The object was loose and held in place by two crocodile clips. When he removed the first, he found that he had a bird's-eye view of Commander Bray at his desk. He was also able to identify the object. It was a microphone bearing the inscription in Gothic script *Telefunken Berlin*. Everything had fallen into place, the unannounced arrival of the dockyard worker, the noise to distract anyone from questioning the work being done, and the camouflaging of the microphones by making them resemble part of the sprinkler system.

He confirmed for himself that all three sprinkler heads were fitted with microphones, and then traced the wires along the recess until he came to a rectangular box, which he identified as a wire recorder, also made by the *Telefunken* company.

He had to move fast. He replaced the floorboard and left the roof void as he'd found it. His next job was to warn Bray and Lucy, both of whom he found in Bray's office.

'Excuse me, Bray, but this is important. I've just inspected the sprinkler system, and it hasn't been touched. You'll probably think I'm out of my mind, but I have to tell you that this building is wired for sound. There are German microphones and a wire recorder up there.'

'Great heavens, Stamford. Are you sure?'

'Absolutely. The dockyard worker you saw is clearly working for the other side. Now, think, Bray. Would you recognise him if you saw him again?'

Bray shook his head. 'I doubt it, old man. I've always thought that one dockyard matey looks very much like another.'

William turned to Lucy, who was in a similar state of disbelief. 'How about you, Marguerite? Would you recognise him again?'

Lucy thought. 'I'm not sure, Commander. He was dark-haired and he had a dark complexion. I thought he had a local accent as well.' She looked apologetic. 'I'm afraid that's about all I can remember.'

'It's better than nothing. I'm going to involve Special Branch. In the meantime, Bray, it's imperative that you don't discuss classified material with anyone in this building. Wireless Station personnel need to be warned as well.'

'Well, I suppose it makes sense, old chap, fantastic though the whole thing sounds, and in no way am I impugning your honesty. You can leave the Wireless Station to me.'

'I'll let you know what's happening just as soon as I know anything, but first, I need to make a telephone call while there's no one up there.'

He went to his own office and asked for Captain Challock at the Admiralty. It took more than two minutes to make the connection, and then Challock came on the line.

'Room Twelve. Captain Challock speaking.'

'It's Stamford, sir, and it's important that we go to Scramble.'

'Okay, Stamford.' There was a pause while they initiated the scrambler system, and then Challock spoke again. 'What's the problem, Stamford?'

'I think we've found *Agent Dohle*, sir, and he's been up to a lot of mischief.' William told him about the spurious dockyard worker and the microphones. 'I thought I'd better leave it to you, sir, to contact Special Branch. Then, we can only hope that, on this occasion, they'll arrest the right man.'

'Quite right, Stamford. Until you hear from me, there's not much you can do apart from keeping an eye out for this chap and making sure no one speaks out of turn.'

'I've warned the only other senior officer in this building, sir. He's in charge of the Wireless Station, so he'll warn everyone else concerned.'

'Good, leave it with me.'

When Challock had rung off, William spoke to Lucy. 'I deliberately didn't include you in the warning,' he said.

'I know. I'm not supposed to know anything.' Looking up at the sprinkler head, she said, 'Do you know what I'd like to do, Percy? I'd like to put a gramophone on this desk, just beneath the microphone, and play the Prelude to Act Three of Lohengrin very loudly indeed. I know the Nazis are fond of Wagner, so they could hardly complain, could they?'

'They could, because they're not reasonable people. Did you know that when the *Bismarck* was sunk the Nazis made a news announcement that she'd been set upon unfairly by eight battleships and about twenty cruisers, and her crew had been obliged to scuttle her as the only way to save her superior equipment from falling into British hands?'

'How pathetic.' She looked up again at the place where the microphone was sighted, clearly relishing the prospect of lowering the needle on Wilhelm Furtwängler and the Berlin Philharmonic Orchestra.

'That's the way with bullies. Give them a taste of their own medicine and they go running to teacher with tears in their eyes.'

'I know, Percy. A hockey stick round the ears has settled accounts with many a bully.'

William winced at the thought of it. 'I'm beginning to worry about you,' he said, 'but it does raise a question. Is that how the term "bully-off" originated?'

'No, a bully-off is a way of restarting a game after a stoppage, whereas what I suggested is a way of stopping someone's game altogether.'

'And that's exactly what we're trying to do with this *Agent Dohle* character.'

In a surprisingly short time, William received two visitors, who turned out to be Detective Sergeant Cobbett and Detective Constable Fawthrop, both of Kent County Constabulary Special Branch. Suspecting that they were sceptical about the reported bugging, he took them up to the roof space so that they could see the equipment for themselves.

Sergeant Cobbett asked, 'What made you suspect this, sir?'

'The man's cover story, that he was replacing the sprinkler system. I was in London while this was happening, but when I returned and heard about it, I looked at the sprinklers and realised he'd done nothing of the sort.'

'Well, we'll keep this building under twenty-four hour surveillance, so that when he comes back to eavesdrop, we'll have him.'

19

Surveillance continued for two weeks, but with no result. Meanwhile, a detective chief inspector called Henderson came to call. He was a tall, spare man with what seemed a permanently woeful expression, and he wore the inevitable trench coat and trilby.

'It seems our Nazi spy has got wind that the place was under surveillance, and he's giving it a wide berth.'

'Quite possibly,' agreed William, who had been unimpressed with the operation from the start, 'and it's hardly surprising, when the building is surrounded by men dressed as detectives. They might just as well be wearing deerstalkers and peering through magnifying glasses for all the incognito their plain clothes afford them in an establishment such as this.'

The DCI gave him a stern look. 'Each to his own, Commander,' he reproved. 'We don't tell you people how to behave onboard ship.'

'It's maybe as well that you don't.'

'One useful thing you can do, Commander, is to prepare a list of dockyard personnel with foreign ancestry.'

William unlocked the safe and took out the list he'd made before he discovered the microphones. 'There you are, Chief Inspector. It's always possible that *Agent Dohle* is an English thoroughbred and a product of Eton and Cambridge, but I agree. Let's start with a list of foreigners.'

'I should be surprised if our man has ever been to Eton or Cambridge. Dockyard workers tend not to move in those circles.'

'Well spotted, Chief Inspector, although you mustn't forget that we're looking for a man with dark hair and a dark complexion.

Mahatma Ghandi answers that description, and he was at University College, London. He practised as a barrister, by the way, but he consorts with revolutionaries and all kinds doubtful company.'

The DCI gave William his disapproving look and said, 'I could find your brand of humour wearing after a while, Commander. At all events, I think you should leave the investigation to those more capable.'

In the interests of harmony, William resisted the temptation to offer the DCI the same advice. Instead, he said, 'When you've narrowed the suspects down to a dozen or so, don't forget that there are two people here who saw him and who may be able to recognise him again.' He doubted Bray's ability to do that, but he had to be included.

'I'm aware of that, Commander.'

William left him to conduct his investigation.

He related the conversation later to Lucy.

'He's like a housemistress we had at school,' she said.

'She must have been ugly.'

'As a matter of fact, she was, but I didn't mean she looked like him. I was referring to his manner. Like her, you see, he has no sense of humour and would never dream of questioning his own methods. Also, he seems to be devoid of imagination.'

Fascinated as usual by Lucy's gems from the venerable pile, he said, 'That must have been a boring house you were in.'

'Yes, it was, although the boring housemistress left during my second year, and we got another. The new one was almost human.'

'Why did the boring one leave?'

'She was invited to leave, in order to avoid a scandal. As far as we could make out, she had a clandestine relationship with a younger mistress, who was also obliged to leave.'

'Not the kind of company parents want their daughters to keep, I imagine.'

'Quite right, Percy. Bunbury prided itself on its traditional values.'

Lucy accepted a mug of tea, transferring it to her left hand so as to avoid drinking from the chipped side. 'Thank you, Thomas.'

'You're welcome, Marguerite. I can't imagine you've spent much time in this part of Chatham. It must be quite an eye-opener for you.'

'What makes you say that?'

He shrugged as if the reason were obvious. 'It's a quarter of the town that's not normally frequented by people of substance.'

She smiled at the typically Irish understatement. 'Well, it's a good idea not to establish a pattern, don't you think?'

'Maybe so.' Changing the subject, he asked, 'How's your *fiancé*? Mr Stamford, isn't it?'

'That's right. He's well, thank you.'

'It's funny. Although I work in the Dockyard, I haven't come across him at all. Mind you, being on the night shift, I don't suppose I would.'

'Of course you wouldn't.' The lie came easily. 'Also, he's an inspector, remember. He doesn't spend all his time in one dockyard. He might be at Chatham one day and Portsmouth the next.'

'Oh, well, I hadn't thought of that.'

'Not many people would, I suppose.' He'd given her cause to think, and she asked, 'Do you have many friends at the Dockyard?'

'Oh, a few. It's difficult not to form friendships in a working environment. Of course, you wouldn't know about that, living where you do.'

'That's true.' She'd been about to say something tactful, but remembered that Marguerite and tact were strangers. 'No,' she said, 'I'm spared that.'

'Does Mr Stamford know what you do?'

'He knows that I'm a secretary at *HMS Pembroke*.'

'But you're still going to marry him in spite of your double existence?'

'The war can't go on forever, and I won't always be an agent.'

'That's true.'

The window of the bedsitter was tiny, but a ray of sunlight released by a passing cloud suddenly caused something to emit a tiny flash beside her foot. She reached down and picked it up to examine it. It turned out to be part of a broken cufflink. At least, the chain had broken, leaving a single gold, or gold-plated, disc bearing the initials *FXM*.

Thomas watched her and asked, 'What have you found?'

'One of your broken cufflinks, I believe.' She handed it to him, saying, 'A jeweller could repair that for you.'

'Oh, this belongs to a friend of mine. I'll keep it safe for him.'

'With cufflinks like that, I don't suppose he's one of your friends from the Dockyard.' It was the kind of insensitive remark Marguerite might have made.

'They don't all wear overalls and flat caps, you know.'

'Don't they? I really wouldn't know.' She finished her tea and stood up. 'Thank you for the tea, Thomas. I must go.' She had to, because she needed to speak to William.

———— ◆I◆ ————

When she reached the office, there was no sign of William, so she went to Commander Bray's office. He wasn't around, either, so she tried the Wireless Station, where she tracked him down.

'Commander Bray,' she said, 'do you know where Commander Stamford is?'

'Yes, my dear. He was called away to the Admiralty this morning. Is it something I can help you with?'

'No, thank you, Commander. I'll speak to him when he returns.'

It was too bad. She'd telephoned Captain Challock when William was in trouble, but even then it was a huge risk, especially when the telephonist had recognised her voice. Also, if Captain Challock wasn't immediately available, Dai would probably answer the telephone, and he would certainly know her voice. It really wasn't worth the risk. She would just have to wait until William returned from London.

———— ◆I◆ ————

'I'm glad you got here when you did, Stamford. I have a full afternoon.' Challock's tone gave the impression that he was not viewing the afternoon's events with any enthusiasm.

'Basically, the situation is that no unauthorised person has been in that building since Special Branch advertised their presence so obviously.'

'What?'

'I'm sorry, sir. That's just the way I see it. The men watching the building couldn't look more like policemen without blowing their whistles and waving their truncheons. Needless to say, the DCI disagrees with me.'

Challock closed his eyes in a gesture of hopelessness. 'Don't fall out with him, Stamford, for goodness' sake,' he implored.

'I'll try not to, sir.'

Reassured, at least to some extent, Challock asked, 'What's the next step?'

'My original idea, sir, a list of personnel with non-British ancestry. The DCI was surprised when I presented him with the list. He thought he was the first to think of it.'

'But you got nowhere with it, as I recall.'

'No, sir, and our culprit may yet be an Englishman with middle-class credentials, although DCI Henderson disagrees. He thinks that everyone who works at the Dockyard wears overalls and boots, smokes Woodbines, drinks tea out of a pint pot, and has bread and dripping for breakfast.'

'Well, at least, as long as *Dohle* gives the Wireless Station a wide berth, he's not eavesdropping on your conversations.'

'No, sir.' William was thankful for that.

'And speaking of eavesdropping, the "Y" station that's monitoring Thomas Gael picked up something last night. Apparently, *Dohle* reported that he's been working on the new RATOG.'

'The new what, sir?'

'Rocket Assisted Take Off Gear. It's a way of getting aircraft into the air where there's limited deck space and they're carrying heavy weapons. He's also given his masters in Berlin a pretty detailed description of it.' Challock looked grim. 'We've got to stop this agent before he delivers more gems of information.'

'So, we know that *Dohle* is working either on the equipment itself or he has access to technical documents relating to it. That could be useful.'

———◂▸◂———

Lucy was waiting in William's office when he returned, and she put the kettle on for tea straight away.

'How's Captain Challock?'

'He's a worried man, but that's not a thing we can discuss here,' he said, gesturing upwards, 'in case our friend's managed to evade the dim-witted detectives and set the machinery in motion.'

'Come outside, Percy. There's something I have to tell you.'

'All right.' He followed her out of the building. 'Right, I'm listening. Thankfully, *Dohle* isn't.'

'When I was at Thomas Gael's place this morning,' she said, 'he was curious about your work in the Dockyard. I told him that, as an inspector, you went from one dockyard to the next, and that was why his friends hadn't come across you.'

'Well done, Marguerite.'

'That's not all. I picked up a broken cufflink, and he said it belonged to a friend.'

'I suppose it might.'

'No, listen, Percy.' She waved her hand impatiently. 'The initials engraved in it were FXM. Now, the only name I can think of that begins with "X" is Xavier, which is the name of a Spanish saint.'

'Is it?'

'Yes, Saint Francis Xavier. I just wonder if there's a man on your list with those initials. If he works at the Dockyard, he should be on it.'

'So he should. Well done, Marguerite.' He considered the next step and then swore.

'What's the matter?'

'Henderson has the list. Wait a minute, though, I still have the names of the ship's company and dockyard personnel. Now I know the name I'm looking for, it shouldn't take all that long to find it.'

———— ▶◀ ————

A call to DCI Henderson resulted in his arrival the next morning. He was curious and impatient.

'What's all this about? I told you to leave the investigation to us, didn't I?'

'Never mind that. I've got Naval Intelligence breathing down my neck, so listen. There's a man called Francis Xavier Moore working in the Dockyard office. He's in communication with a double agent based in Chatham, and I think you should bring him in for questioning.'

'What makes you say that?'

'Intelligence received. I can't reveal its source, but we know that an enemy agent has been working either on special equipment for carrier-based aircraft or somewhere where he can lay his hands on the technical data.'

Henderson was still impatient. 'I need to know more than that.'

'And you will know more when you've questioned him. You may like to let the two witnesses have a look at him as well. They may be able to identify him as the chap who claimed to be working on the sprinklers. In fact, I'm prepared to put a sizeable bet on it.'

———— ▶◀ ————

William saw and heard nothing from DCI Henderson until after the weekend, when he knocked on William's door and entered without waiting to be invited.

'We've brought Francis Moore in for interrogation, and we asked your colleague Commander Bray to take a look at him. Unfortunately, he doesn't recall him well enough for identification.'

'What about Miss Werner?'

Henderson wrinkled his brow. 'Who's Miss Werner?'

'The other witness.'

'Oh, the secretary.' He didn't sound impressed.

'She's a witness, Henderson.' He lowered his voice to say, 'And she's probably a more reliable witness than Commander Bray.'

'All right, round her up and bring her down to Chatham Police Station. I'm going back there now, if you want a lift.'

'Thank you.' William wasn't keen to spend more time in Henderson's company than he had to, but a lift was a lift.

He found Lucy in her office and explained what was happening.

'I think he's foul,' she said, 'not including me in the identification process.'

'I'm not impressed with any of them. In fact, I can't see what's so special about Special Branch. I think we'd achieve a great deal more if we were dealing with honest coppers.'

They joined Henderson outside the building and took their places on the back seat of his Wolsley.

William spoke to Henderson as they set off. 'Will you ask your sergeant to stop at the main gate? We need to inform them that we're going ashore.'

Henderson gave his sergeant a sly look. 'Did you hear that, Sergeant Cobbett? We're going ashore.'

'Right you are, sir.' Cobbett pulled in at the main gate, and William showed his identity card and Lucy's to the quartermaster.

As they resumed their short journey, William said, 'I've no doubt the police, and particularly Special Branch, have jargon that outsiders might well find arcane and amusing, if not uproarious. Live and let live, Chief Inspector.'

Henderson made no response, but maintained a dour silence until the car pulled into the police station carpark, where he simply beckoned to them to follow him.

Henderson checked in at the desk and ordered the prisoner to be taken to an interview room, whereupon a uniformed constable was sent down to the cells to perform the task. Henderson led William and Lucy to an interview room and invited them to be seated.

'Moore was born to a Spanish mother and an English father, who deserted them when Moore was very young. He spent some time in Germany before the war as well as joining the British Union of Fascists here. That,' he said, 'is as much as we know.'

'And those details seem to have passed notice when he was vetted for work in the Dockyard,' observed William.

'You have to blame MI Five for that,' said Henderson, not without satisfaction.

There was the sound of footsteps in the passage, and the constable arrived at the door with a dark, swarthy man dressed in a two-piece suit.

'Bring him in,' said Henderson.

The constable motioned to the prisoner to enter the room and stood behind him.

'Now, miss,' said Henderson, 'do you recognise this man?'

'Yes, I do. He's dressed differently today, but he's the man who came to work on the sprinklers.'

A momentary look of fear crossed Moore's features before he composed himself.

Henderson asked, 'Are you sure, miss?'

'Yes, I recognise him all right, and he's wearing the same hair oil as he wore then.'

'What's that, miss?'

'His hair oil is scented with Parma violets. It's most unusual for a man to wear something like that.'

'Some men wear lavender Brilliantine.'

'But he's wearing hair oil. You can see how it glistens, and it does smell of Parma violets.'

William had been silent until then, but he had been studying Moore's shirt cuffs. 'Let me see your cufflinks,' he said.

Moore held out his arms for William to look. The outer disc was missing from the right cufflink, which was held in place by a broken matchstick.

Lucy asked, 'Is the other cufflink engraved with his initials?'

William looked and nodded. ' "FXM",' he confirmed.

'The other is in Thomas Gael's possession.'

Moore's eyes flashed briefly at the mention of Gael, and then he resumed his deadpan look.

Henderson asked him, 'What have you got to say for yourself, Moore?'

The prisoner gave Lucy a casual look and said, 'I've never seen this woman in my life, and I don't know what she's talking about. I broke my cufflink getting off a train, and the missing part fell on the platform. The train had started. There was no time for me to get out and pick it up.'

Henderson was not impressed by his story. 'Francis Xavier Moore,' he said, 'I'm charging you with treason under the Treachery Act, Nineteen-Forty.'

20

Back at HMS Pembroke, Lucy said, 'That was most unpleasant. I know he's most likely guilty, but he'll be hanged, and it's all down to the fact that I identified him.'

'Not all of it, Marguerite. I'm sure they'll find out a lot more. In any case, you did no more than your duty, and no one can criticise you for that.' They were nearing the Wireless Station, and even with Moore in custody, he was inclined to be careful. 'It's not likely that he'll be hanged,' he assured her, 'but let's say no more until I've checked the roof space.'

'Do you think there might be someone up there?'

'I don't know, but it's worth a look. There's always the chance that Moore wasn't working alone.' He left her and took the ladder up to the roof space. As far as he could make out, nothing had been disturbed. Special Branch would be returning with a photographer to provide evidence for Moore's trial, so he left the arrangement untouched and returned to his office, where he found Lucy waiting for him.

'All clear,' he reported.

'Good. Why did you say Moore wouldn't be hanged?'

'I said it wasn't likely. If they can turn him, he'll be okay.' He sat back, relieved that the task seemed to be over, but still puzzled about one thing. 'It was quite remarkable how you remembered Moore's hair oil,' he said.

'Not really. It's a strong scent, and as I said earlier, most men don't use that sort of thing. I'd forgotten about it, though, until I saw him at the police station.'

'I hardly noticed it until you drew our attention to it.'

'Most men wouldn't notice.' It was as if she'd always known it but hadn't really considered it, because she said thoughtfully, 'Men are not good at detail, I've found.'

'Go on, Marguerite, enlighten me before I speak to Captain Challock.'

'All right. Ask a man to describe a woman, and he might say that she was pretty, that she had fair hair and that she was wearing a green dress.'

'What's wrong with that?'

'It's too vague to be called a description. A woman would say something like, "She had the kind of playful prettiness that can lead a man to all kinds of indiscretion. Her hair was fair, not quite blonde, and it was cut in the popular, Veronica Lake style. Her dress was emerald green satin and with a halter neck and it ended just below the knee." '

'All I can say is that women have too much time on their hands.' He picked up the telephone and asked for the Admiralty. When he got through to Captain Challock, they initiated the scrambler.

'Tell me it's good news, Stamford.'

'Excellent news, sir. The man arrested yesterday has been positively identified as the spurious dockyard fitter who pretended to be working on the sprinklers. Miss Pendleton identified him from his facial features and his hair oil.'

'Good God. Well done, Miss Pendleton.'

'Women are good at noticing details, sir.' He winked at Lucy, who gave him a dismissive look.

'At all events, sir, we believe this man is *Agent Dohle*.'

'Well done, Stamford.'

'It wasn't just my doing, sir. Miss Pendleton found a broken cufflink at Thomas Gael's bedsitter. She became curious when she read the initial "X" on it. It turned out to belong to Francis Xavier Moore, a draughtsman of Spanish extraction, who's been working in the Dockyard drawing office for the past two months.'

'So that's how he came by details of the new RATOG.'

'Presumably, sir.'

'Well done to you and Miss Pendleton.'

'Thank you, sir. I'll pass your message on to her.'

'Good. Is she there?'

'Yes, sir.'

'Put her on, will you?'

William handed the receiver to Lucy and walked to the door. Her conversation with Captain Challock would be official business, but it somehow seemed wrong for him to stay in the office when they were talking.

After a while, she called him and handed him the telephone. 'The Captain wants a word,' she explained.

'Stamford here, sir.'

'I've just told Miss Pendleton to say nothing about Moore and *Agent Dohle* when she speaks to Gael. We'll keep him guessing, and with any luck, he'll confirm that the two are the same.'

'I see, sir.'

'Well done again, Stamford. Carry on.'

'Aye-aye, sir.'

'Well,' said William, putting the telephone down, 'with that little job done, I suppose we should get back to bamboozling the enemy. I've been wondering about your idea of senior officers being photographed in divers places, and I wonder how feasible that might be. I imagine they're all pretty busy just now.' He noticed that Lucy wasn't looking in his direction. Instead, she seemed to be fascinated by something in the region of the skirting board. 'Marguerite, did you hear what I was saying?'

'I'm sorry, Percy. I was watching that spider.'

'That puts me in my place, doesn't it? Less interesting than a spider.'

'No, you're not,' she assured him. 'It was no more than a fleeting interest. I just wondered if insects can tell each other apart. I mean, one looks so much like another.'

'I suppose they do,' he agreed, trying to contain his excitement, 'and you may not have been paying attention, Marguerite, but you've just given me a brilliant idea.'

━━━◆I◆━━━

Captain Challock was in conference when William arrived, so he spent some time chatting with Dai and then wandered up to Bea's office to pay his respects. He found her tidying her hair.

'You've caught me in a state of disarray,' she said. 'I've just been ashore on an errand for the Admiral, and it's blowing a gale out there. It's still lovely to see you, though.'

'Who would have known it, Bea? You're as elegant as ever. It's my belief that you could walk through a thunderstorm and arrive at your destination unflustered and untouched.'

'Thank you, William, although I disagree entirely.' Reflecting for a moment, she said, 'At the same time, though, I wish you'd spend some time teaching your Welsh friend how to pay compliments. He compared me recently with the ruined Harlech Castle, believe it or not.'

William tried not to laugh. 'What made him say that, Bea?'

'He says it's because of my unchanging splendour and the fact that I remind him of noble things.'

'The main thing is that he's devoted to you, and no words can be a substitute for that.'

'That's true, William. I must remember that.'

The adjoining door opened, and a voice said, 'Who's engaging my secretary in idle conversation?'

'It's Commander Stamford, sir.'

Vice-Admiral Davies opened the door further and saw William. 'Stamford, my boy. Come into my office. Coffee, please, Bea.'

'Aye-aye, sir. There's some that was made only a short time ago.'

William saluted and took the seat the admiral offered him.

'How are you, my boy?'

'I'm well, thank you, sir. And you?'

'Well enough, thank you. I heard about your part in apprehending *Agent Dohle*. Really well done.'

'Thank you, sir, but I wasn't the only one.'

'I know. I believe the admirable Miss Pendleton was partly responsible, and it came as no surprise.'

'She's a remarkable girl, sir.'

'Who's a remarkable girl?' The question came from Bea, who carried the coffee things in and placed the tray on the admiral's desk.

'You are, my dear.' The admiral favoured her with a rare on-watch smile.

'I thought you hadn't noticed, sir.'

'Be off with you and stop fishing for compliments.' He waited until Bea was out of the office before asking, 'What brings you here on this occasion, Stamford?'

'I came to see Captain Challock, sir. I have an idea to put to him, but he's in conference.'

'Tell me your idea.'

'Very well, sir. As usual, it's in connection with misleading the enemy as to the planned location of the invasion. My assistant put forward the idea of having prominent senior officers photographed in certain places, but I can't see them fitting in with our plans when so much is afoot. However, you know, sir, how everyone has a double—'

'Stop there, Stamford.' The admiral raised a cautionary hand. 'There must be no further talk of doubles.' Relaxing a little, he went on to explain. 'As we speak, an actor, who is physically identical to a very senior army officer, is being trained to take that officer's place for the purpose of deception. This thing is so critically important that there must be no reference to anything relating to it. That's why I stopped you.'

'I see, sir. Someone has pilfered my idea, and not for the first time.'

'There's every likelihood that he had the idea before you, Stamford. It happens to the best of brains, you know.'

—◆◆◆—

'It's very important,' said Captain Challock, 'that Miss Pendleton keeps the matter of *Agent Dohle* under her hat.'

'You can rely on her, sir.'

'Good.'

William was struggling. 'I find it all baffling, sir.'

'What's that, Stamford?'

'Gael believes Marguerite to be a committed Nazi agent.'

'Correct.'

'In that case, why shouldn't she know about *Agent Dohle*?'

'If you think about it long enough, you'll work it out for yourself, Stamford, but just to get you started, Gael knew about *Dohle*, but he said nothing about him to Marguerite.'

'Of course.' It began to make sense.

'In this world of agents and double agents, no one trusts anyone, so they're bound to keep secrets from each other.'

'It's a funny kind of comradeship, sir.'

'Even lovers have secrets, or so I'm told.'

'I believe so, sir.'

'Also,' and Challock lowered his voice as a warning, 'it's quite possible that *Dohle* was sent to find out if the information Marguerite had been sending was genuine.'

It was a frightening scenario.

———◆I◆———

Lucy's first question was, 'How are Bea and Dai?'

'They're fine. Dai has pretty well got over his disappointment at being deskbound for the remainder of the war, and Bea is still breathing a long sigh of relief.'

'I miss them both, but Bea in particular.'

William smiled at the memory of his conversation with her. 'She wants me to tutor Dai in the art of romantic blandishment,' he told her.

'Oh?'

'Dai's compliments are genuine enough, but they can be clumsy. He actually likened her to the ruins of Harlech Castle.'

'No, really?'

'Yes, he said it was because of her permanent splendour and because she reminded him of noble things.'

Lucy grimaced. 'As you said, well-meant but clumsy.'

'I don't know so much about that, Marguerite. I can see his point. I mean, you remind me of the entrance to Headingley Cricket Ground.'

'This had better be good,' she said, narrowing her eyes.

'You'll like it. You see, it's a familiar and welcome sight, and I enter it knowing I'm going to have a good time.'

Her eyes flashed in mock outrage. 'You're every bit as bad as Dai, you awful man. You'll have to atone in some way.'

'What would you like?'

'Oh.' She pretended to think and then held up one finger. 'I know.'

'Don't keep it to yourself. Share it with me, Marguerite.'

'Do you think we could go back to my flat tonight, and have a William and Lucy night?'

'Is that what you'd like?'

'Mm. Wouldn't you?'

'Why not?' He studied her from various angles.

'What are you doing?'

'I'm visualising you with a sign over your head, saying, "Yorkshire County Cricket Club".'

Lucy scowled. 'If I had a cricket ball handy,' she said, 'I'd use it to practise leg theory on you.' She held up a hand to forestall his response, adding, 'And don't think I couldn't.'

21

MAY

William and Lucy half-expected to be called as witnesses in the case against Francis Moore, but several weeks passed with no word from DCI Henderson. In fact, the next news came from Captain Challock during one of William's visits to the Admiralty.

'Dohle is proving to be most helpful,' he said. 'The alternative is usually sufficient to make them amenable.'

'It's not what I'd call a difficult decision, sir.'

'Nor I.' Challock looked thoughtful and said, 'You know, his reason for joining Hitler's gang was pettish and illogical. He hated his father for deserting the family home, and his father was an Englishman, so he hated the English. It's possible he still does, but he believes the odds are now in our favour, so it makes sense for him to co-operate with us.'

It made a great deal of sense, but only to someone faced with that stark choice. Meanwhile, another question had been waiting for an answer. 'Are we sure, now, that Moore is *Agent Dohle*, sir?'

'Yes, we've intercepted a message from Gael to Berlin, reporting that *Dohle* had not been in contact with him since the twenty-ninth of March, and he feared that he'd been caught. For that reason, we can't use him as a double agent, although he will continue to have his uses.' Bearing in mind William's more personal concern, he said, 'I've notified Miss Pendleton, by the way.'

'Thank you for that, sir. It seems to me that the most powerful weapon in our armoury is our ability to decrypt Nazi signals.'

'You can say that again, Stamford. It's saved our bacon in the Atlantic and it continues to give sterling service.'

'And, as far as we know, the enemy have never suspected a thing.'

Challock rolled his eyes. 'Long may it last.' He seemed about to bring the meeting to its close, and then hesitated. 'There's something else I've been meaning to speak to you about.'

'Yes, sir?'

'Do you possess a motor car, Stamford?'

'No, sir.' It seemed a strange question. 'Should I?'

'I think so. It would make things easier for you in Chatham.'

'To be honest, sir, I'd set all thoughts of motoring aside until after the war, when petrol will hopefully no longer be rationed.'

'Oh, you'd get an allocation for service use. I do.'

William remembered Challock picking him up outside New Scotland Yard. 'Of course, sir.'

'How are you fixed for funds?'

'It shouldn't be a problem, sir. People are selling cars at ridiculously low prices, simply because they're an embarrassment.'

'Well, think about it, Stamford.'

'Aye-aye, sir.'

Challock stood up and offered his hand. 'I'll keep you informed of any developments.'

———◆I◆———

'What are you doing with *The Chatham News*, Percy? Have you decided to go native?'

'No, I'm looking for a car.'

Lucy assimilated the information. 'It's possibly not the best time to take up motoring, Percy, but I expect you know best.'

'That's very loyal of you, Marguerite. Actually, Captain Challock says that, as it will be serving, so to speak, under the white ensign, I'll get an official allocation of petrol for it.'

'Oh, shiver me timbers. What sort of car are you looking for?'

'A modest one that won't break the bank.' He peered more closely at one advertisement and said, 'This sounds promising.'

'It may sound promising to you, Percy, but I can't hear a thing.'

'I'm sorry. It's a Morris Eight saloon and it's within my limited budget.'

'Don't forget that help is never far away.'

'That's very generous of you, Marguerite, but I can manage this without falling back on the Pendleton fortune.'

Lucy shrugged. 'Have it your own way.' Then, reverting to curiosity, she asked, 'May I come with you when you go to inspect it?'

'Of course, but we won't be able to drive it away immediately, even supposing it's suitable. I'll have to arrange insurance, and very likely buy a road fund licence.'

'Yes, I'd forgotten about all the grown-up things that have to be done.'

'It's a grown-up world, Marguerite,' he said, lifting the telephone to ask for an outside line, 'but if I can arrange to view the car in the early evening, I'll take you out for a treat afterwards.'

The vendor of the car was a Mrs Wilmshurst, who lived in a quiet street off Maidstone Road. William had arranged to be there for six-thirty. The taxi dropped them at a little after six twenty-five, and they saw the car on the drive.

'Gosh,' said Lucy, 'it looks rather fetching.' She joined William at the front door, where he rang the bell and waited for less than half a minute, before Mrs Wilmshurst came to the door.

'Good evening, Mrs Wilmshurst,' said William. 'I'm William Stamford and this is my assistant Miss Werner.'

'Oh, you've come about the car. Well, there it is, on the drive. I'll get the keys.' She disappeared into the house, and William said quietly, 'She's a friendly soul, isn't she?'

'I'd hate to be around during one of her brusque spells,' agreed Lucy.

Mrs Wilmshurst returned with the keys to the car. 'It's not insured, so you can't take it anywhere,' she said.

'I'd like to run the engine,' said William.

'Oh well, go ahead. I suppose you could run it up and down the drive if you want to. The engine was running about an hour ago, so it should start on the button.' She handed him the keys. 'No further than the end of the drive,' she warned.

'I'll stay here as a precaution,' offered Lucy. She thought 'precaution' sounded better than 'hostage'. 'He can't go anywhere without me,' she explained.

Mrs Wilmshurst looked at her sharply. 'Can't he?'

'No, he has absolutely no sense of direction. Why they made him a navigator is a complete mystery.'

Mrs Wilmshurst looked blank and asked of no one in particular, 'How do they expect to win this war?' Then, as William reversed up to the garage doors and then changed into first gear to make the return trip, she said, 'In case you're wondering why my husband's not here, he's a prisoner-of-war.'

Lucy hadn't wondered at all. It seemed quite normal in wartime for husbands to be absent from home, but she felt she should offer her sympathy in this case. 'I'm sorry to hear it,' she said.

'I'm divorcing him. I'm selling everything and we're going to divide the proceeds between us.'

'Ah.' There wasn't much else Lucy could say.

'We talked about it before he was captured, and now the whole thing can be done through the Red Cross,' she said. 'He has a roving eye, you know.' She nodded, as if confirming the fact. 'And that's not all.'

Lucy was left wondering about the extent of Mr Wilmshurst's transgressions, because just then, William stopped the engine, locked the car and re-joined them on the drive.

'I believe you said eighty pounds, Mrs Wilmshurst.'

'That's right. No bargaining. Take it or leave it.'

'I'm satisfied. He counted out the money and took the log book from her. Inside, he found a receipt already signed over a twopenny stamp. It seemed that Mrs Wilmshurst had been confident of a quick sale. 'I'll fix up the insurance and road fund licence tomorrow,' he said.

'That's fine. Take the keys and then when you come you'll be able to drive the car away even if I'm not at home. There's petrol in the tank, although I don't know how much.'

'Thank you, Mrs Wilmshurst.' William offered his hand, which she ignored.

'Goodbye, Mrs Wilmshurst,' said Lucy. 'I hope the rest of the sale goes as smoothly, and good luck with the divorce.'

William gave her a strange look, but said nothing until they were clear of the house and almost at the bus stop, when he asked, 'What was that about?'

'She's divorcing her husband. He's a prisoner-of-war, so the Red Cross are handling everything. It's one of the services they provide nowadays. I imagine they send a little man and he does it all for you.'

'Just like Harrods?'

'Well, maybe not with quite the same flair.'

William considered the news. 'I don't know the first thing about Mr Wilmshurst,' he said, 'but he has my sympathy, and not just because he was taken prisoner.'

'He has a roving eye.'

'Well, it won't be much use to him in a PoW camp, unless he... you know.'

'Unless he what?'

'Turns out for the other side.'

'What? Oh, I see. I suppose it's always possible. Oh, look, here's the bus.'

The bus stopped for them, and they took their seats. At that time of the evening, they were spared the usual crowds.

'Fares, please.' The conductress stood beside them with her thumb poised over the lever of her ticket machine.

'Two to the Estuary Restaurant, please,' requested William.

'This ain't a taxi, Lord Nelson, and the Estuary Restaurant ain't a bus stop or even a fare stage, neiver. It's between the devil and the deep blue sea.'

'In that case, if you can suggest a bus stop fairly close to it, I'll be guided by you.'

'That'll be eightpence.'

William counted out the fare and handed it to her, taking the tickets.

'It's a pity we couldn't call at my flat,' said Lucy. 'I don't make a habit of dining out in my office clothes.'

'We're going somewhere that's between the devil and the deep blue sea,' William reminded her, 'and no one will mind. I know, because I've been there.' He leaned closer to whisper, 'And for what it's worth, I find you equally inviting in any item of your wardrobe.'

The bus lurched onward, until the conductress called, 'Your stop coming up, Admiral.' She threw him a mock salute, which he returned.

'Thank you.' He and Lucy got off the bus and looked ahead, where the Estuary Restaurant was clearly visible.

'It's just a short walk,' said William. 'Will you be all right in your high heels, or would you like me to carry you?'

'I'll manage, thank you.'

He gave her his arm, and they walked to the restaurant.

———— ◆◆ ————

Later, Lucy let them into her flat. As she did so, she said, 'That was a very good meal by wartime standards.'

'It was pretty good,' he agreed, removing his jacket and hanging his tie over the back of a chair, 'but every meal I have with you affects me the same way.'

She beckoned to him to follow her into the bedroom. 'Which way is that?'

'I find myself consumed with lust.'

She nodded. 'I thought you were leering a bit over the main course. I put it down to the excitement of buying a car. I'm told it takes some men that way.' She drew up her skirts provocatively and unfastened first one suspender, and then the other, narrowing her eyes at him as she allowed her stocking to fall. 'Are you going to join in, or must I do all the undressing around here?' She repeated the process with the other stocking, and then he regained his composure and began undressing.

'Back in a jiffy.' She left the room, returning after a short time, during which he finished undressing and hopped into bed.

'Ah,' she said, 'it's that strange man again in my bed. I suppose I'll have to acquiesce to your vile demands, as usual.' She pulled her dress over her head and hung it in the wardrobe.

'You've never complained in the past.'

'Well, one gets used to it after a while.' She shed the rest of her clothes, creating a neat pile of lingerie and finally stood naked in front of him. 'Go on, take me,' she said, holding her arms wide. 'You know you want to.'

'Another time, you know, I really must organise some music for you to disrobe to.

'Is there no limit to your debauchery?'

'If there is, I haven't discovered it yet.' He took her in his arms and kissed her unhurriedly.

'You know, there can't be many admirals who kiss as well as you. It compensates in some way for your appalling grammar.'

'Thank you, but what prompted you to say that?

'You ended a sentence with a preposition. You said, "disrobe to".'

'I meant your reference to "many admirals".'

'The bus conductress thought you were an admiral.'

'She thought I was Lord Nelson before that, and he was a hopeless kisser.'

'How do you know?' It was more a query than a challenge.

'It was in one of my schoolboy diaries. Every week, there was a useful gem of general knowledge. I think the leaking of Lord Nelson's secret occurred on the twenty-first of October.'

'You have a good memory.'

'No, it's the date of the Battle of Trafalgar, when he defeated the French and Spanish fleets. The action, believe it or not, took place in a configuration not unlike the female anatomy. The French were here, you see.' He demonstrated by planting a languorous kiss on her left breast. 'And the Spanish were here.' He transferred his attention to her right breast.

'And where was Lord Nelson?'

'Just here.' He journeyed downward to her flat tummy. 'That's why this thing is called the navel,' he explained. 'I should point out that spelling was quite arbitrary in eighteen-oh-five.'

'You seem to know a great deal about the Battle of Trafalgar.'

'I'm an acknowledged expert. I'll show you. First, Nelson opened fire on the Spanish.' He delivered a cluster of tiny kisses on her right breast. 'And then on the French.' Again, he showered her with kisses, this time favouring the left. 'The remnants of the Spanish and French fleets formed a line of battle together, but Nelson broke through it and won the day.' He traced the passage of Nelson's fleet with a series of tiny kisses, finally celebrating at length on her lips.

Eventually, she managed to say somewhat breathlessly, 'I request the pleasure of Lord Nelson's company on board at his earliest convenience.'

'His Lordship is pleased to accept your invitation.'

Lucy caught her breath and shuddered. 'Oh, welcome aboard, Admiral.'

———— ▸◂ ————

As they took their seats on the bus to *HMS Pembroke* the next morning, Lucy said, 'There goes Thomas.'

William turned away from the window. 'Gael?'

'Yes. I wonder what he's doing in this neck of the woods.'

'Do you think he saw us?'

'He may have caught sight of me, but I can't imagine he saw you. Not with me in the way.'

'The last thing we want is for him to see me in uniform.'

The conductress came to take their fares. When she'd gone, Lucy said, 'I think we're safe, but we mustn't take any more chances.'

22

Captain Challock agreed that it would be much better for William to go about his duties in civilian clothing, at least when he was in Chatham, and he wrote the order accordingly. Meanwhile, the task of misleading the Nazis remained, and William was determined to keep up the flow of disinformation. He'd been giving the invasion, and one aspect of it in particular, a great deal of thought.

'We've been inclined to look at the operation from one side,' he said.

'Our side, of course.' Lucy nodded approvingly. 'Let the Nazis worry about their part in it.'

'I mean that we've only considered it as a successful operation with absolutely no hitches. We haven't considered casualties at all, and there are bound to be a great many.'

Lucy stared bleakly through the window. 'What a horrible thought.'

'I know, Marguerite, but if we're to pull the wool over the enemy's eyes, we have to be realistic.'

Shifting her gaze from the window, she gave him her full attention and asked, 'What kind of thing have you in mind?'

'For all we know, hospitals all over the south of England must be preparing for the influx of casualties. I just think we should let it slip that civilian patients are being moved out to make beds available in hospitals in the south-east.'

'And the south, surely? If you remember, we agreed that we should work on two possibilities, the Low Countries and the Pas de Calais.'

William smiled knowingly. 'I get the impression from Captain

Challock that our best ideas have already been appropriated by the others. It makes sense, I suppose.'

'We're all in it together, and we all want the same thing to happen,' agreed Lucy. Then, adopting a business-like expression, she said, 'Maybe we should make a start. Do you want me to type it?'

'No, thank you, Marguerite. I'll do it.'

'It's probably the wisest course.'

'You should learn to type, you know. You could do it in your own time and at your own pace.'

'I *can* type, Percy, but not always with the right letters, and when I do get the letters right, they sometimes find their way into the wrong part of the word.'

'All right, take this down in longhand, and I'll type it later.'

'That's what I call an excellent arrangement.'

———◆◆———

At the RAF listening station in Chatham, a WAAF sergeant was keeping watch on Thomas Gael's frequency. His transmissions and those intended for him occurred at various set times, although not every day. The circuit had to be monitored, however; everyone was aware of its importance, and Corporal Angela Gibson was determined to miss nothing.

Suddenly, the tedium was broken. The operator on the circuit was calling the station listed on the sheet pinned to Angela's desk. She pulled a message pad towards her and took down the slow stream of coded groups. She had no idea who was transmitting or to whom. All she knew was that it was vital that every transmission was read and logged, and the intercept sent by motorcycle to Station 'X' at Bletchley Park.

———◆◆———

The first William knew about the signal was when Captain Challock summoned him urgently to his office.

'I've received a decrypt from Station "X",' he said. 'You can read it for yourself. It was sent by Berlin to Thomas Gael yesterday.'

'I'm afraid my German only stretched as far as School Certificate, sir. I rely on Miss Pendleton for anything more demanding than the fairly basic.'

'At least you're honest, Stamford. I'll translate for you. It says, "Expect *Agent Bachsteltze* on the twenty-ninth of May. *Treffpunkt*" – that's "Rendezvous" – seventeen thirty-five Euston." The cunning blighters. Special Branch will be there to keep them under surveillance, but anything could happen in the rush-hour.'

'I imagine he's coming via Ireland, sir.'

'That's right, and Liverpool.'

'Why Liverpool, I wonder. It's way up north.'

'All the ports that handle Irish traffic are about the same distance from London. Also, with the large Irish population in Liverpool, they'll have no shortage of contacts.' Challock got up and placed the decrypt in his safe. 'The likelihood is that *Bachsteltze* is *Dohle*'s replacement, and it's further likely that his first job will be to ascertain Miss Pendleton's *bona fides*.' He looked at William sharply and said, 'You should carry a pistol, Stamford.'

'I have a Webley four-five-five semi-automatic, sir.'

The disclosure caused Challock to raise his eyebrows. 'How did you come by that?'

'It was in nineteen-forty, sir, when things were a trifle uncertain. No one asked me for it, so I never returned it.'

'Tut, tut. It's far too big for you to carry around, anyway. Turn it in and take something smaller. I'll arrange things with the armoury.'

It all sounded very dire to William. He said, 'I take it you're expecting trouble, sir?'

'Not expecting trouble, so much as taking precautions. I'll be honest. If the Nazis suspect that Miss Pendleton is anything other than their agent, things could become unpleasant, and that's quite apart from the future of *Operation Overlord*.'

William was uneasy. 'With regard to my pistol, sir,' he said, 'I've always reckoned that anything less than forty-five calibre, or thirty-eight at the very least, lacks stopping power as well as being inaccurate.'

'I was a gunnery officer too, Stamford, so don't try blinding me with science. In any case, if things do get confrontational, you'll be at close quarters, and a small calibre pistol will be quite adequate, as you'll discover if the enemy uses one first.'

'Yes, sir.'

'Is there anything else?'

'Yes, sir. Just out of interest, I imagine the *Bachsteltze*, like the other agents' codenames, is a bird. Do you know what kind?'

'I haven't a clue, Stamford. You'll have to ask Miss Pendleton.'

———— ◆◄◆ ————

Back at *HMS Pembroke*, Lucy found him cleaning his old Webley pistol.

'Why are you playing with that gun, Percy?'

'I'm not playing with it. I'm making sure it goes back to the armoury in pristine condition. I've been told to return it.' It was as much as he was prepared to tell her about firearms. He had no wish to frighten her.

'Why do you have to return it?'

'I don't know, Marguerite, but orders are orders. Actually,' he said, laying the pistol down on his desk, 'there's something you need to know. Gael is meeting a new agent on the twenty-ninth, codename *Bachsteltze*. He's coming via Ireland and Liverpool, and Gael will be meeting him at Euston Station.'

Lucy nodded slowly. 'Are you certain this *Bachsteltze* is a man and not a woman?'

'He was referred to in the signal from Berlin as "*Agent*", rather than "*Agentin*". You may get to meet him, although it would be better if you didn't.'

'Some things just can't be avoided, Percy.'

'Just be careful.'

'I will.' She blew him a kiss across the desk.

'Marguerite?'

'Mm?'

'What does "*Bachsteltze*" mean?'

' "Wagtail". I asked you if he was male or female because it's a feminine noun.'

'Oh, we went through all that with *Dohle*. The enemy don't seem to differentiate between the sexes nowadays.'

'They're running out of birds with masculine names, I shouldn't wonder.'

————— ▸◂ —————

Lucy was naturally interested in *Agent Bachsteltze* and she was keen to know more. She hadn't long to wait, because the telephone rang within half-an-hour of her return. She'd only just left *Pembroke*, so it couldn't be William. The only other possibility was Gael, who confirmed her suspicion a moment later, when she heard him press button 'A'.

'Marguerite, it's Thomas. I have important information for you. Is it convenient if I come now?'

'I suppose so.'

'I'm in the telephone kiosk at the end of Manor Road. I'll be with you shortly.'

She imagined he wanted to tell her about *Agent Bachsteltze*. She would soon know.

Less than five minutes later, the doorbell rang, and she went down to let him in. She found him sheltering from the rain as best he could in the doorway.

'It would be a lot easier if I had a key,' he said.

'There's no spare key,' she told him. Neither had she any intention of obtaining one for him. William had the other key, and that was how it would stay. 'Anyway, you'd better come up to the flat.'

Gael followed her upstairs.

'I must say, this sounds very mysterious,' she said, closing the door behind him. 'What's it all about?'

'I'm afraid the British have captured *Agent Dohle*,' he said.

'*Agent* who?'

'Dohle. He was working at the Dockyard.'

'Ah.'

'It was most unfortunate, but they're sending an agent to replace him.'

'Oh?' Rather than feign surprise, she said, 'I was about to make tea. Would you like some?'

'Yes, please. That would be very nice.'

'Carry on talking to me while I put the kettle on.' It was better than being face to face with him at such a time.

'Yes, the agent they're sending is codenamed *Agent Bachsteltze*.'

'How quaint.'

'That's not all. You and he are old acquaintances. You knew him as Gerhardt Edelmann. I believe you trained together.'

The shock triggered a release of adrenalin, and Lucy felt the icy rush of blood leave her extremities, but she had to respond. Adjusting quickly to the situation, she turned and said, 'How marvellous. I haven't seen Gert since before the war. Will he be based locally?'

'For a while.' His tone was guarded.

It seemed to her that Gael was keeping something back, some secret he didn't want her to know.

'When is he arriving?'

'Next Monday. I have to meet him at Euston Station. You could come too if you like.'

'If only it were so easy, Thomas. Time off is precious and seldom granted. No, you meet him. I've no doubt his path and mine will cross eventually.'

◆◆◆

'Apparently, Gerhardt Edelmann and Marguerite Werner trained together before the war. I don't know how much time they spent together, and an absence of five years is quite a long time, so I may still pass for her physically, but that's not what's worrying me.'

William nodded, but let her continue.

'It would be easy for me to say something that would give the game away. I know absolutely nothing about him.'

'Let's ask Captain Challock what he can find out. I'm going up to London again. He may be able to come up with something in the meantime.' William picked up the telephone and asked to be connected to the Admiralty.

———•┤◄———

Challock was in a meeting when William arrived, so he went down to the armoury, which was his other reason for being in London.

The chief petty officer had been advised of his visit and was waiting with what William could only call a respectful rap on the knuckles.

'You should have handed that Webley in three years ago, sir.'

'I would have, Chief, but nobody asked me for it.' As he spoke, he realised it was what the lower deck called an 'OD's excuse'. An ordinary seaman was the lowest form of messdeck life, and was expected to offer feeble excuses. William was expected to know better.

The CPO let it pass, saying instead, 'There was a lot going on at the time, sir.'

'Yes, I was conscious of a certain level of excitement. Anyway, Chief, what are you going to trust me with?'

The CPO studied the message from Captain Challock and said, 'It says here that the weapon should be easily concealed and carried, sir. Let me see.' He referred to his records.

'Nothing too puny, I hope. I need to rely on it.'

The CPO picked up a short-barrelled Colt revolver and said, 'If you carried this, sir, you'd be telling the whole of London you were armed. It's the width of the cylinder, you see. It would stick out a mile and spoil the cut of your uniform into the bargain.'

'All right, Chief, I'll be guided by you.'

The CPO picked up a Webley and Scott thirty-two calibre semi-automatic and handed it to William, who checked that the gun was empty, weighed it in his hand and squinted down the sights. Finally, he said, 'It's a handbag gun, Chief.'

'A pocket pistol, actually, sir, but it's the best I can do in view of my orders. You're a commander, fair enough, sir, but I've got a captain breathing down my neck, and he says I have to arm you with a small calibre, easily concealed weapon, a shoulder holster and two spare magazines.' He swivelled the book in front of him for William's convenience and said, 'Sign here, please, sir.'

———◆◄◆———

'It seems to me, sir,' said William, 'that however much gold braid we have thrust upon us, a chief petty officer can still cut us down to size.'

Challock smiled briefly. 'That's what they're for, Stamford, and we couldn't function without them. How did CPO Harding upset you?'

'By giving me a handbag gun, sir.'

'That's a gross exaggeration. In the last war, infantry officers purchased the same weapon for use in trench raids. It gave them an additional eight rounds to those they carried in their service revolvers. Some officers carry them to this day, and for what it's worth, I defy you to find a ladies' handbag sufficiently free of disorganised clutter that it could accommodate such a weapon.'

William thought of Lucy searching her bag for her house key, and had to agree. 'I stand corrected, sir.'

'Good. In any case, CPO Harding was acting on my orders.' Opening the file before him, he went on to say, 'I've had a group photograph copied. It's of Edelmann's class at the intelligence school at Quenzsee. You'll see where he's been identified, and you'll probably recognise Marguerite Werner as well.' He handed the photograph to William.

'Good grief. She really does look very much like Miss Pendleton.'

Challock nodded. 'Also, our colleagues in MI Five are trying to find out what they can about Edelmann from the real Miss Werner. I shall let you know as soon as I can what they discover.'

23

At safe house *Kestrel*, Lieutenant Colonel Selby accepted a cup of tea from Marguerite Werner, who sat opposite him, on the sofa.

'Thank you, Miss Werner.'

'You're welcome, Colonel. Which detail of my past life do you want me to repeat today?'

'Essentially, none of them.' He put his cup and saucer down on the occasional table and said, 'I'd like to know more about your training in Germany. I don't believe we've discussed that in any kind of detail.'

'How careless of you, Colonel.' Her eyes teased him. 'You know, of course, that I was trained at Quentzsee, near Brandenburg, but then, who wasn't?'

'Yes, I've known several of your colleagues who underwent training at Quenzsee. How long were you there?'

'Three months.'

'And what did you learn?'

'Very little.' Seemingly rewarded by the look of surprise on Selby's features, she said, 'My German-born comrades spent a great deal of time learning English and about the British way of life, a superfluous part of the course as far as I was concerned.'

'Quite, but what *did* you learn?'

'Oh, wireless telegraphy, cryptography, photography... the usual things that I've no doubt British intelligence agents also learn.' Her tone was dismissive, which was not surprising after five months' interrogation.

Selby sat back comfortably in the armchair to encourage her to relax. She was possibly wise to it by that time, but it was always a good idea, and for Selby, it had become a habit.

'Three months with the same people,' he commented. 'You must have got to know them well.'

'Not all of them. There were some I didn't want to know.' Suddenly, her eyes flashed with suspicion. 'Who have you caught now?'

'Mm? Oh, a chap called Francis Moore, otherwise known as *Agent Dohle*.'

'I've never heard of him. He certainly wasn't in my class.' Her dismissive tone sounded genuine.

'I imagine you made friends, though. Three months is a long time.'

'Five months is longer, Colonel, and it seems interminable when it's spent in custody and under interrogation. When will you people accept my word that I'm prepared to work for you?'

'I think we're getting there, Miss Werner. In the meantime, I'd like you to tell me about some of the people you knew in your class at Quentzsee.'

'To enable you to identify them, I suppose?'

'Can you think of a better way to convince me that your offer to work for us is genuine?'

'Maybe not.' She picked up the teapot and strainer. 'More tea, Colonel?'

'Yes, please. Do you recall Gerhardt Edelmann?'

At the mention of his name, her eyes showed instant recognition. 'What dealings have you had with him?'

'Our paths have crossed, actually in North Africa, but he managed somehow to stay one step ahead of us.'

'He would.' Her satisfaction was evident in the way she uttered those two words.

'You knew him well, then?'

'Colonel, you know perfectly well that he and I were close. Someone's told you, obviously.'

Selby had no such idea, but he was grateful for the information. It was rare that Marguerite Werner lowered her guard, and the subject was worth pursuing. 'It's my business to find out these things, Miss Werner. How close were you to Gerhardt Edelmann? I mean, you were obviously on "Gert" and "Marguerite" terms, but were you lovers?'

She looked at him as she might view a half-wit. 'There's a limit to what two people under training in National Socialist Germany can get up to, Colonel. Let's just say that, had circumstances been different, our relationship might easily have blossomed in the usual way.'

'The situation must have been very trying for you.'

'Well, this war won't last forever, and if we both survive it, who knows what might happen?'

'Do you imagine he still has the same feelings for you that you evidently have for him?'

'We were and are committed to each other, Colonel.' Unexpectedly, she gave a quick smile. 'There is one thing I'll tell you about him,' she said, 'although it will be of no help to you in finding him.'

'Oh?' It was unusual for her to be so forthcoming. Maybe memories of their relationship had made her careless. At all events, Selby was grateful for any detail.

'You spoke about our being on "Gert" and "Marguerite" terms, I recall.'

'That's right.'

'No one ever addresses Gerhardt as "Gert". He dislikes diminutives, especially of his own name. His father and grandfather were called Gerhardt, so the name means a great deal to him, and he insists on being addressed and referred to correctly.'

That was interesting, but Selby needed more information. 'Have you a photograph of him, Miss Werner?'

'If I had, your people would have found it by now. Unfortunately, we were parted before we could exchange photos.'

'So he has no photograph either. That's most unfortunate. Still, you're a most attractive woman, Miss Werner. I doubt if he'd ever forget your face.'

'I sincerely hope not, Colonel.'

On the other hand, Selby hoped he would. He also hoped that Captain Challock might somehow elicit more information from Miss Werner.

———◆◆———

Captain Challock refused William's offer of a chair. 'No,' he said. 'Thank you, Stamford, but I've just driven from a safe house in Surrey, where I've been in conversation with the real Marguerite Werner. Miss Pendleton, I think you'd better sit down to hear what I've got to say.'

'Oh, dear.' Lucy obediently lowered herself on to her usual chair.

'Special Branch are going to maintain a twenty-four-hour surveillance of your flat,' he told her. 'They're also watching Gael's bedsitter. Now, it's possible that Edelmann will be taken in. He hasn't seen Miss Werner for almost five years and, as far as she knows, he has no photograph of her to remind him of her appearance. They will each have their memories, of course. Miss Werner told me that he has a kind of earthy, rough-hewn attraction that she found appealing after the effete Englishmen she'd known. Be that as it may, however, there is every chance you will pass muster.'

'That's a relief.' William's words lacked feeling. 'Might I be allowed to stay in Miss Pendleton's flat, sir? She needs protection.'

'She does, Stamford, but no. Just as Special Branch are watching the flat, you can bet Gael's doing the same thing, and if he saw you, he might smell a rat. No, we don't want to lose Edelmann.'

'There's the telephone,' said William, 'but it takes time to get through the switchboard to my office, and in emergency, that time would be crucial.'

'You're saying that Miss Pendleton needs a second line of defence. I'm sure we can rely on Special Branch to protect her, but just to set your mind at rest, let me see if the "boffins", as our RAF colleagues call them, can find some way of raising the alarm.'

'Thank you, sir.'

'Not at all, Stamford.' Challock waved his gratitude aside. 'Miss Pendleton, I would never knowingly have put you into a dangerous situation, but Edelmann's arrival has come as a surprise. Be assured, though, that your safety is my concern.' Taking a card from his wallet, he handed it to William and said, 'There's my home telephone number, Stamford. If you need me outside working hours, you'll find me there.'

'Thank you, sir.'

'Oh, there's one more thing we learned about Edelmann. On the face of it, it doesn't sound important, but you may as well know, Miss Pendleton, that he doesn't like his name to be shortened. I don't know how it might be shortened, but there it is.'

' "Gert" is the usual form,' she told him, 'but if I meet him, I'll be careful not to call him that. Thank you, Captain Challock.'

'You're welcome, my dear. Don't get up, Stamford. I'll see myself out.'

'Goodbye, sir.'

'Goodbye, Captain.'

'Goodbye, both of you. I'll see you soon.' Challock left the office and went to his car.

Lucy watched him go and said, 'If I'm to be brought face to face with earthy, rough-hewn, Teutonic manhood, Percy, I need comfort.'

'In that case, come away from the window.'

Obediently, she left the window to join him in their private corner. 'I'd really like a re-enactment of the Battle of Trafalgar tonight, just to calm my nerves. Do you think it's possible?'

'I don't have to stay away from your flat until Monday, which means that I may just be able to provide the sedative you need.' He put his arms round her and drew her closer. 'On second thoughts,' he said, 'away with false modesty. I know I can provide it.' They kissed by way of celebration. 'Actually,' he said, 'I don't see why we shouldn't throw in the Battles of Copenhagen and the Nile as a bonus.'

———◆◄◆———

'I wonder if that was what Lord Nelson and Emma Hamilton used to do.'

'Of course,' he assured her. 'It was popular even then.'

'I'm talking about re-enacting his battles, William. 'At least, all except one. He couldn't really include Trafalgar.'

He raised himself on one elbow to remonstrate with her. 'I've shown you what Horatio and Emma used to get up to. You really must pay attention.'

'Oh, I was paying attention. Didn't you hear me?'

'I think half of Chatham must have heard you. It would be enough to make Thomas Gael green with envy.'

For a moment, Lucy looked anxious. 'Oh, don't talk about him, William. Just for this evening, I was trying to forget him.'

'I'm sorry, darling. Honestly, you've nothing to worry about.'

She snuggled closer. 'Let's talk about afterwards,' she said.

'After what?'

'After this thing is all over, and you and I can return to normal life and make plans.'

'All right.' William turned to face her. 'How many children do you want?'

'Two, three, perhaps four or more. I haven't decided.'

'Maybe we should get started. I mean, there's no time to be lost.'

'I think we should get married first, and that quite soon.'

'Before the first baby comes tumbling down the chute, yes. Wouldn't it be marvellous if we could produce a cricket team? The Stamford Eleven.' His face was suffused with enthusiasm.

'Seriously, William, when can we get married?'

'As soon as you're back in your normal job, as far as I'm concerned. I don't want them to put you on special duties again.'

'Would being married give me exemption, like a reserved occupation?'

'I'm sure they'd take marital status into account.'

Having introduced the subject, Lucy was keen to explore it further. 'I'd like to be married in white. Do you think that would be dishonest of me?'

'Who would know the truth? If you can keep a secret, so can I, but bear in mind that if you start boasting to your friends about your sexual adventures, I'll disclaim all knowledge of them.'

After a moment, she said, 'My parents will want a huge, lavish wedding.'

'You didn't tell me they were planning to get married as well. We could have a double wedding.'

'No, I meant that they would want us to have an elaborate wedding, although I suppose that might be difficult in wartime.'

'If you don't want a big wedding,' he said, touching her nose with his, 'you needn't have one.'

'Oh?'

'No.' He kissed her slowly. 'All you have to do is tell Grandpa how you feel, and he'll unmake all the arrangements.'

'That's true. In no time at all, you've put your finger on the Pendleton family secret.'

'Is this where you keep it?'

She wriggled. 'You'll make the words come out all jumbled again,' she warned him. Then, reverting to an earlier subject, she said, 'I'm still not sure about being married in white. I believe a bride has to answer all kinds of questions put to her by the vicar, minister, priest or whatever. He'll want to know how long I've lived in the parish, and that sort of thing.'

'I've heard that the bride has to fill in a form, but I don't think it includes "Maidenhead Status: intact/otherwise. Delete as appropriate".'

'I hope not. Mine was inappropriately deleted some time ago, as you know. I could hardly say it happened by accident.'

'They say that riding can rob a girl of her credibility.'

'Really? I've done a lot of riding.'

'Well, then. It could have happened over a five-bar gate or simply hoisting yourself into the saddle.'

'You're a great comfort to me, William, as well as a distraction when you do that down there. Are you saying that Lord Nelson wants to come aboard again?'

'He's waiting to be piped aboard.'

'Oh, let's just dispense with the formalities.'

24

Thomas Gael was uneasy. He'd always imagined that the British trusted him; so far, there had been no suggestion that things were otherwise, so why, he wondered, did he keep seeing men in trench coats and trilbies with little to do apart from stand on street corners or read newspapers in unlikely places? It was possible that they were watching someone else. Mistrust was widespread. He had already decided that he no longer trusted Marguerite Werner entirely. She always shied away from talking about her time at Quentzsee, and that was very suspect. Gael was also convinced he'd seen Marguerite board a bus outside her flat with a naval officer who bore a remarkable resemblance to Mr Stamford, previously introduced as a dockyard inspector. He could, of course, be mistaken; there was always that possibility, but if and when he had real evidence, he would notify Berlin, hopefully before he could be taken for questioning about his own activities.

———◆◀————

Captain Challock's next visit was unannounced. He came into William's office with two webbing cases, both of which he placed on William's desk.

'The SCR 536 two-way radio,' he announced, 'is currently known, for some reason best known to its American users, as the "Handie Talkie". It has a maximum range of about a mile over land, always provided nothing gets in the way. The distance between Miss Pendleton's flat and this office is less than a mile and the signal crosses part of the Medway, which is a good thing.'

'Why is it a good thing, sir?' William had seized gratefully on a pause in Challock's delivery, to ask the question.

'Because the range increases over water. Another good thing is that Miss Pendleton's flat is on the first floor of the building. That gives the signal a clearer path than it might otherwise have had.'

'Let me see if Miss Pendleton is free, sir.'

'That's a good idea.' Challock moved out of the way so that William could open the door.

He found Lucy in her office, typing. 'Take a break from that, Marguerite,' said William. 'Captain Challock is here with a new toy to show you.'

'Oh, goody.' She treated her typing to a look of distaste and followed him to his office.

'Good morning, my dear.' Challock offered his hand.

'Good morning, Captain.' She stopped short of the desk and asked, 'What on earth is that?'

'It's a two-way radio, a means of communicating with Commander Stamford from your flat. I want you to test it this morning.'

Lucy stared at the contraption and asked, 'How does it work, Captain?'

'It couldn't be simpler. To switch it on, just pull out the antenna.' He demonstrated. 'Then press the "Press to Talk Switch", and say what you have to say. When you've said it, release the switch and I have no doubt at all that Commander Stamford will speak reassuring words to you. When you've finished, push the antenna back into the chassis, like this, and you'll conserve the batteries.'

'How marvellous. Thank you, Captain. I feel safer already.'

Challock smiled at her childlike trust. 'So that you feel even safer, I want you to take it to your flat. Commander Stamford will go with you, I'll stay here, and we'll make sure it works properly. Off you go, Stamford and call me as soon as you arrive.'

'Aye-aye, sir.'

———◆◈◆———

Lucy unlocked the door of the flat and opened it. 'It's a pity I can't tell my brothers about this, Percy,' she said.

'You're not allowed to tell anyone about it,' he reminded her, 'but why your brothers, particularly?'

'Because when they were boys, they sometimes played with tin can telephones, but they never let me join in.'

'Bad luck, Marguerite, but now we're here, let's test this bag of tricks. Take it.' He offered her the set, which she took gingerly. 'Pull the antenna out.'

'Right.' She seized the button on the antenna and drew it out to its fullest extent.

'Okay,' he told her, 'it won't come out any further. Now press the button and speak to Captain Challock.'

'What shall I say?'

'Anything you like, but for security reasons, don't use his name.'

'Okay.' She looked uncertain, but pressed the switch and was rewarded by a crackling noise. 'Hello, Captain?'

'Release the switch.'

'Sorry.'

The distant voice said, 'Hello, my dear. Well done. You can return now.'

More confidently than before, she pressed the switch and said, 'Thank you, Captain.'

'Right,' said William, 'push the antenna back inside the case to save the batteries.'

'That was fun.'

'Better than tin can telephones, I imagine. Let's hide this thing.'

Lucy took the radio and placed it in a drawer. 'I could never understand how they worked.'

'Tin can telephones? The string had to be taut,' he explained, 'and the sound of the person's voice caused it to vibrate. The tin can acted as a resonating chamber.'

'You make it sound so basic.'

'That's because it is.' He stood on the landing while she locked the door again. 'Next time you think of your brothers not letting you play with their tin can telephones, just remind yourself that you were possibly the first woman to operate a Handie Talkie set.'

'The name sounds Chinese.'

'There are lots of Chinese in America, where it came from,' he assured her, 'but I don't think they gave it its name.'

———◆◆———

At 0800 the following morning, Captain Challock received two more decrypts from Station 'X'. The first read:

Strongly suspect am being watched by English. Request further orders. Buchfink.

The signal had been transmitted at 1830 the previous day. *Buchfink* was Thomas Gael's codename. It seemed, then, that Special Branch had not been sufficiently careful in keeping undercover. He turned to the other decrypt, timed at 2016, London time. It read:

Rendezvous with Bachsteltze *as ordered. Hand over radio and equipment to him. Will advise further. Adler.*

Challock made two scrambled telephone calls. One was to Special Branch in Maidstone, the other to William.

———◆◆———

'Gael's got the wind up,' William told Lucy. 'He knows Special Branch are watching him, and as far as Captain Challock can see, he's asking Berlin to let him return. Whether it's to Germany or just to Ireland, we don't know. Either way, he'd be impossible to find. They'll have to catch him before he leaves the country.'

'What have they said?'

'They've told him to meet Edelmann and hand over the radio and coding stuff to him, so it rather looks as if they're going to pull him out.'

Lucy was thoughtful. Eventually, she asked, 'what would happen to him if they arrested him now?'

'There'd be no second chances. A "guilty" verdict would most likely result in the death penalty, but they won't arrest him yet. They'll wait until he's handed over to Edelmann.'

Lucy remained as preoccupied as ever. 'It's an awful business,' she said. 'I know he's working for the enemy, but the knowledge that someone I've known quite well is going to be hanged as a spy is too awful for words.'

'I know, but think of the thousands of allied soldiers who'll form the invasion force when *Overlord* goes ahead, and what might happen to them if Gael reaches Berlin and tells them he has doubts about you and about the intelligence you've been passing to him.'

'That puts it in perspective,' she agreed. 'It's no less grisly, but it makes sense. Even so, I'll be glad when this awful business is over.'

'Two days from now, Gael and Edelmann will be arrested, and the whole sordid business will come to an end.'

——◆◆——

In his hotel in Dublin, Gerhardt Edelmann was looking forward to arriving in England, and particularly to seeing Marguerite for the first time since graduating from Quentzsee. He was confident that she was still spying for the Fatherland. Those idiots in Berlin had their doubts, but he had his doubts about some of them. At all events, he looked forward to confirming to them how wrong they had been. Marguerite would never have been foolish enough to let herself be captured by the English, and next Monday, he would prove it.

25

Edelmann thought of himself as a proud man, although others might have called him vain. Physically, he was impressive, being well over six feet tall and powerfully built, but that was not all; he had graduated from Quenzsee with a special commendation from the *Kommandant*, an honour that would come automatically to the attention of the *Führer* himself. He had acquitted himself with great success in North Africa and then in Italy, and after discharging his current duty in England, he expected to survive the war and accept the plaudits due to him. There were those, he believed, who were born to succeed, just as there were lesser mortals who fell by the wayside. He naturally saw himself in the former category.

He had been surprised to find so much of Liverpool still standing. There were signs of bomb damage, it was true, but the vast hectares of desolation that Dr Goebbels had described were well hidden. He wondered if perhaps the English had learned somehow to hide their war damage behind false *façades*.

He found Lime Street Station without difficulty, and was surprised again to find it whole and functioning. It had been reported that the station had been rebuilt twice after the *Luftwaffe*'s bombing, replaced each time by a pathetic, temporary enclosure. Again, the English had disguised the damage most effectively.

He headed for the ticket office, where he found a free window.

'Good morning,' he said. 'I should like a single ticket to London, please.' He slid a one-pound note under the screen. 'I have here my National Registration Identity Card.'

'Quite right, love. You keep that safe.'

'You do not wish to see it?'

'Not really, love. When you've seen one, you've seen 'em all, I say. London single, third class, you said. That's fourteen and ninepence.' She handed him a ticket with five shillings and threepence change.

'Thank you. I see you have repaired all the damage.'

The clerk blinked. 'What damage was that, like?'

'The damage to the station.'

'Oh, that. It was only a bit of glass, like, off the roof. That's all this station got in the Blitz. We were very lucky.'

'Really? Thank you, anyway.'

'It's no trouble. You want Platform Four an' it leaves a' twenny past, like.'

'Thank you.' Edelmann looked around for Platform Four, wondering why the people of Liverpool found the English language so difficult, when, as a German, he had learned to speak it correctly in a matter of months. As if to reinforce his impression, a voice on the public address system made an announcement with the same distorted vowels and guttural consonants as those of the ticket clerk.

'Due to works on the line, the train from London Euston will be approximately twenty-five minutes late arriving. We apologise for the delay.'

Edelmann could only wonder why the railway company should apologise for a twenty-five-minute delay. In Germany, people suffered longer delays than that and simply got on with their lives. They knew better than to complain.

To fill in time, he went to the buffet, and when the woman behind the counter came to serve him, he said, 'I should like a cup of tea, please.' Everyone knew that the English drank tea, always provided they could still get it.

'A cuppa char, love? Right you are.'

'No, I said, "tea".'

'''Course you did, love, but we're not all as posh as you. There you are.' Despite the misunderstanding, she handed him a cup of tea. 'Sugar's in front of you. Two sugars per person only. Help yourself, like, and that'll be fruppence when you're ready.'

'How much?'

'It may seem a lot, but you're lucky to get it at all. What have you got there?' She looked at the change in his hand. 'Give me that fruppenny bit an' we'll call it quits, an' don't try passing them Irish coins in England or you'll have the law after you, like, y' know.' She took the threepenny bit from his hand. 'Where are you from, like? You've gorra funny accent.'

'Dublin.'

'You don't sound Irish.'

'I've spent a lot of time abroad.'

'Have you now? Well, in that case, you'll be ready for a cuppa char. Sorry, I should say "tea", shouldn't I?'

Edelmann took his tea to the nearest free table and sat down. His conversation with the tea seller had been difficult, and all the time, he'd been distracted by a stack of sandwiches beneath a glass dome. They appeared, incredibly, to have been made with white bread. At least, the bread was more grey than white, but it was much closer to white bread than anything that was available in Germany. Also, ridiculous though it seemed, the sandwiches appeared to contain butter. On a whim, he got up again and attracted the attention of the tea seller.

'Is that butter in the sandwiches?' As he asked the question, he realised how foolish it must sound.

'Where have you been livin', love? Cloud Cuckoo Land? We only get two ounces of butter per person per week. After that, we 'ave to make do with margarine, like everybody else. The bread's National Loaf an' all, but beggars can't be choosers, like, y' know.'

'Nevertheless, I should like a sandwich, please,' he said.

'What kind, love? There's cheese or Spam.'

He had no idea what Spam was, so he opted for cheese.

'Very wise, love. I wonder, sometimes, what goes into that Spam.' Using a pair of tongs, she lifted a sandwich and put it on a plate for him. 'It's Government Cheddar, but we're all in the same boat, aren't we?'

He could only agree, having no idea what she meant. He only knew that, according to the English Language Manual, the answer to 'aren't we' was usually 'yes'. He paid an additional fourpence, took the sandwich back to his table and examined it briefly before trying it, unable to believe that he was about to eat white bread. When he bit into it, he became aware of the inviting aromas of cheese, white bread and the *ersatz* butter the tea seller had mentioned. Even that melted on the tongue, and he made the decision that, come the long-overdue invasion of England, he would alert the armies of the *Reich* to his latest epicurean discovery: railway buffet sandwiches made with white bread, and a kind of *ersatz* tea the English called 'char', but which tasted no different from the real thing and was sweetened with real sugar. He also mused briefly about the way the tea seller had repeatedly addressed him, a complete stranger, as 'love'. It seemed that the stories he'd heard about the decadent and promiscuous English were true after all.

————▸◂————

Prepared as he was for a lengthy journey along wayside routes, Edelmann was surprised when the train pulled into Euston only three hours and twenty minutes after leaving Liverpool, and he was even more surprised when a fellow passenger told him that the journey had been very much shorter in peacetime.

The train halted, and Edelmann joined the other passengers as they made their way on to the platform. Most of them seemed remarkably patient, and some were even courteous. He followed the crowd along the platform towards the ticket barrier, where he surrendered his ticket to a female ticket collector, who called him 'dear'.

Once outside the ticket barriers, he made himself less conspicuous by studying a large wall timetable.

After a few minutes, he became conscious of someone close by. The person in question then spoke to him.

'Excuse me. Would you have a light, by any chance?' The accent was unmistakably Irish.

Edelmann's pulse quickened. 'I'm afraid I do not smoke,' he said.

'Very wise. That way, you're less likely to burst into flames. At least, that's how I look at it.'

Edelmann turned and looked the newcomer in the face. 'I am pleased to meet you, Gael.'

'And I to meet you, O' Neill. Let's get a tube train to Charing

Cross before we attract unwelcome interest. He led the way to the tube station, where he bought two tickets for Charing Cross.

As they took the downward escalator, Gael said, 'I have to hand over my radio and codebooks to you. I'm waiting for orders to leave this damned country for good.'

'I'm not here for long, Gael, but I will need to contact Berlin.'

'Okay.' The escalator reached the lower floor, and they stepped off it. 'That's enough talk for now. You never know who may be listening.' It was a fact that so many of the passengers waiting for the next train wore the ubiquitous trench coat and trilby, so that it would have been impossible to tell a detective from a debt collector.

Before long, the familiar howling noise coming from the tunnel warned that a train was approaching. It was one thing, at least, that Edelmann recognised. The only difference he'd noticed so far was that the *U-Bahn* was inevitably cleaner than its British equivalent.

They boarded the train, but found that all the seats were taken, and they were obliged to hold on to the straps that hung from the ceiling. As the train continued on its way, Edelmann saw a man stand up, lift his hat and surrender his seat to a woman. He asked Gael, 'Is it normal for a man to do that?'

'Yes, these people are not completely uncivilised.'

They travelled on in silence, until they came eventually to Charing Cross Underground Station, where Gael led the way up to the main line station.

'I already have the tickets,' said Gael, 'but the next train's not due for another half-hour. Shall we go to the buffet?'

'Yes, I should welcome a cup of char.'

Gael looked at him in disbelief. 'You'd better keep quiet,' he advised, 'or you'll give yourself away in no time at all.'

Gael went to the counter and asked for two cups of tea. Edelmann suppressed his surprise and asked, 'May I have a cheese sandwich, please?'

'Why not? It's your funeral.'

The buffet assistant gave him a look of passing resentment, but put a sandwich on a plate for him. 'That'll be tenpence.'

Gael handed over the money, and they sat down.

Edelmann viewed the sandwich with overt reverence whilst Gael eyed Edelmann with disbelief.

———◆◄◆———

They eventually reached Gael's bedsitter in Chatham and Gael produced a cup of tea. 'It's real tea,' he told Edelmann. ' "Char" is a Hindustani word that the British use as slang.'

'They are a strange people,' observed Edelmann.

'You'll have to sleep on the floor until I leave,' said Gael.

'That is of no consequence as I am here only for two nights.'

Gael nodded. 'It's just as well. There's not a lot of food in the place.'

'Again, that is of no consequence.'

Gael was curious. 'If you're only going to be here two nights, what do you hope to achieve?'

'My orders are to make contact with Marguerite. When I have confirmed for Berlin that she is *Agentin Elster*, I shall be free to return to Germany.'

'You sound confident, O' Neill.'

Edelmann smiled. 'It has been some time since I lived under an assumed name.'

'Well, you'd better get used to it, even for two nights. You just can't take chances. I'm only too well aware that the British are on the lookout.'

'They are fools. I outwitted them easily in North Africa and in Italy.'

'You won't find it so easy in their own backyard.'

'We shall see, but firstly, why do you say that I sound confident that Marguerite is the woman I know?'

Gael looked uneasy. 'I have my doubts, O' Neill. I've had them for some time, but I've never found any real evidence.'

'Why do you doubt her?' It was clear from his tone that Edelmann had already taken offence.

'Calm down, O' Neill, and listen to what I have to tell you.'

'I am listening.'

'From time to time, I've tried drawing her into conversation about Quentzsee, and each time, she's refused to be drawn.'

'Maybe she considers idle reminiscence a waste of time when there are more important matters to which she must attend.'

'That's what she says.'

Edelmann merely shrugged.

'I think you should also know that she's engaged to be married to a man who claims to be an inspector at the dockyard.'

'What?'

'There's a chance, of course, that their engagement is phoney. I can't swear to it, but I'm fairly sure I saw him with her on a bus, and he was in the uniform of a naval officer.'

'I see.'

'We'll go and see her tonight. At least, you will, and the truth will be for you to discover. Meanwhile,' he said, looking at his watch, 'I must call Berlin. Come, and I'll show you where I keep the radio.'

Gael took out the small suitcase that contained the transmitter and receiver and extended the aerial so as to get the correct wavelength. 'Have you used this model, O' Neill?'

'Of course I have.'

'All right, I'm only trying to be helpful.' He tuned the receiver and loaded the transmitter coil. When the minute hand on his watch reached the hour, he began calling. His call was answered immediately, and he sent the code *T E*, for *Treffpunkt erfolgreich*, 'Rendezvous successful'. The operator receipted his message and told him to stand by. An important message was on its way. Gael picked up his pencil to take down the coded groups.

Finally, he receipted the message and signed off before beginning the process of decoding it.

Edelmann asked, 'What have they told you?'

'Give me a chance to decode the damned thing, O' Neill.'

'Very well, but you are slow.'

Gael eventually decoded the last group and read the signal. 'My orders are to guide you to Marguerite's address. I am then to take the train from London at ten-fifteen tomorrow morning to Liverpool. *Agent Rabe* is coming from Dublin to meet me with a ticket for the Ferry leaving Liverpool at sixteen hundred tomorrow afternoon. We shall return to Ireland together.'

Edelmann nodded in his usual way. 'You have served the Fatherland well,' he said.

'Listen, O' Neill. It's absolutely vital that you make no mistake when you see Marguerite. If she's the woman you know, there's no problem, but if the British have caught her and substituted one of their agents, as I suspect they have, she will have taken the opportunity to pass countless items of false information to Berlin. It could be catastrophic for the *Reich*.'

'I, of all people, know her well enough to be sure.'

'Even after five years?'

'Even after five years,' Edelmann assured him.

26

Lucy stepped off the bus and let herself into the building. She understood that Special Branch were keeping the flat under surveillance, but she knew better than to look for them. She only wished the whole business were over. It had been exciting and even amusing at first, but now that her life was in danger it was the wrong kind of excitement and not at all amusing.

She unlocked the flat and put the kettle on for tea, unable to face eating. Having lit the gas, she checked that the radio was in its place. There was no reason for it not to be, but that was a measure of her anxiety.

———◆◄———

A little way down the hill and on the other side of the road, Detective Constable Stewart of Special Branch kept watch from behind a copy of the Daily Express. He was watching number seventy-six, an easy task, as the address was situated in the line of sight between his right-hand page and the door pillar of the car. He had to be careful, however. It was easy to lose concentration during a long surveillance.

———◆◄———

William sat in his car with the Handie-Talkie switched on. He was assured that the batteries were good for twelve hours' active use. Nervously, he checked the Webley and Scott pistol, maybe for the third time. It was loaded with a full magazine. He returned it to the shoulder holster, having checked that the safety catch behind the hammer was in the 'on' position.

Nothing could be allowed to go wrong with the operation. So much depended on it, although his fear, for the moment, was for Lucy's safety. At the first intimation that Edelmann had arrived at her flat, William would be on his way, and to shorten that journey, he had already left the main gate and was parked just beyond it.

———◆◆◆———

DC Stewart maintained his surveillance. From time to time, he shifted in his car seat to make himself comfortable. He had sometimes emerged from long periods of surveillance with creases in his behind. They didn't tell recruits about that in training. Neither did they warn them about unpleasant characters like DI Colman, recently transferred from the Metropolitan force after, it was believed, a disciplinary hearing and demotion to DI. He wished he knew more, because, whilst DCI Henderson was in overall control of the operation, the actual surveillance was being carried out under Colman's supervision.

Absolutely nothing was happening, so Stewart looked more closely at a story about Croydon, his home town. It even involved someone he knew, a lad he remembered from school, who had evidently embarked on a life of crime. Recalling his schooldays, Stewart was hardly surprised, but he read on, fascinated by the story and, for the time being, so completely distracted that he failed to see two men approach number 76.

———◆◆◆———

Lucy poured the tea away, unable to drink it. Her stomach felt as if it had been tied in knots, and her mouth was as dry as sand.

As she emptied the teapot, she looked out of the window and saw two men, one of whom was Thomas Gael. She saw Gael turn and say something to his companion before turning and walking back the way he had come. The other man was heading purposefully for the door of the house.

She picked up the radio and pressed the button, but there was no crackle, as there had been the other day, when they tested it. She tried again. The doorbell was ringing. Her hands were shaking now, but she remembered the antenna and pulled it out. The doorbell rang again.

'William!' She remembered to release the switch.

'What's the matter, Lucy?'

'He's here! He's downstairs!' She put the radio down and heard William say, 'I'm on my way.'

She started down the stairs, forcing herself to breathe normally, but her heart was pounding. When she reached the bottom, she had to steel herself to open the door.

The man who stood on her doorstep was tall and powerfully built, but that was the limit of his *Übermensch* credentials, because far from having blonde hair and high cheek bones, he was dark, and his features were mean and pinched. It was evident, as well, that he'd not shaved, probably since early morning. He spoke first.

'Marguerite,' he said with a smile that revealed a set of uneven teeth, 'aren't you going to invite me in?'

'Of course, Gerhardt. It was the suddenness of seeing you after so long. Come this way.' As she spoke, she wondered frantically where Special Branch were, and when William would arrive.

When they reached the top of the stairs, and she opened the door to the flat, Edelmann lost no time in taking her in his arms. 'Five years,' he said, 'five whole years.'

'I know.' She made herself return his hug.

He stood back to look at her. 'You've hardly changed,' he said.

'Neither have you. You're still the same Gerhardt I knew all those years ago.'

'So, have you a kiss for me?'

'Of course.' She braced herself, holding her breath as his wet lips smothered hers.

'What a time we shall have tonight,' he said, squeezing her buttocks between his huge hands. 'I shall make love to you all night long, now that we are no longer apart. It will be worth the wait of five years.' Moving her over to the sofa, he kissed her again. The foulness of his breath made her stomach heave, so that she was afraid she might vomit.

'What is the matter, Marguerite? You used to like the way I kissed you.' He was looking at her oddly. 'Don't you remember?' It was as if his suspicions were suddenly aroused.

'Of course I do, Gerhardt, but why the hurry? Surely, we can take things a little more slowly.'

'Why should we?' He ran his hand playfully beneath her skirt and squeezed her thigh. 'I am surprised,' he said, that you are able to find stockings in England,' and he celebrated the novelty by toying with the welt of her stocking before exploring further.

'Wait,' she said, standing up. 'This is far too sudden after all this time.' She wondered what else she could say, and then fell back on convention. 'Let me get you a cup of tea.'

'Oh, if you insist,' he sighed. 'All the English ever do is drink tea. I have learned that they now call it "char", a word they have taken from the primitive language of one of their subject races.' Shaking his head, he said, 'I cannot understand why they should wish to imitate the ways of an inferior people.'

Lucy filled the kettle with shaking hands, still nauseated by his obscene physical intrusion.

Edelmann said, 'As you know, I always preferred coffee before *ersatz* became the only kind available in Germany. It must be impossible, also, to find real coffee in England.'

'It's not easy,' she confirmed.

'So why should we not forget tea and go to your bed? We can get to know each other all over again, as you English say.'

'Do I have to remind you that I'm half-German? I feel the same as you about the English.'

'So the past five years have not softened your attitude towards them?' There was an edge to his voice. It seemed he was testing her.

'I'm as loyal to the *Führer* as I ever was,' she told him.

'More loyal than ever, it seems, as you now refer to him by his correct title. You only ever used it when you could be overheard by higher authority. Do you not remember that?'

Lucy sidestepped the question by saying dismissively, 'Oh, that was a long time ago.'

'But you remember how *frech* you were.'

Lucy would never have described Marguerite as 'cheeky', but she felt obliged to say, 'I was very young.'

'Don't you remember what you said about the *Führer's* moustache? It earned you a severe reprimand on one occasion, didn't it?'

'Of course I do. Who could forget a thing like that? But I am still loyal to the Fatherland and the *Führer*, and I still despise the British.'

He came to watch her. 'The English are clever in some ways,' he said in the same measured tone.

'What ways are they?' She was determined to keep him talking until help arrived. It was infinitely better than being slobbered over and pawed by him.

'Their doctors are clever,' he said, stroking the side of her neck with his forefinger. 'I see someone has removed the large birthmark from here. He did it very expertly, because there's no sign of it now.'

Lucy tried unsuccessfully to recall such a blemish on Marguerite's neck. As she remembered it, her classmate's complexion had been almost flawless. It was one of the physical qualities of which, during her silly moments, she had been nauseatingly proud. She decided to hedge. 'Oh, that,' she said. 'It wasn't such a large one, but it cost me a fortune to have it removed. They used a new and expensive process.'

'Is that so? Tell me, how is your brother. What is his name? Harry, isn't it?'

Lucy tried frantically to remember anything about Marguerite's family. She couldn't recall a brother, so she prevaricated. 'Oh, I believe he's very well, but I haven't seen him for quite a long time.'

'Yes,' he said, moving closer, 'English doctors are remarkable. They can even remove a birthmark that never existed.'

Lucy could only stare at him, open-mouthed.

'Also, Marguerite has neither a brother nor a sister, and she only ever spoke of the *Führer* loyally and with the respect due to him.' Suddenly, he was openly hostile. 'Who are you, and where is Marguerite?'

'I don't know what you're taking about.'

He struck her hard across the face with the flat of his huge hand. 'Yes, you do. You're an English agent.' His voice became louder with each sentence. 'They have captured Marguerite, haven't they? Tell me where she is.'

Her ear was ringing from the blow. 'I don't know.'

He hit her again. 'Have they executed her or is she in prison? Tell me.'

'I don't know.' She'd been determined not to show weakness, but the second blow had brought tears to her eyes.

His voice became level, but no less menacing. 'You're going to pay for this, you English whore, and then you're going to die. Whore is what you are, isn't it? You're an English whore, and I shall treat you as one. Take off your clothes.'

'No.'

He hit her again. 'Remove your clothes,' he demanded. 'I shall help you.' Grasping the 'V' neck of her blouse, he tore it apart and then seized the straps of her brassiere.

'Get off me, you savage!'

Edelmann took her by the throat, 'What did you call me?'

Lucy struggled, but he was far too strong for her. She was fighting for breath.

'You will give yourself to me. Do you understand?'

She saw his loathsome features through a red mist and feared she was about to lose consciousness. Desperately, she fought to dislodge his fingers from her throat.

———— ◆◗◀ ————

William swore. From *Pembroke*'s gates to Lucy's flat was hardly any distance, but two vehicles had collided and the road was blocked. There wasn't even enough room to turn in the road. Further along, a policeman was holding up traffic. It was hopeless. William got out of the car and took to the pavement.

'Hey, you can't leave your car there!' The policeman was pointing angrily to where William's car stood. 'If you'll only wait a minute, I'll let you through.'

Without bothering to reply, William sprinted along the footpath to the end of Manor Road, surprised and thankful that his weak leg was holding up. A car was parked a little short of the flat, and as William approached it, its driver got out. He looked guilty.

'If you're Special Branch,' shouted William, 'come with me!'

The driver leaned into his car and spoke into a handset.

The outer door was unlocked. William ran up the stairs, drew his pistol and flung open the door. Lucy stood, facing him, her clothes torn and in disarray. At her feet, a man lay writhing and clutching himself. From the noises he was making, he appeared to be in great pain.

'William,' said Lucy in a voice that was little more than a croak. 'Oh, thank God!' Her face and neck bore the red marks of an assault, and her face was drenched with tears. She threw her arms round him and buried her face against his chest, sobbing uncontrollably.

William held her with his left arm, keeping his pistol trained on Edelmann's jack-knifed body. 'What have you done to her, you bastard? I've a bloody good mind to shoot you now and save the hangman a job.'

Edelmann merely groaned and continued to clutch his private parts.

The young detective who had been in the car came into the room, also wielding a pistol, and William lost no time in venting his anger. 'Where were your people when this bastard arrived?'

Before the hapless officer could reply, a groan from Edelmann prompted William to say, 'I don't care how much it hurts. Stand up! Get your hands up! Go on, *Hände hoch*, you bastard!'

'I didn't see him arrive, sir.' The shamefaced detective looked at William uncertainly, as if waiting for orders.

'Well, maybe you'd like to make yourself useful now and arrest him. I'll cover you while you handcuff him.'

Hearing the outer door, the constable looked down the staircase and said, 'The DI's here now, sir. He'll want to do it himself.'

'About bloody time.'

Edelmann was now standing with his hands raised, his earlier discomfort evidently eased, at least to some extent, and now his eyes moved alternately between William and the detective. He was possibly waiting and looking for an opportunity to escape. William kept his eyes on him, resolved to shoot him if necessary. Speaking to Lucy, he said, 'You'd better find something to cover yourself with, darling.'

She nodded mutely and went to the bedroom, holding her torn blouse together.

The face that emerged from the landing was one that William recognised immediately, but it was no more welcome for that.

'Oh, hell,' he said. 'No wonder the operation's fallen flat on its arse. It's DCI Colman.'

'Just "DI" now,' admitted Colman.

'Right, Colman, here's your prisoner. His name's Gerhardt Edelmann, also known as *"Agent Bachsteltze"*.'

Colman took a pair of handcuffs from the pocket of his trench coat. As he moved in front of William to handcuff Edelmann, the German seized his chance, hurling his massive frame at Colman, who cannoned into William, trapping him momentarily against an armchair. Then, with surprising agility for a man recently, if temporarily, disabled, he leapt through the open door and took to the stairs.

'Out of my way, you bloody fool!' It was William's turn to shove Colman aside and make for the staircase. Edelmann was already turning the front doorknob when William fired three times. In his haste, he hit the doorframe with his first shot, but the second and third found their target, and Edelmann fell against the door, gasping with pain.

'Now you can arrest him, Colman, and try not to let the bastard escape this time.'

DI Colman descended the stairs and bent over Edelmann. 'He's going to need an ambulance,' he said. 'He's bleeding like hell from a leg wound, and it looks as if you got him in the unmentionables as well.'

'Well, see to it, but don't let him get away, whatever you do.' Considering the prisoner's injuries, there was little risk of that, but William was feeling no better disposed towards Colman than when he'd last seen him in New Scotland Yard. Turning to the young detective, he said, 'Use the telephone in the flat to call an ambulance.'

'Very good, sir.'

He left both of them with Edelmann, and went looking for Lucy. He found her in the bathroom, on her knees and retching into the WC pan. He poured some water into a tumbler and took it to her.

After several minutes, she got to her feet and let him take her to the bedroom, where she clung to him, sobbing.

'Don't say anything yet,' he told her. 'I'll get you some ice for your face.' Outside, a bell signalled the approach of an ambulance. William heard Colman issuing orders to his subordinate, and he imagined the ambulance must be the one the detective had called. His guess was proved right when the ringing rose in volume until it came from the street, directly below. He took ice from the refrigerator and wrapped it in two towels, which he took back to the bedroom.

Presently, Lucy's tears dried up and she began to recover, but her breath was coming in involuntary shudders.

'You have some cognac, I know.' William remembered bringing it from the wardroom of *HMS Pembroke*.

'I'm not... keen... on cognac,' she croaked.

'It'll do you good,' he said taking it from the drinks cupboard. 'You don't have to enjoy it.' He poured two glasses and gave her one.

'You just... wanted one... yourself.'

'Of course.'

Lucy sipped and grimaced in turn. 'He was... a brute,' she said.

'It's all over now.'

'I know.' She closed her eyes as if to banish the memory, but then she spoke again. 'He called... me a... whore. He was going to... you know, and then he was... going to kill me.'

William held her close, hating even the thought of it.

'I upset him. I called him... a savage, and then... he tried to strangle me.'

'I can see that. I should have shot him when I arrived.'

'It was the only thing I could do.'

'What was?'

'I kicked him,' she said, adding, '*in testes*.'

'Only you could defend yourself in Latin, darling, but I'm glad you did. I'm only sorry you had to.'

'I kneed him first and then I kicked him to make sure.'

He held her even closer, berating himself for not arriving sooner. 'If it makes you feel any better,' he said, 'I shot him in the same place when he tried to escape.'

'I heard the shots, but I couldn't move.'

'I know. You'd be in shock, and no wonder after what you'd been through.'

'Were you aiming for his... you know?'

'No, I'm not that good a shot, but I'm glad I hit him there. From what you've just told me, it was poetic justice.'

There was a tentative knock on the door of the flat, and William got up to answer it. When he opened the door he saw a woman, possibly in her twenties. She looked frightened. She asked, 'Is everything all right? I heard... I think someone fired a gun, and then an ambulance came and took someone away.'

'Everything's fine,' he assured her. 'The police have arrested the culprit and taken him into custody. No one here has been hurt, but there's an awful mess at the bottom of the stairs.' He thought it wise to warn her. 'Someone will come along to clean the place up.' Unless Special Branch were totally stupid, they would see to that rather than leave it to excite people's imagination and encourage gossip. 'As it's a police matter,' he explained, 'they've asked that people keep quiet about it.'

'Oh, of course. I was just worried about Marguerite.'

'Marguerite's fine. I'm going to take her away for a day or so, and she'll be as right as rain.'

The woman began to relax. 'Oh, thank you for telling me that. I was very worried.'

'Not at all. Goodnight.'

'Goodnight.' She returned to her own flat.

When William re-joined Lucy, she asked, 'Was that Emily from the second floor?'

'A young woman with light-brown hair?'

'Yes.'

'In that case, it most likely was. She came to make sure you were all right.'

'Poor Emily. She must have heard everything. She'd be scared out of her wits.'

'Don't worry about her. She'll be all right now.'

They sat together for some time, half-an-hour or more, until Lucy was calmer, and then William motioned towards her glass. 'Drink up while I telephone Captain Challock.'

He dialled Challock's home number and got him immediately.

'Stamford, how is the young lady?' His concern was unmistakably genuine.

'Very shaken, sir, but recovering. You've evidently been told about it.'

'We should bear in mind that we're on an insecure telephone line and we need to be guarded, but yes, the DCI spoke to me less than ten minutes ago. Well done, Stamford. It's as well you got there when you did.'

'I'd have been here sooner but for a traffic incident.'

'Well, don't blame yourself for that.'

'No, sir.' He was trying not to.

'By the way, our visitor didn't make it to hospital. Loss of blood, apparently. I told you that thing was more dangerous than you thought.'

'Well, at least even Colman can't let him escape again.'

'Oh, was he involved?'

'I'm afraid so.'

'Bad luck, but listen, Stamford. Our Celtic friend has been ordered to catch the ten-fifteen from Euston to Liverpool tomorrow. The snag is that, when our colleagues arrived at his place tonight, he'd already done a bunk. Still, he can't sail until sixteen hundred tomorrow, so they'll have a chance to intercept him before he can board the ferry.'

It was leaving an awful lot to chance. 'After all that's happened, sir, I don't trust them not to bungle it. I'm going to get the overnight train from Euston.'

'All right, Stamford, I'll see you on the train.'

'Goodnight, sir.'

'Goodnight, Stamford.'

William found Lucy much more settled. 'It's time to change into something decent, darling,' he told her. 'If you can face it, I'm going to make you something to eat, and then we have a train to catch.'

'Why?'

'Gael's made a dash for Liverpool, but he can't sail until tomorrow afternoon, so we're going up there. Captain Challock's coming as well.'

'But, why me?'

'I can't leave you here on your own after all that's happened. In any case,' he said, remembering the blood-soaked linoleum and doormat, 'the place is a complete pot-mess.'

'Have I time for a quick bath? I feel dirty.'

'It's not you that's dirty, but I do understand. Yes, go and have a bath. Also, have you a pair of sun glasses?'

'Yes, what do I need them for?'

'To hide the bruises. A headscarf might be a good idea as well. I'll pack an overnight bag and then I'll get first-class tickets, so you'll have a comfortable ride up. When we get to Liverpool, I'll leave you in a hotel, to catch up on your beauty sleep. Best of all, when it's all over, I'm going to speak to Captain Challock and ask him for a big favour.'

27

Captain Challock was difficult to spot at first, dressed as he was in civilian clothes, but he recognised them at the same time as they discovered him, at the newspaper stall.

'Miss Pendleton,' he said, clearly shocked by her appearance, 'I didn't expect to see you here.'

'In view of everything, I couldn't leave her behind, sir, and her flat's not fit for habitation.'

'Of course, Stamford. Stupid of me. My dear,' he said, taking Lucy's hand between his, 'if I'd had any idea something like this would happen, I should never have asked you to do the job in the first place.'

'I'm all right now, thank you, Captain.'

'Are you sure? Your voice....'

'It's improving,' she assured him. 'I was croaking earlier.'

'You poor girl. Have you eaten? There'll be no buffet service on the train, but you could get something before we set off.'

'I had something before we left the flat, thank you.'

'I hope you bought first-class tickets, Stamford. You're a senior officer, after all, and you'll be able to claim it on expenses.'

'Yes, sir. I intend to book Miss Pendleton into a hotel when we arrive. Maybe I can claim that as well.'

'I imagine Vice-Admiral Davies will have no hesitation in arguing your case.' Looking around him, he said, 'Let's find a little space where we can talk, and I'll fill you in on what's happening. It'll be too crowded on the train for us to talk.' They moved away from the crowd of sailors, soldiers, airmen and their relations, and then, satisfied that they would not be overheard, he said, 'Special Branch are watching Liverpool Lime street Station and the Cunard

Ferry Terminal. MI Five also have someone at the Terminal, because we're after *Agent Rabe* as well. We've been after him for some time, so this could be quite a coup.'

William was only half-impressed. 'I'm glad MI Five will be there, sir. I've never worked with them, but they can't be as inept as Special Branch. That would be impossible.'

Challock smiled. 'They're usually much better than this, Stamford. You've been unfortunate enough to encounter Colman and that drip of a constable who was supposed to be watching Miss Pendleton's flat, but I assure you that those two are an extreme example.'

'That's of some comfort, sir.' The memory of finding Lucy bruised and abused was still brutally fresh. 'Apparently, they'd already reduced Colman to Detective Inspector, although, frankly, I wouldn't trust him on point duty in a quiet village, but what will they do to the constable, I wonder?'

'I expect he'll be hauled over the coals, Stamford. Everyone is entitled to a second chance, as you know only too well.' Challock's half-smile was a friendly reminder of the earlier incident, when Bonnington had demanded William's return to the fleet.

Lucy, who had been quiet for some time, came to his defence by saying, 'That was below the belt, Captain.'

'It was, Miss Pendleton, I admit.' Then, still concerned for her well-being, he asked, 'Are you sure you're all right?'

'I'm perfectly sure, thank you, Captain. Else Müller's Academy for Ladies produced a doughty kind of damsel.' Her voice, along with her spirits, was returning to normal.

'I now see you in a new light, my dear.' Had he said more, it would have been lost in the noise of an approaching train and the announcement that accompanied it.

'The train now arriving at Platform Two is the eleven-twenty to Liverpool Lime Street, stopping at Stafford, Runcorn, Crewe, Manchester Piccadilly and Liverpool Lime Street. Passengers for Newcastle-under-Lyme, Stoke-on-Trent and Nantwich change at Crewe.'

'Hurrah,' said Captain Challock, 'and only twenty-five minutes late. Follow me, children.'

Obediently, William and Lucy followed him on to the train and into a first-class compartment. Three passengers already occupied the compartment.

'That was masterly, sir,' said William.

'Put it down to years of practice.'

William lifted Lucy's bag and his on to the rack while she removed her coat.

The door to the corridor opened again, and a second lieutenant in the Royal Marines called to someone outside, 'It's all right, there are two in here.'

'There most certainly are not, Lieutenant,' said Captain Challock. 'This lady is waiting to be seated, as is this senior officer. Newly-commissioned you may be, but that is no excuse for slovenly manners.'

The young officer gaped momentarily, and then said, 'I'm terribly sorry, sir. I didn't realise that.'

'Evidently.' Challock pointed towards the corridor. 'Go and sin no more.'

'Yes, sir. Goodnight, sir.' The second lieutenant beat an embarrassed retreat.

An elderly man with a waxed moustache and a regimental tie gave Challock an approving look. 'Well said, sir.'

'I'm glad you approve, sir.'

In the dim safety light of the compartment, Challock sat back and closed his eyes. William looked around at his fellow passengers, none of whom looked particularly interesting, until the events of the day proved too tiring, and he closed his eyes too, vaguely conscious of Lucy's head against his shoulder.

———◆◆———

When the train rumbled into Liverpool Lime Street at ten-past four, Lucy, William and Captain Challock emerged with dry, sleepless eyes and stiff necks, and showed their tickets at the barrier.

'Let's try the Lord Nelson Hotel,' said Challock. 'I think Miss Pendleton would benefit from a proper sleep, and I know we'd all appreciate coffee and breakfast.' He checked the time and corrected himself. 'It will have to be just coffee for now, I think.'

He led them to a Victorian building that was happily close by, as their arrival had coincided with a heavy shower. The building turned out to be the Lord Nelson Hotel. A member of the night staff saw them enter, and offered his services.

'We've just arrived in Liverpool,' Challock told him. My young friend, here, wishes to make a reservation, and we'd all appreciate coffee, if that can be arranged.'

'Of course, sir. Will you take coffee in the lounge?'

'Yes, please.' He tapped William on the forearm and said, 'Book yourselves in for tonight. I'll be returning to London, so I'll wait in the lounge.'

'Aye-aye, sir.'

The desk clerk returned from ordering coffee and asked, 'How else can I help you, sir?'

'I'd like to reserve two single rooms, if possible, for tonight, and I should be grateful if the lady could take one of them as a day booking as well. She's travelled a long way and she's feeling the effects.' As he would be claiming the cost of the hotel bills on his return, a double room was out of the question.

'I think that might be arranged, sir. What are the names?'

'Commander W. F. Stamford – that's with an "m" – and Miss L. J. Pendleton. Our joint address is Room Thirty-Three, The Admiralty, London SW One, but I'll pay in cash when we leave.'

—◆I◆—

Lucy slept for much of the day, whilst William and Captain Challock made contact with the various Special Branch and MI5 officers involved in preparation for the main event. They now waited at the Terminal. So far, there had been no sign of Gael.

William said, 'The ferry's been there for ages, sir. Whatever do they find to do between sailings?' A team of deckhands working in a leisurely manner had rigged an accommodation ladder secured on both sides by heavy ropes tied to mooring bollards, but there had been no other activity.

'Crossing the Irish Sea, as they do,' said Challock, 'I imagine they spend quite a lot of time swabbing out after seasick passengers. Other than that, you have to remember that they're the merchant service, and time is more plentiful for them than it is for us.' A movement beyond the barrier alerted Challock, and he said, 'They're going to embark passengers now. Come on.' Showing his identity card to the seamen on the gate, he took his place just inside the barrier. William positioned himself on the other side.

It made sense that the wanted men would try to board the ferry as soon as they could, and William wasn't surprised when, scanning the queue of passengers, he saw two men looking particularly guarded. Both wore flat caps low on their foreheads, either for concealment or against the persistent rain, and one of them was definitely Gael.

'Five rows back, sir,' he told Challock, 'in a grubby, beige mackintosh and a cloth cap.'

Challock signalled discreetly to one of the waiting officers, and as the two approached the gate, they closed in. Meanwhile, a steady stream of passengers climbed the accommodation ladder and joined the ship between decks.

Two MI5 officers joined the Special Branch detectives and formed a barrier between the two men and the gate.

One of the officers asked, 'May I see your identification, gentlemen?'

Gael looked alarmed, but his companion felt calmly in his pocket. Then, shoving the nearest of his captors roughly aside, he made a dash for the dock gates, and might have made it, but two other officers appeared from within the crowd and restrained him, handcuffing him.

With one of the wanted men detained, a Special Branch officer asked William, 'Which one is Gael?'

'The one you're holding.'

'All right, Gael,' said the detective, 'the game's up. Come with us.'

Wildly, Gael wrenched himself free and dashed into the crowd, barging passengers on either side in his bid to evade his captors.

Two of the MI5 officers raced after him. One of them caught him, holding him doggedly by the arm. Above them, passengers halted on the ladder, fascinated by the drama being enacted below.

William tried to grab Gael's free arm, which he was flailing desperately as he tried to break free of the arresting officer, but without success. The second MI5 man also reached out for it, falling victim to a blow to the face that burst his nose and possibly broke it as well.

With the strength born of desperation, Gael tore his arm free, and the released momentum sent him lurching backwards towards the edge of the dock. It seemed that he might steady himself, but then he stumbled against a mooring bollard and fell backwards. For several seconds, he fought to recover his balance, but then tumbled over the kerb, clawing frantically at the wet, moss-covered stone before falling into the foul waters below.

Captain Challock yelled to the crew members on the ladder, 'Throw a lifebelt, quickly! There's a man overboard!'

Gael was shouting, 'Help! I can't swim!' His head disappeared beneath the surface and then re-emerged as he made panic-stricken efforts to stay afloat. William found a coil of heavy-duty hemp rope and dragged it to the dockside. As he attempted to pay it out, a seaman appeared above with one of the ship's lifebelts.

Challock shouted, 'Here!' Catching it, he dropped it into the water and yelled to Gael to grab it. Choking and crying hysterically for help, Gael reached for it desperately before his head disappeared beneath the oily surface for the last time.

William was suddenly conscious of the screams and shouts of the passengers, and the efforts of the crew to calm them, but he didn't care. All the passengers knew was that a man had lost his life. They had no way of knowing the truth. Meanwhile, the senior Special Branch officer would explain matters to the local police. Then, when Gael's body was recovered from the dock, William would be required to identify it. After the frantic urgency and pandemonium of the past few minutes, normal procedure would be observed and followed, and he would identify the dead man as Thomas Michael Gael, dockyard labourer, of Castlebar, County Mayo in the Republic of Ireland.

28

Lucy was up and about by the time they returned to the hotel. Not surprisingly, she was fresher than either of them. She asked, 'Did they arrest Gael?'

'Yes,' Challock told her truthfully.

'Will he be hanged?'

'No, my dear. He won't be hanged.'

'I shouldn't say it, but I'm glad. Hanging's a dreadful fate.'

Both William and Challock merely nodded in agreement. They were taking tea in the hotel lounge, and Challock had just joined them after making a series of telephone calls.

'I shall return to London tonight,' he told them, but before I do, I should like you both to join me for dinner.'

'That's very kind of you, sir. Thank you.'

'Yes. Thank you, Captain.'

'It's the very least I can do in the circumstances. Of course, you'll both be staying the night here, and then, in the morning, you must make your own arrangements.'

'For what, Captain?'

'I have just spoken to Vice Admiral Davies, who is naturally relieved and delighted with the outcome of the operation. He is so delighted, in fact, that he has granted Commander Stamford's request and has insisted that you both take seventy-two hours' leave with effect from oh-eight-hundred tomorrow. Your home being a stone's throw from here, Miss Pendleton, you might easily take your leave there.' Adopting a suitably stern look, he added, 'Normal security restrictions will naturally apply.'

'We shan't breathe a word,' promised Lucy, almost tearful in her joy.

'I know you won't, but you will need a cover story for your bruises. I imagine Commander Stamford will take care of that.'

Lucy looked appealingly to William.

'It happened in London,' he suggested. 'A lorry carrying an insecure load of used tyres drove past you. Some of them fell on to the road, and one bounced straight at you. It hit you squarely on the bridge of your nose, blackening both your eyes.'

Challock shook his head in admiration and wonder.

'I just regret that the incident took place,' said William.

Lucy squeezed his hand reassuringly. 'It wasn't your fault, William.'

'No,' agreed Challock, 'we know who was to blame, and he's paid the ultimate penalty for it.' He held up his hands to forestall further discussion. 'After your leave,' he said, 'you are to return to Room Thirty-Three at the Admiralty. Chatham is now a closed chapter.'

'That's a relief,' said William, 'even though I have a Morris Eight that's now standing idle.'

'Mothball it,' advised Challock. 'The war can't last forever.' Then, remembering an earlier indiscretion, he added, 'You should return your pistol to the armoury, however. You're not going to need that again.'

'It's just as well, sir. I was sorely tempted to shoot Colman as well as Edelmann.'

Challock smiled. Then, returning to the original subject, he said, 'As the real Marguerite Werner has satisfied everyone concerned that she will only ever be an odious Nazi sympathiser, word will be passed via the usual channels that Agents *Elster*, *Bachsteltze* and *Buchfink* have all been captured. We'll keep quiet about *Rabe* in case we manage to turn him. At all events, it should give our friends in Berlin something to think about for a while, whereas I understand the Prime Minister will want to see you both on your return, and I suspect you may be offered a token of the nation's gratitude.'

Lucy stirred uncomfortably. 'I don't know about Will... Commander Stamford, Captain, but I don't want them to go mad over this. I mean, we did what we had to, and we did it in secret, so that's surely how it must remain.'

'And I agree with the future Mrs Stamford, sir.'

'It will remain a secret for a very long time,' he assured them, 'but, you know, I'm sure something will be forthcoming, and I'm not just talking about your wedding. I must congratulate you, by the way. This *is* a surprise. When is it to be, or haven't you decided yet?'

'We need to discuss it with our families, sir, but we'll let you know.'

'See that you do. In spite of all current constraints, my wife remains a dab hand at finding wedding presents.'

29

S even days later, on the 6th June, the BBC made the following announcement:

Early this morning, allied forces landed on a number of beaches in Normandy. There was some opposition but the enemy were taken largely by surprise, and our forces are now making progress inland.

30

PARK AVENUE CRICKET GROUND, BRADFORD
YORKSHIRE v NEW ZEALAND

1949

Vice-Admiral Sir Henry Challock KBE, RN (retired) and his wife made their way into the Members' Enclosure. The tour match was a popular one, and the ground was filling rapidly.

'Have you seen them yet, darling?' Like her husband, Lady Challock had been scanning the seats in the enclosure, but so far without success. She was an elegant woman with a fair complexion and bright blue eyes, giving her a friendly, engaging appearance that mirrored her personality. Now that her husband was retired, she accompanied him to cricket matches, which she watched in a detached, uninformed sort of way. She had a special reason for attending on that day, however, because they had arranged to meet the parents of their two godchildren.

'Here they are. Over here, you two.'

'Henry,' said Lady Challock, 'do try to stop giving orders. Remember you're retired now.'

'I'm sorry, darling, it's a lifelong....' He broke off to welcome the newcomers. 'Lucy and William, how are you both?' He bent to kiss Lucy's upturned cheek and extended his hand to William. 'And how are the children?'

'They're well, thank you, Sir Henry. Julia is talking non-stop, now she's got the hang of it, and David's walking, albeit a little drunkenly. Their great-grandpa is spoiling them to death today.'

'We're glad to hear it, and no more of that "Sir Henry" nonsense. I've told you before, it's "Henry", now that we're, as it were, related.'

Lady Challock shook her head at her husband's nonsense and asked, 'How is the book coming along, William?'

'It's still at the planning stage, Frances.'

'He has to be sure of his facts,' said Lucy with a knowing look. 'In fact, he's quite fussy about the detail.'

'Actually, Henry,' said William, still feeling a degree of awkwardness at using the familiar form of address, 'I wonder if, at some time, I might tap into your knowledge of naval life during the first war.'

Henry looked surprised. 'It's an ever-open door, my dear fellow, but you must bear in mind that, until nineteen-seventeen, I was a midshipman, the lowest of the low. I imagine from your request that your story is set during the Great War?'

'Yes, it's about two music-hall comedians, a cross-talk act, who become inadvertently involved in a naval espionage operation.'

Frances beamed at the idea. 'What are you going to call them, William?'

'I thought maybe "Doddington and Doyle". One is a scheming clown whose plans always come undone because Doyle, who seldom knows which way to turn, usually ends up washing his hands of the whole thing and leaving his partner high and dry.'

'Of course.' Feeling her husband shake with suppressed laughter, she asked, 'What's the big joke, darling?'

'Are they, by any chance, related to Bonnington and Boyle, William?'

'Well, I wanted names for a pair of blundering idiots, and I thought immediately of those two, but I didn't want to make it too obvious.'

'I don't think either of them will want to draw attention to their past misdemeanours, so you should be all right.' Looking at his watch, he said, 'We're going for a saunter, just to speak to a few people, but we'll be back to join you before the match begins. I must say I'm rather disappointed. I was hoping to see the new fast bowler. What's his name, again?'

'Trueman.'

'Yes, apparently he's not included in the side. I can't think why not.'

'I believe he's been called up by the RAF for National Service.'

'Oh, well, we can't argue with that. Anyway,' he said, giving Frances his arm, 'we'll see you both later.'

As they walked down the steps to the front of the enclosure, Frances said, 'What a lovely couple they are, Henry.'

'Indeed, a truly remarkable pair. I wish I could tell you more about them, but their story, like mine, must remain a mystery until nineteen ninety-five, would you believe? And by that time, they will both be quite elderly, and neither of us is likely to be around.'

'But you were all there when you were needed, darling, and that's the main thing.'

———◆◆———

Lucy took William's hand and said, 'Isn't it wonderful that Henry and Frances have moved back to Stamford Bridge?'

'Yes, he'll be able to get to the Scarborough matches now.'

His glib remark was lost on Lucy, who said, 'I feel sorry for Frances.'

'Why?'

'I mean, having to tag along to matches when she's completely in the dark about cricket.'

William thought about it and said, 'As far as she's concerned, it's a social occasion, and she does them ever so well.'

Suddenly, Lucy put her hand to her mouth. 'Oh, there's something I forgot to tell you. A letter came this morning. You were in the bath at the time, so I couldn't tell you then.'

'End the suspense, Lucy. I don't think I can cope with it.'

'Silly. It was from Bea. She and Dai want to visit us next month.'

'If it comes to that, we could put them up.'

She nodded. 'That's what I suggested. Bea speaks Welsh like a native now, by the way.'

'Whereas Dai still talks nonsense like an idiot. Do you remember when Bea complained about his heavy-handed wooing?'

'Yes, but they're in love, so it doesn't matter.'

'I must remember that when I need an excuse.'

Absently, she said, 'Don't you dare.' It was clear that she was already thinking about something else, which she proceeded to do for several minutes.

Eventually, he said, 'A penny for 'em.'

'I was just thinking how wonderful it is that so many of the couples we know are perfectly matched and happy together.' She began counting on her fingers. 'There's Bea and Dai, Frances and Henry, and there's us as well....'

'Don't forget Lord Nelson and Emma Hamilton.'

'Hush.' She put a finger to her lips. 'Someone might hear you.'

'But no one would know what we mean.'

'I suppose not. I imagine lots of people must have their own names for... you know... *it*.'

'Including "*it*".'

'Well, you know what I mean.'

'Not really. You'll have to show me later.'

She treated him to a look of mock-severity. 'You never miss a trick, do you?'

'I try not to,' he admitted. 'I'm still planning on having a cricket team. I believe I mentioned it to you on one occasion.'

'You did, but it's a lot to ask.'

'I suppose so.' As he looked around the ground, spectators were still arriving, all keen to see the touring side and their county in action. Their sheer number made him think. 'You know,' he said, 'I dare bet no more than a handful of people in this ground has ever heard of "Nelson's bridge for boarding first-raters".'

She looked at him blankly. 'If it comes to that, darling, neither have I.'

'I'll demonstrate it to you tonight,' he promised.

THE END

www.ingramcontent.com/pod-product-compliance
Lightning Source LLC
Chambersburg PA
CBHW021331070726
47496CB00016B/699